LITTLE MILL
ON
BEAVER CREEK

A Historical Novel

By Jackie Jobe Haines

Copyright © 2017 by Jackie Jobe Haines

Published by Mai Tai's Book Shack

ISBN Number: 978-1-64008-705-7

DEDICATION

This book is dedicated with loving memory to my husband, Marion Haines, who always encouraged me to write and to reach for my dream.

I also dedicate this in loving memory of my maternal Grandmother, Virginia Gorrell Medlin, and my parents, Garland and Martha Ann Jobe, who instilled in me a love of local history and taught me so much about "how things used to be" in rural Guilford County, North Carolina.

Table of Contents:

To Adam,
Enjoy the story!
"To God be all the glory, honor,
and praise!"
Love, Jackie Haines

PROLOGUE: *My Personal Family History.*

I was born in Greensboro, North Carolina, raised on land that was part of the farm where my mother, Martha Ann Medlin Jobe, had grown up. Mama's great-grandparents had built a home out of hewn logs from their own woods in the 1800's. It sits on a foundation built of stones brought from the stream just down the hill.

The Gorrell family had moved into this area southeast of what is now Greensboro along with many other Scotch-Irish settlers in the middle 1700's. The farm may originally have had ninety or one hundred acres when it was settled, but by the time my great-grandparents inherited the farm, it consisted of eighty acres, with two streams crossing the land. In that area of southeast Guilford County, in the northern Piedmont of North Carolina, the land consists of red clay, rock, gently-rolling hills, swamps, open grassy areas, and thick woodlands. On their farm, a spring house was built near the barn in the 1800's.

The Gorrells raised cattle, hogs, and horses, and their fields grew clover, hay, seed corn, barley, wheat, and oats. At least one field was used for growing cotton when my Grandmother Virginia Gorrell was a little girl. She told me stories about how hard she worked in her girlhood. The blazing hot sun gave her huge freckles with lots of wrinkles on her arms and on her face. She implored my parents, "Keep that little girl out of the sun! Protect her fair skin. I don't want this to happen to her."

Early in the farm's history, several fields were devoted to raising tobacco; that ended when my mother was young. By the time I came along, a Mr. Carter leased three of our fields and raised tobacco, curing the leaves in two tobacco barns built of wood covered with tin and topped with tin roofs. An oil furnace in the barns was used to cure his tobacco; it had heat outlets all around the perimeter. When I was young, five large fields still remained on my grandparents' farm.

Adjacent to the farmhouse, my grandparents tended three garden plots. Surprisingly, the garden soil was a rich chocolate color, not the red clay found everywhere else. Apparently, the Gorrells must have known how rich that one section of soil was and situated the house nearby, to take advantage of that soil for their gardens, which grew magnificent white potatoes, sweet potatoes, tomatoes, small round "Sugar Baby" watermelons, cantaloupes, okra, watercress, Crowder peas, turnips, cabbage, lettuce, green beans, butter peas, butter beans, green peas, corn (which sometimes grew taller than my grandfather), radishes, squash, cucumbers, and my Daddy's favorite: black-eyed peas.

When the settlers first arrived, they must have marveled at the amazing variety of trees on their land: wild cherry, red bud, sweet gum, red cedar, black walnut, chestnut oak, black oak, blackjack oak, white oak, willow oak, red oak, red maple, holly, tulip poplar, several species of pine, persimmons, sassafras, dogwood, wild plum, sycamore, hickory, and locust. Blackberry and muscadine vines were abundant in the woods.

The pioneers quickly planted blueberry bushes, grape vines, and fruit trees: pear, tart June apples (best applesauce ever!), red apples, and cooking cherries. Scuppernongs and strawberries grew very well in this soil. The women of my family planted crepe myrtle, gardenias, lilacs, mock orange, wisteria, hydrangea, pyracantha, quince, and forsythia. My grandmother planted beds of bearded iris in a variety of colors, as well as larkspurs, sunflowers, roses, and gorgeous dahlias.

Like all farmhouses, the kitchen was the heart of the home, with its wood-burning stove and the warmth and wonderful smells of the meals that were made on that stove. Beneath the house was a root cellar where my great-grandparents and, later my grandmother, stored jars of canned vegetables. This cellar kept the food at an even temperature year-round. Dug eight feet deep in the red clay, this cellar was accessed by lifting a heavy wooden door below the dining room window and walking down several large stones placed strategically in the red clay as it slants down the hill under the home.

The foundation of the entire house sits on rocks gathered from the large creek below the house and from the nearby fields. Because this foundation was never sealed, groundhogs and even an occasional fox have made their homes underneath the house. Though wood clapboards later covered the log structure and additions were built on either side of the original cabin, the logs were exposed in the attic and in this cellar. The largest and strongest logs were on the bottom row just above the root cellar; in the attic, the logs were smaller. Wooden pegs and mud mortar kept the logs securely in place through the generations. The logs were notched to fit into each other and secured with wooden pegs instead of nails. Concrete mixed with mud from the creek down the hill provided the chinking.

I cannot visualize how one had entered this house when it was first built, because now additions stretch on either side of the log structure and a screened porch has three doors into the house. On a very warm summer evening, all these doors and the windows were opened to allow breezes to flow through the entire house. The porch was furnished with heavy wooden chairs, a wooden bench, and heavy rocking chairs, all painted dark green. My grandmother used to read book after book to my brother and to me as we sat with her out there. It was a very peaceful and happy place 'way off the road and so very close to the woods.

Nowadays, one door from the porch leads into the original log structure—the front became the dining room. If you step up and pass through a very small doorway—less than six feet high—and make an immediate left, you proceed up very narrow, very steep steps to the attic. I imagine that in the earliest years, this could have served as a bedroom. Many interesting antiques were stored there, as I discovered when I explored the attic as a child.

Exiting the dining room on the right, we entered the living room, which has two windows. I'm sure a fireplace was positioned between them in the original log structure, but in my childhood, a large oil circulating heater sat on what would have been the flat concrete hearth; the electric fans inside the circulator did a good job of moving the heated air around the large room, whose walls are now covered in knotty pine paneling. During my childhood, this room was where we watched television and used the telephone.

On the wall behind the oil circulator, a large Regulator clock tick-tocked, the type that was wound with a key. This gift to my grandfather came with a story. In the latter 1920's, just after J. C. Medlin married Virginia Gorrell, he was working in the city and accumulated a bit of money in the bank, which he lent to friends who promised to pay him back. The Stock Market crashed around this time, and the Depression began. No one could repay J.C. Medlin, but a hotel was so grateful to my future grandfather for the work he had done for them that they gave him the hotel clock. Through the years, though the motor no longer worked, the clock was still beautiful; it was sold in 2011 at the Jobe estate sale.

The flooring on the main floor of the Gorrell/Medlin house is truly beautiful. In my estimation, the most valuable things about this home are the logs in the original section and these red oak floors. Mr. J.C. Medlin laid these red oak planks himself in the 1940's, but they still look new.

The door to the right of the living room leads to the parlor, which was closed off in the winter. Here my grandmother used to entertain the women in her church circle. In the summer, I sometimes joined these women during their meetings because my mother and Granny Medlin wanted me to learn "social graces". The parlor was furnished with the old upright piano and overstuffed horsehair chairs ornamented with crocheted and tatted doilies on the backs and the arms. Doilies also covered the tables. This room is also accessed from that screened-in front porch. Its little stove may have used coal.

One more room can be found to the right of this parlor; it was used as a guest bedroom when my brother and I were little. I believe this was my Mama's bedroom when she was a girl, but it was turned into a den at some point after Mama moved out. I found photos in my family album of a casket lying in this room under the end window. Here the body of my mother's grandmother, Mrs. Mary Burnsides Gorrell, laid in state for several days. People used to have the "viewing" of their dead loved ones in their own homes before funeral parlors appeared in communities.

The parlor and guest room have mantles back-to-back, on opposite sides of the wall, which makes me think that once there were two small fireplaces. On top of the mantle in the end room, Granny always displayed a Chinese vase; I have it now in my town house. As my mother's best friend, Thelma Anderson Greeson (still going strong in

2017, I'm delighted to say!) told me, when the girls would get together and play, my Granny Medlin would come to this doorway to say, "Y'all play and have fun, but mind that you don't break that vase. It's the most valuable thing in this house!" An antique clock was displayed on the other mantle; Granny wound it with a key. I remember it made the loveliest sound when it bonged the hour. Doors from that bedroom as well as the parlor open onto the screened front porch.

On the opposite side of the dining room is another "new" wing. From the dining room, walk through that door, stepping carefully down because the level is three or four inches lower than the other part of the house, and you enter the "new" kitchen. I have no idea where the Gorrells used to cook and eat before my mother was born, but this kitchen/ eating room is now the main entrance to the house.

A wood cook stove stood on the front outside wall beside a little window. Granny worked with few built-in cabinets, but near the wood stove (replaced by electric around 1961) was a one-piece unit that was on tiny wheels. Some call it a Hoosier. It had a large flour storage canister with sifter built under it, drawers for storage, a bread box, and a roll-down door to hide items. It was well-used.

We always ate and laughed and talked at the little table, which was surrounded by four chairs. Around the corner near a small oil circulator heater, Granny kept her butter churn, butter mold, and "pie safe" storage cabinet. All of these have found a home in my town house, along with the Singer treadle sewing machine from her living room.

Just to the left of the pie safe, a little door opened into a room just large enough for a double bed. No other furniture fit here. This is where my grandparents slept, in a room with three doors: one that entered the kitchen, one that passed the oil circulator and pie safe on its way to the bathroom, and one beside the head of the bed, which opened into the living room.

One additional door in the kitchen stayed shut almost all the time. My grandmother called this the "milk room," and it gave me the shivers. It was basically a storage room where she kept Mason jars. It held an ancient chest freezer with two doors on top—that's what scared me. It was big and noisy (it quit running when I was young), and sometimes mice ran out from hiding places underneath. Granny Medlin's upright General Electric washing machine (with the reels on top to squeeze water out of clothes after rinsing) was also in this room, whose best feature was the view of the fields from the windows. The very best view in the entire house, however, was from the windows over the kitchen sink, which surveyed the garden, the pond, the barns, the corncrib/shed and the pastures and woods off in the distance.

The very last room in this home was literally an add-on. In 1961, when my Grand Daddy Medlin was ailing, he decided the outhouse, located thirty yards down the driveway, needed to be augmented, even though they had a "chamber pot" for night use. Grand Daddy reluctantly decided that they needed a little indoor bathroom, with a toilet, sink, and shower. This was quite simple, but it was a luxury.

The Family

John David Gorrell and Mary Burnsides Gorrell had five girls, no boys. One of these was Virginia ("Jenny") Gorrell, who taught school and then worked in an insurance office. She was the only daughter who remained on the family farm, although one sister, Mamie, moved back after a divorce to a small house within walking distance of the old home place. The ninety-some acres of Gorrell land became eighty acres of

Medlin property in 1929, when Virginia Gorrell married a widower named John Columbus Medlin, who was originally from South Carolina. They had one child, Martha Ann Medlin; my future mother would marry Garland Jobe on December 22, 1951.

My grandfather, John Columbus Medlin, was tall and thin. I was only eight years old when he died, but I'll do my best to describe him. Grand Daddy probably stood two or three inches above six feet. I have a photograph of him standing beside some of his best corn, which was taller than he was. He was quite thin, perhaps 160 or 170 pounds. He was a quiet man, not one for long conversations. Instead, he spoke to others through deeds of kindness. Until the end of his life in 1962, Grand Daddy drove a black Ford pickup truck built around 1950. Since he was so thin, Mr. J.C. Medlin wore suspenders to keep his pants up. He was most often seen wearing an old grey fedora hat; I can't even tell you what color his hair really was Mr. Medlin was known for having a dry sense of humor, yet I just can't remember seeing him smiling. He expressed his opinions of his two precious grandchildren to my parents with a smile in his voice, not around his mouth.

Once I heard him say, "That Jackie could be a writer or a storyteller because she goes on and on and remembers lots of details. Or, possibly, she should be a lawyer because she loves to talk so much. She could argue with anyone, even the Devil himself!"

My grandmother, Virginia Gorrell Medlin, was a bit taller and heavier than an average woman for that time. She probably stood five feet, eight inches tall. Everyone loved her for her wit, her smile, her sense of humor, and how much she cared about her family, her church, her community, and her neighbors. She could carry on a conversation with just about everyone. Miss Jenny, as the neighbors called her, had attended a Normal School and taught for at least ten years before her marriage. She had a life-long thirst for knowledge and did well in school. It was obvious that she had been a teacher, because she often encouraged my brother and me to get a good education, and she was very patient when we did our homework at her house. When I didn't understand something about math, Granny Medlin often had a fun way of helping me remember.

As I had mentioned earlier, Granny had red hair. Unlike me, however, Jenny Medlin's hair had been a shade of brassy red on the orange side. Granny cried when she first saw me as a newborn, because the summer sun made my hair look like it was on fire. "It's all my fault!" she wept. She was actually more pleased each year with my hair, because it became a deep shade of red, nearly auburn. Though she never liked her own hair when she was young, my Granny Medlin had a very special hair color when I knew her: somewhere between a strawberry-blonde and a light yellow. Also, I was fascinated by what she could do with her long hair. Usually, Granny braided her hair and wore it in a bun on the back of her head. At night, she removed the hairpins and brushed it out. I loved watching her braid her hair without even having to look. Her eyes were hazel in color, and she always wore glasses. (Grand Daddy Medlin never wore glasses.)

Although my grandfather didn't often attend church on Sunday mornings, Granny was always there. She was definitely "Old-School Southern Lady." She dressed properly to go to church, with heels and stockings, a dress, and a hat to complement it or match the dress perfectly; the ensemble was complete when she pulled on her white or black gloves.

She didn't like seeing women wearing pants at business or to church—and Granny was never shy about telling someone her opinion about that, or anything else. However, she drove all around the city of Greensboro by herself, shopping, going to the Court House or bank on business. She sold fresh vegetables, eggs, and home-churned butter to a man who ran a market on the southeast side of Greensboro.

As I said, John C. Medlin spoke through kindness and hard work. When my mother was attending college at "W.C.," he and his wife discussed downsizing from the large farm. They bought a small lot on what is now Presbyterian Road, on the corner of the Gaither Welker farm (in the concluding chapter of my book, this will be the Foust Farm). Grand Daddy Medlin was a skilled craftsman; he built a simple two-bedroom, one bath, two-story white frame house with a full upstairs that could be turned into living areas in the future. He finished this sometime in 1951, though for some reason, he and Virginia Gorrell Medlin had not packed anything for their move. Around Thanksgiving of 1951, Garland Jobe came to them, asking permission to marry Martha Ann. They gave the young people their blessing, and then that night, J.C. and Virginia Medlin had another conversation. He and Granny Medlin invited Garland over for supper soon afterwards and suggested, "Why don't Jenny and I just stay here on the farm and you two kids buy the white house I just built?"

The arrangement worked beautifully. The Jobes lived there from the time they returned from their honeymoon until they decided to build a three-bedroom, two-bathroom home in the early 1960's on the southeast corner of the Medlin farm "for peace and quiet and privacy." It offered them a big basement workshop, garden, and a lot of room for the "young 'uns" to play. Ironically, just before the brick home was completed, Mom and Dad sold our little white house on Presbyterian Road and within the month, John Medlin died.

On the southeast corner of the farm, our new home with more elbow room was placed near a lovely meadow that was a short walk from this brick house. The smaller of two creeks ran through it. On the other side of the stream, where the meadow ended, a very steep bank led up to a large pasture. Dad made terraces on this hill to keep it from washing away.

Every Christmas Eve after Grand Daddy passed away, we picked Granny Medlin up at her home with her overnight bag, and she spent the night at our home. After sharing a happy Christmas morning with us (she loved watching all of us open presents and laugh and talk), we had a nice breakfast together.

Granny did pretty well living alone for ten years after her husband died, but a broken hip led to complications, and she died two weeks before my high school graduation in May, 1972. I owe my love for expressing myself to my grandmother; she had always encouraged me when I wrote little poems or long letters or "news stories" about family events. She would be proud that I have continued writing.

Family Memories

Even though electricity was introduced to most of the rural southeast Guilford County by the beginning of World War II, this was not the case on the Medlin farm. It was located so far off the road that they were last family in that area to have a pole erected and wires strung so they could enjoy the luxury of electric lights. The year was 1948, the same year that my mother graduated from Alamance High School. Up until that time, the Medlins didn't consider living without electricity a problem or a challenge. It was their way of life.

Electricity provided lights, but it wasn't until 1961 that my grandmother relinquished her wood-burning stove. I often wondered how she could create such delicious food on a stove that burned wood. How did she control the heat? She loved this stove, but she finally allowed my Dad to haul the wood stove out and install an electric stove in its place. Twenty years later, my Dad regretted his decision to junk the wood stove; by that time they were valuable antique commodities. Plus, a wood-burning stove was reliable when electricity was out.

Like all outbuildings on the farm, the tobacco barns were built of logs and topped with metal roofs. According to my mother, during her childhood, the farm relied upon two huge, gentle, intelligent work horses to pull the tobacco skids for people working in the fields. When the skid was full of tobacco leaves, the worker would speak to the horse named Toby, commanding Toby and his partner to pull the skid up to the tobacco drying barns---and they would do so. Then, when the skid was once again empty, the tobacco barn workers would tell the horses to return to the field for another load. They would do this several times in a day, with water breaks and oats in between trips.

I enjoyed watching Granny churn butter by hand and press it into the wooden mold. She let me churn sometimes, a chore I enjoyed because I loved the smell of fresh butter. I still have that crockery butter churn and wooden butter press. At one time, butter, milk, and cream would be stored in the spring house near the barn. I don't remember it, but Mama told me that the cold water bubbling out of the ground kept the food fresh year-round. That spring was converted into a pond when I was a little girl; I remember the day they stocked the pond with tiny bass and sun fish.

My Granny Medlin had a treadle Singer sewing machine. I loved watching her sew. Sometimes she let me kneel down and push the treadle mechanism up and down with my hands as she sewed. I still cherish this machine (either a 127-3 or a 128-3). It was also the one on which my mother learned to sew. Mama became an excellent seamstress, making most of my clothes until I was married. She even made my wedding dress, hand-sewing each bead that adorned the dress and the veil.

My grandmother was one of the few women I know who could tat. How I wish that I had paid attention and learned that lost art from a special woman who was so talented. My mother could crochet, do candlewicking, and make quilt squares, but not tat.

Education was very important in our family, and Granny's love of learning was passed down to my mother. Martha Ann graduated from The Woman's College of The University of North Carolina in 1952. (The same school will be mentioned in my book as The North Carolina State Normal and Industrial College.) On December 22, 1951, she married Garland Jobe, a graduate of North Carolina State College of Agriculture and Engineering. My brother, Robert Jobe (Bob), graduated from the same school a quarter-century later, after the school had been renamed North Carolina State University. (In this book it goes by the name North Carolina State College.) I graduated from the University of North Carolina at Chapel Hill. Founded in 1789, it is the first state-supported university in the United States. These three universities were all part of the original University of North Carolina system.

After Granny Medlin died in May 1972, my father hired a professional survey crew to survey the entire farm, mark every corner with large iron posts, and make an official map (plat), which is in the Guilford County Records Department in Greensboro. Old survey maps are fascinating. To mark property borders back in the 1700's, corners of property were noted as "Ten chains west of the large rocks" or "The chestnut oak that boundaries the Gladson property" or "Where the stream turns suddenly south" or "Iron fence post." Many things can happen over two hundred years, my family learned when the land was officially surveyed. Even in my lifetime, the creeks' channels have changed slightly, especially the large stream.

New sandbars have formed, and those I played on have disappeared. The large creek had huge rocks in it when I married in 1984; I could hop from one rock to another without making a splash. This has changed so much in thirty-two years that I can no longer find an easy way to cross. My nephew, who now lives in the home my parents built on the southeast corner of the farm in 1963, said "Forget that!" and bought a powerful four-wheel-drive Polarias ATV to take him from the brick house across the small creek, up the hill, through the woods to the large stream, over that rocky crossing and up a hill behind the barn and onwards, either to the old farmhouse or to the fields.

Around 1961, my mother and father bought ten hilltop acres of land from her parents on the southeast corner of the big farm, quiet, secluded, and private. At that time, Alamance Road was very narrow and had an extremely sharp curve beside the cemetery of Alamance Presbyterian Church. The entrance to the property was on the southeast edge of the church property, at least a third of a mile from where the property lay. There was already a dirt driveway continuing on past the church, down a hill, and then up a steeper hill past a few parcels of land of pine and other trees, weeds and thickets; this land was not buildable because the acreage wouldn't pass the perk test for septic tanks. Past that point, the land was the Gorrell/Medlin farm.

I was eight at the time our new house was completed. My family moved in on New Year's Eve, 1962. Around 1964, the North Carolina Roads Department made the wise decision to widen Alamance Road, taking out the dangerous curve. However, instead of the gentle incline up the hill that had originally led from the church to the Jobe property, our driveway now was up a very steep hill.

The house is completely hidden from the road. That hill is so shaded by trees that ice and snow take forever to melt, and the driveway offers challenges in these conditions. There were a few times during heavy snows when we walked the half-mile trek to church. (Services were only cancelled once during my lifetime.) The walk was actually quite nice when we wore boots and warm clothes; instead of the steep driveway, we used the gentler hill through the grass.

I cannot say what the farm looked like in the 1700's, but many of the things built in the 1800's are still on the farm. First of all, there used to be only one road leading to this farm from Alamance Church Road, and it is probably more than a quarter-mile long. Dad used his tractor to spread tons of gravel trucked in from the nearby rock quarry, so this new surface wouldn't wash away. Many types of fences have been built on the farm over the years, to corral cows, horses, mules, and pigs. As time passed, more and more of the land was used for grazing cattle and for fields of hay, so more fencing was necessary. Cows require different fencing than horses. The last horse disappeared from the farm when my mother was in high school, so more barbed-wire fences were required to keep the cows inside the pastures—they love to wander out to where the grass is greener on the other side.

The fences kept the cows inside our property, out of my grandmother's garden, and out of our garden. Daddy designed the fencing so the farm had four or five areas that could be shut off by closing gates. Therefore, he could rotate his small herd of cattle (never more than twenty-five) from one location on the farm to another, allowing grass to grow back after it had been foraged. Cows need water, so each section either includes a creek or the pond. When my grandparents built the pond using the spring as source of the water, I enjoyed watching the construction, especially when it was finished and stocked with baby fish.

Although my father was a gifted mechanical engineer and worked for Bell Labs many years, he loved nothing better than working on the farm, growing things and preserving land that had been in his wife's family for a century. He reversed much of the damage from erosion caused by folks raising tobacco and cotton on the same soil for years; he made terraces and planted rye, oats, clover, and other crops that would restore the land to a better condition. Dad was an incredible mechanic, too, repairing his own cars (until computers became standard in the cars of the 1980s) and his farm equipment. He would often machine or weld his own parts---and on a farm, something always needs repairing.

The Antique Gasoline Engine Bug bit Garland Jobe, in 1970. My father brought home a very old, box-like cast-iron contraption with the name **Fairbanks-Morse** and two wheels (also cast-iron) on either side. I had no idea what this machine was, and it delighted him to explain how this engine worked and what it had been used for—almost as much as it delighted him to restore it to running condition. My father's new hobby gave him lots of opportunities to work with machinery in his basement. He found satisfaction in taking something that was broken, rusted, and missing important parts, and then restoring it until it was running again.

I learned a lot about the history of farming and the way it used to be done through trips with Mama and Dad to countless antique farm equipment shows in the 1970's and 1980's. At the Southeast Old Thresher's Reunion in Denton, North Carolina, I watched farmers thresh wheat using steam engine power, horse power, and tractor power. I watched avidly as old tractors drove through a wheat field with reaper-binder machines behind them. Those machines cut the wheat with rolling sickle blades and then tied the stalks in little bundles. I studied steam shovels, hit-and-miss gasoline engines that could do many different tasks, stationary steam engines sawing logs, antique bulldozers; and generations of tractors, beginning with old steel-wheel tractors and ending with those huge tractors made today with power steering and air-conditioned cabs that do the work of numerous farm hands on enormous farms.

From 1970 until my mother's death in 2006, my parents had many happy times in their motor home, traveling to farm shows and fairs where they could display their antique gasoline engines. They traveled all over North Carolina, as far south as Zolfo Springs and Avon Park, Florida, and as far north as Portland, Indiana, home to one of the largest antique farm equipment shows in the United States.

My dear mother died in July of 2006, and my father died in March 2009. His will stated that my brother and I were to share this land. Bob and I decided to split the old farm evenly. I had no desire to repair and deal with old outbuildings, so my brother and I came to a peaceful agreement. Bob got the old farm house, the barn, and the outbuildings. I inherited the back part of the property that not many people have seen, with woods and pastures. Since we both loved the pond, there is an "invisible line" drawn on the survey map, right through the pond.

Old mills have always held a special fascination for me. So many roads in my own community outside Greensboro even today contain the word "mill" in their name, a mute testimony to the number of mills that once flourished in our region. We have Woody Mill, Young's Mill, Brookhaven Mill, Company Mill, Millpoint, and Millstream. The grist mill here outside Greensboro at Guilford, which natives call the Old Mill, was built in the late eighteenth century. When travelling on the Blue Ridge Parkway in southern Virginia, I always make a point of visiting Mabry Mill, a one-of-a-kind. Mabry Mill is not only a grist mill, it is also a saw mill. Each time I've visited, I've watched the demonstrations closely, and I always learn something new. The water-powered mills are very old technology, yet to my amazement, they continue to do their work very well.

I am a life-long member of Alamance Presbyterian Church in Greensboro. Alamance is the second-oldest Presbyterian Church in Guilford County. (Buffalo, founded in 1756, is the oldest). Mrs. Edna Smith Jobe (wife of Lee Jobe, was my Dad's third cousin) wrote *A History of Alamance Presbyterian Church 1762-2000 Her People and Their Stories,* which relates the story of a settler named William Cusach who donated land for a church in 1759, on a beautiful knoll beside a small stream. A small group of Scotch-Irish families began worshipping on the spot in the outdoors and the congregation became known as Alamance Church, most likely named for the nearby Alamance Creek. In 1762, men came with axes to clear the land to build a log church building. Andrew Finley, one of the worship leaders in this group, asked the band of men to kneel and pray before the axe was wielded for the first stroke. He pleaded with the Lord God that, on that hill where they knelt, a house of worship would be built *where God's Word would be preached so long as the world should stand.*

This first church building, made of logs, was built in 1762, and lasted until about 1800. When it was torn down, a larger building took its place on exactly the same spot. The story is told that the Alamance congregation worshipped outside under the trees during the entire time of construction, and not once were they rained upon. On the first Sunday they moved worship into the brand-new frame building lovingly called The Old Yellow Church, it poured!

This yellow church was three stories tall, with two rows of large windows that allowed daylight to illuminate even the balcony areas, which ringed the sanctuary on three sides. This magnificent building could hold nearly one thousand people, and sometimes it was filled. The main floor had five sections of seating; the east corner was reserved for African-Americans, who often came with the landowners to worship. A solid black walnut pulpit was built by a parishioner; beautifully carved, it stood ten feet tall, high enough for the minister to address people up in the balconies easily. The minister had to climb a lovely stairway with a baluster to get there.

Though this building was in good shape, in 1844, it was torn down and another church was erected across the street, closer to the creek. This was poorly constructed of bad materials and didn't last long. The next church building was constructed back on the beloved knoll again, and this fourth building lasted until my parents were married there in 1951. Soon after that, the present Alamance Presbyterian Church building was erected, and it has been our house of worship since 1953. There have been several renovations over the years: a new Sunday school building in the 1950's, the children's education building in 1966, and a connector joining this with the original Sunday school building. Housing a new kitchen, classrooms, offices, and an elevator, the connector was completed in 2006.

The oldest church in Guilford County is Friedens Lutheran Church in Gibsonville, founded in 1741. The other very old congregations in Piedmont North Carolina are the Quaker (Society of Friends) churches built during the 1750's, and the Moravian churches in Winston-Salem. (Bethabara was founded in 1753.)

Walking through the cemeteries of these churches is like walking through a page in a history book. One of my ancestors, Ralph Gorrell, Jr., was a private in the Revolutionary War. In 1808, Ralph Jr. sold forty-two acres of land for $98; this land became Greensboro, North Carolina. There is a monument remembering him in a small cemetery at the Historical Museum in downtown Greensboro; he is buried in the Alamance Church Cemetery beside his "Consort" (wife).

His grandson, also named Ralph Gorrell, was a lawyer and a businessman known for his honesty, devotion to principle, and his reliability. He was a devoted husband to Mary Jennings Chisholm. They had ten children; unfortunately, seven of them died. I didn't realize until researching family history that one member of this branch of the Gorrell family served in the Civil War. Captain Henry Clay Gorrell, one of Ralph and Mary's sons, was killed leading his troops into battle. The only child who lived to marry and bear children was one of the daughters, Anne Eliza Gorrell, who married Joseph Fariss in 1869.

I am convinced that a Mr. John T. Gorrell and his wife, Virginia Jane Andrews Gorrell, were the settlers who built the original log home on the Gorrell farm. At that time it consisted of eighty acres near Alamance Presbyterian Church. Their son, John David Gorrell, married Mary Florence Burnsides on February 24, 1887. They had five girls, one of them Virginia Gorrell, who married John C. Medlin on August 10, 1929. Their daughter, Martha Ann, was born on March 5, 1931. Garland

and Martha Ann Medlin Jobe had two children: Robert Allen Jobe, Sr., born October 12, 1952, and Jackie Carol Jobe (me!), born July 5, 1954. I married Marion Delbert Haines, Jr. on April 28, 1984, and our son Benjamin was born in 1990. My brother Bob married Marlene Sosnoski on December 2, 1988; their son, Robert A. Jobe, Jr., was also born in 1990.

My father was in charge of the Alamance Church Cemetery map from the time he carefully drew this map in 1958 until he died in 2009. He showed me on this blueprint-size map, and later in the cemetery itself, a section with no marker stones. An historical marker indicates that Native Americans were buried in this part of the cemetery. Garland Jobe drew a circle on the map indicating that future generations should keep the spot open and untouched, noting, "Do not bury anyone in here or disturb. There are bodies already there." He was also convinced that several slaves were buried in the cemetery. This section of Alamance Church Cemetery is considered sacred, though the names of the dead are unknown.

The Novel Begins

What gave me the idea for this book? The idea took root as early as 1984, when I married a wonderful man named Marion Haines. He served in the U.S. Air Force at Patrick Air Force Base in Cocoa Beach, Florida for much of his active duty; we lived forty miles away on the mainland. When he retired in 1989, he landed a job with Brevard County, Florida, as a networking specialist for the county's computer system. When our family arrived in Greensboro for Dad's eightieth birthday, in August of 2008, Marion and I drove to the old family farm, which Dad owned. We decided to build a retirement house there, near the pond. His plan was to retire sometime in 2011. Sadly, one month after our happy visit with Dad, Marion was diagnosed with advanced pancreatic cancer. My husband died October 31, 2008, at the age of fifty-nine.

Marion's death devastated me. I did not know what God wanted me to do next. I was only fifty-four. I dearly love my friends and our church family in Florida, but North Carolina was home. My first decision was to downsize. I put our family-size home in Florida on the market in 2009, and bought a small apartment in a complex beside our church. My father died suddenly as all this was going on.

When I visited Greensboro the summer of 2009, I stayed in the dark-and-quiet Jobe family home, empty for the first time since New Year's Day 1963. This home and the farm needed to stay in our family, but I discovered I was not comfortable living in such an isolated place by myself. My brother, the executor of our parents' estate, hired the same surveying company our parents had used when Granny Medlin had died in 1972, and we carefully divided the farm. I found a place of my own nearby, and Bob bought my share of our parents' home. I'm pleased to say that his son lives in the 1963 Jobe home today, so our farm has remained in the family into the fifth and sixth generations. The old farmhouse on the other side of the property lies empty, left to its memories.

Three years after I lost my husband, my brother died at age fifty-nine, and I realized that I was the only family member who remains to tell the story of our family history.

A new community of single-family homes and town homes was built only a mile-and-a-half from where my family had lived "up on the hill." I looked at two homes during my search; across from the first sat thick hedges at the edge of a sharp drop-off down to the woods. I knew a large stream meandered through the land back there because a bridge on this road crosses this creek and my school bus crossed that bridge on the way to my high school. The homeowner said, "After a heavy rain, you can hear water going over the dam."

"WHAT dam?" I asked. I had lived in this area all my life and never knew there was a dam here. Shortly after considering this home, I found another on the same street. I am certain that God directed me to this place, because the builder was moving on to other projects, and this was the very last new home he completed. It became my permanent residence in July of 2010, although I still own the small apartment in Florida that serves as my winter residence.

Back to the dam. Asking around at church, I was amazed to discover that one of our church members who was in her eighties had grown up on this very land. Her father was a farmer; later the farm was owned by other relatives, also named Smith, who owned the tract when I was growing up. They farmed it until 2000, when D.R. Horton started developing the property for a planned community. Two outlets lead onto a major thoroughfare, and in the rear, the neighborhood joins Forest Oaks North.

Soon after moving in. I took my camera, wiggled my way through those hedges, and carefully descended the hill, then ventured into the woods. A short walk took me to the rock dam. Fascinated, I took photographs and thought about the people who had hoisted those large granite rocks on top of each other so long ago. The mortar they mixed by hand and applied must have been terrific, because the dam remains in great condition except for the top, where vandalism has occurred.

My friend's son Bill told me that when he was young and visiting the farm, he'd put on boots and walk down from the dam and around a bend in the creek, to explore the foundations of the old saw mill.

I was amazed once again. I had lived in this community most of my life, but never knew that a saw mill once operated on this creek. I wasn't surprised that the old building had rotted away years before I searched for it, but I didn't discover the foundations of the old mill *until…*

The Department of Transportation decided that the bridge needed to be replaced in 2014. The work began that summer while I was in Greensboro. Because the road was shut down, there was no traffic at the bridge. Many times I walked to the end of my community and around the corner to check on the progress of the removal of the old bridge and the work to create a new larger, safer bridge. I pulled back a few limbs of a sycamore tree and peered down into the shadows of thick woods. There, about ten feet below me, I glimpsed the very top of the foundation of what used to be a saw mill. When I explored further, I discovered that the actual base of this foundation was located another eight feet down beside the creek, which meanders peacefully as it flows under the bridge. That is as close as I could get to the foundation of the mill from where I stood. Another two steps and I may have caught my feet in small tree roots and plunged more than fifteen feet down a steep bank, landing on granite rock.

The granite foundation was hauntingly beautiful, and started me thinking about the people who had once lived here and built this dam and the mill. Also I thought about those people who, for many years, came here to get logs cut or to have them turned into lumber. What was the owner's name? I wondered. I found the answer in the Greensboro Public

Library, by looking on an 1897 map of Southeast Guilford County. The mill was known as Hanners' Mill. But, who was the man who ran the mill?

As I was proofreading my book, I decided I needed information about the first Big Meeting services held at Alamance Presbyterian Church. I flipped through Mrs. Jobe's *A History of Alamance Church 1762-2000*, but I didn't find the answer to my question until Lynn May, our church's administrative secretary, helped me. I almost dropped the book later that day in absolute surprise when I read these two sentences: *Lottie Watkins said she remembers when the first high school was built. Her father, Henry Lee Hanner, sawed lumber and hauled it to the school to use in the new building.* I strongly believe that Mr. Henry Lee Hanner was the third generation of sawyers at Hanners' Mill. I went through my work and gave the grandfather the name Lee, to make the story more authentic.

I learned a lot about the City of Greensboro at the turn of the twentieth century during my research in the Greensboro Public Library. I read about the famous and beloved educator Dr. Charles McIver, who rode on a campaign train from Raleigh to Greensboro with William Jennings Bryan in 1906, when Bryan was preparing to run for the Democratic candidacy for president of the United States. The stop in Greensboro turned into a very somber event, however, because Dr. McIver had suffered a massive stroke on the train and died.

Other prominent local names were discovered in the library, and I was happy to mention them in my story; among them are Lunsford Richardson and William Henry "O Henry" Porter. Greensboro is proud to have launched the product Vicks Vapor Rub. (Now the company is owned by Proctor and Gamble.) Greensboro also once boasted the world's largest manufacturing plant for denim: Cone Mills, founded by Herman, Moses, and Ceasar Cone. And what high school student could forget O Henry's masterpiece, *The Gift of the Magi*? I lingered over photographs of downtown Greensboro in 1913, and I tried to mention some of the buildings present that year when I began writing.

I was startled to discover that the railroad tracks once ran down Elm Street. I knew that South Elm Street was Main Street and that trolley cars ran on Elm and Market, but to see photographs of the steam-powered train with familiar store buildings in the background amazed me. The former passenger terminal still stands on South Elm, where train tracks come together and on other side of street and near what is now Natty Greene's Pub and Brewing Company. I recognized its dark red brick and the turrets from the old photo in the library book. I love the sanctuary of the West Market Street United Methodist Church, built in 1892. For those local readers who wonder why I didn't mention the Kress Building or the Jefferson Standard Life Insurance Building, I learned they were both either on the drawing board or under construction during 1913.

Lastly, I tried to honor Native Americans in my story by mentioning their importance in this part of North Carolina. I have stood beside Beaver Creek and pondered these proud people, who lived here so many years before white settlers came and eventually forced them out. Arrowheads and other artifacts are still found in our region, though this is now a rare occurrence. My son found a stone axe head on my parent's farm somewhere around 2006. In 1948, Alamance High School, when my mother belonged to the first graduating class, chose as its mascot the name Indians. That team name remained for generations, until the 1990's, when someone on the school board petitioned for a name change, suggesting that "Indians" could be considered degrading to Native Americans. We had always tried to honor the Native Americans who had lived in this community. Students attending Alamance Elementary School now are called the Alamance Wolves, although some of us older alumni are proud to say that we were Alamance Indians.

Enjoy my book! I take you back to the year 1913, to the land where a fictional rural family lived, loved, laughed, and worked around a little sawmill on a stream I now know as Beaver Creek.

Jackie Jobe Haines

Little Mill on Beaver Creek

CHAPTER ONE: *IT'S A RIGHT CHILLY DAY TO BE SAWIN' LOGS*
Saturday, February 22, 1913

"Sure hate to put this warm coffee mug down," sighed Samuel Gilmer to his father-in-law, Lee Hanner, as he pushed himself back from the table. "I really don't feel like leavin' here and walkin' down that hill to the mill again on a Saturday. I'm sorry we promised Will Granger that lumber today. The *Farmer's Almanac* wrote that this arctic blast wouldn't arrive until next Wednesday. But, four days early, it's already movin' in."

"Well, mid- and late February can be counted on for a surprise or two," Lee reminded him, grunting. The gray-haired gentleman in his late sixties touched a checkered napkin to his handlebar mustache and groaned as he struggled to push himself up to a standing position. "Dadgum arthritis! Usually I get along, but this damp cold is really giving me the misery."

Samuel moved quickly to his side and gently put his hands under Lee's elbows to give him the boost he needed to rise out of the chair. Samuel knew his father-in-law was not one to complain, so when Lee willingly accepted his help, it was a sign that he really was in pain on this chilly February day.

When the two men opened the door, winter slammed them in the face. The wind had gained strength and velocity since they made the fifty-yard trek up the hill just over an hour earlier. Now large flakes of snow were falling, and the temperature had plummeted into the low teens. Samuel walked silently at Lee's side, ready to catch him if Lee stumbled. Lee broke the silence by chiding the younger man, perhaps to call attention away from the sight of him hobbling so awkwardly.

"Samuel, I announced three days ago that the arthritis in my hip was predicting a bad winter storm on the way, and you kept waving that *Farmer's Almanac* at me, arguing that we were going to have nice weather for one more week. Because Will Granger had been by twice already asking when his pine lumber would be ready, you thought we could squeeze in the work before the weather changed. But I've told you before, Sam, when there's a difference of opinion between that magazine and my hip, my hip is right."

"I'll remember to trust your hip from now on, sir," Samuel said soothingly, pulling his wool cap lower on his forehead and bending his head against the wind until his chin practically grazed his chest.

Lee raised his voice so he could be heard above the gusts of wind. "When I was nearly your age, a log I was sliding onto the log carriage slipped, knocking me to the floor of that mill and pinning my right leg underneath."

Samuel grinned. He had heard the story a dozen times over the years.

"It took four other men to pull that blasted log off me. Nothing was broke, but soon after that, arthritis settled in that hip. I feel the cold and damp 'fore it even gits here." Lee saw his son-in-law nod an acknowledgement before he raced forward to open the mill door.

The small wooden door on the side of Hanners' Mill was difficult even for a young and solid thirty-six-year-old man to open on this day.

The wind sounded like a gang of angry demons pounding against it with such force that the younger man threw all his might against the door to keep it open wide enough for Lee to stumble through. When he managed to follow him, the winds shoved Samuel into the dark interior as the door slammed shut with a vicious bang.

The gusts were howling through the cracks in the old mill building, through places where the mud "chinking" had dried and fallen out. Small streams of snowflakes followed in their wake. Samuel quickly made his way to the coal bin, shoveled a pail full of the stuff, and threw it into the little stove, which stood near one of the mill windows. As he pumped the bellows, a fire sprang to life from the banked coals left from the morning's work. Samuel swept his snow-soaked hat off his head to reveal a thick crop of dark curls and stood in front of the stove after closing the lid, long enough to rub his hands vigorously over its warmth and stamp his feet on the floor in a vain attempt to warm them. "Did we ever think about getting a bigger heater? This pipsqueak can't do much against such bitter cold," he said, shivering.

Lee Hanner was still catching his breath, leaning against the wall of the drafty mill before he spoke. When he did, he ignored Samuel's question.

"What do we do now, son? You want to get on the horse and ride over to tell Will to wait another week? What's he gonna say 'bout that? Huh?"

When Samuel shrugged, Lee continued, "You got us into this, and we'll just have to finish the job. A man always keeps his promise. I guess I'm fine now that I'm walking, but if this snow keeps up, you may have to pull me or carry me back up the hill. If we hadn't had to replace the saw blade this morning, we'd have been done with that last log and sittin' by the fire warming our feet by now."

"Well, we've got two hours before Will gets here—if he does, considerin' the storm outside," Samuel said.

"I don't know why you young bucks have to be so stubborn," Lee muttered under his breath.

Samuel patted the older man on the shoulder as he tossed off his jacket, rolled up the sleeves of his flannel shirt, and turned to the saw. "I'm sorry, Lee. I had to make a decision, and I did. It was just the wrong decision this time." He hesitated, then continued the conversation with a grin, "But you're just as stubborn as I am. I told you the first time we dealt with Will Granger that it should be the last time. I didn't want him as a customer ever again. He yelled and swore at me when I gave him his bill. Made me feel like I was holding a gun to his head and robbin' him of his last nickel. I told you that night as soon as he left that I'd never again do business with the son-of-a-gun. And here we are, sawin' logs in a blizzard, just to make our neighbor happy."

Lee shook his head as he limped to the massive log, letting his son-in-law air his grievances.

Samuel continued, "But you said that since Will is one of our neighbors and he's only been here a few years, we should give him another chance—at least until we find out more about him. You were the one who threw *Love thy neighbor* in my face. I know the Lord says to love our neighbors, but in Will Granger's case, that's kind of hard to do."

"Well, what's done is done." Lee wiped his nose with a red handkerchief and prepared to get down to work. "If I know Will, he'll be here to pick up that lumber today, storm or no storm. Let's get going."

The men grunted with exertion as they began to move Granger's last log onto the log carriage with the help of a strong chain hoist. When Lee groaned, Samuel looked over at his father-in-law with concern, "Lee, I've never tried to run that saw and move the log hoist around when my hands have been this cold. We need to be extra careful today. This is when I wish we had a crew of four helping us."

A sudden pounding on the mill's side door startled the men. Lee grabbed at the galluses of his bibbed overalls, "Heavens to Betsy! That can't be Will Granger so soon."

The door squealed open only a few inches, so Samuel guessed that the wind gusts were even stronger now, preventing whoever was outside from opening the door sufficiently. When Samuel put his shoulder to the wooden planks and shoved the door outward, in blew his ten-year-old son, Jake.

"Thanks, Pa! What a storm, huh? How much snow do you think we'll get? Up to the rooftops, you reckon?" Jake Gilmer was taller and stronger than many boys his age, indicating that he'd inherited his father's and grandfather's height. "Wow! It's warm in here now. Feels good." Jake unbuttoned the heavy wool coat that not so long ago had belonged to his father, and then he tossed off the crocheted wool beanie hat that had been a Christmas gift from his older sister.

"Hi, Pa. Hi, Pap-Paw. Mom sent me out. I've already fed the chickens, closed the cows in the barn, fed them, and milked them. I've put the milk in the springhouse and given oats to the horses. She said Will Granger is coming for his lumber, so I wondered if you needed some help."

"Do we ever!" Lee exclaimed. Samuel put a strong hand on his son's shoulder and nodded. Without another word, Lee handed Jake a thick pair of gloves. Together, the two men positioned the log to remove the bark and square it off. When his father nodded, Jake pulled the lever, letting a rush of ice-cold water flow from the dam through the flume to start the waterwheel turning. The three generations of men worked on one side of the log, turned it, and evened out all four sides before starting the vertical saw to make twelve-foot-long boards. Jake and Samuel piled the boards carefully on top of the other lumber waiting for Will Granger in a stack under one of the windows.

When the last board was finished, Lee immediately shoved the lever to stop the saw blade, and Samuel closed the lever to stop the flow of water over the wheel. At that instant, they heard hammering thuds land on the mill's side door. Samuel rolled his eyes at his father-in-law, cleared his throat, and walked to the door. Jake looked at his grandfather quizzically. Lee Hanner put his finger to his lips for silence and motioned for Jake to come stand beside him.

With Samuel's help, the door groaned open. A flurry of wind blew gusts of snow into the mill, along with two men who were covered in snow. They had to stamp their feet and brush the white coating off their woolen pants and outerwear before they could be identified.

The first man had coal-black skin. Thin and nearly as tall as Samuel, he wore a threadbare work jacket, a plaid scarf wrapped tightly around his neck and lower face, gloves, old boots, and a very old greasy-dirty fedora. Following close on his heels was a massive man whose cheeks were bright red from the cold. His heavy coat had been worn through many winters, Jake noticed, and it was missing the top two buttons.

"Solomon," Samuel first greeted Will Granger's sharecropper, ignoring his customer for a moment. "Good to see you again." He held out his gloved hand, but the man only nodded shyly, then stepped back beside the pile of lumber.

Only then did Samuel turned to his neighbor. "Will, this weather's rough, ain't it? Considerin' the storm, we weren't sure whether you'd make the trek here to pick it up this afternoon, but we finished the last of your lumber."

Will snorted, "Yeah the weather's bad. That's why I need the lumber now. Y'all know how old and rundown that farm of mine is. Three years after I moved here, I'm still workin' on repairs. The barn where I keep my livestock and their hay has rotten clapboards all along the bottom, and I need to fix the barn before plantin' season." He looked belligerently at the mill owners. "I told y'all I'd be here, and I kep' my word. I need to commence work on the barn tomorrow, snow or no snow."

Samuel pointed to the stack of twelve-foot-long planks. "Well, then, I can fix you right up. Jake can help the three of us load it up. Did you back your wagon to the loadin' doors?"

Will Granger nodded, running strong grimy hands through his black, unkempt hair. He spat a stream of tobacco juice, missing the spittoon and hitting the floor. "Right outside that carriage door," he grunted.

Jake studied the man curiously. He was sporting at least a three-days' growth of beard, and his large dark eyes were almost obscured by bushy eyebrows that protruded from under the shapeless hat he slapped onto his head. Jake sniffed, guessing that Will had skipped several Saturday night baths in a row. Samuel caught a whiff of strong corn whiskey and turned his head, preferring the warm, rich smell of newly sawn woodchips.

Samuel and Jake slid open the large double doors, which were, fortunately, on the side of the mill away from howling winds and blizzard. Under the roof extension, Will Granger had backed his empty wagon; his two draft horses were stomping their feet and snorting, obviously anxious to return to their barn and dinner.

As Samuel threw on his coat and drew on his gloves, he gave directions. "Will, you and I get on either end of the boards. Sol, you and Jake can work together." The three men and one boy took their positions and carried the hefty pine boards one by one to the long wagon. They slid the bottom layer of boards as far back as they would go, then carefully began stacking the others on top. When the pile reached shoulder height, Jake and Solomon climbed up onto the trailer and finished the stacking as Samuel and Will handed up the final boards. In twenty minutes, all the lumber was positioned and secured with ropes.

When the men returned to the comparative warmth of the mill, Samuel glanced around the floor and discovered the pile of scrap wood remaining after the logs had been squared. He groaned, "Oh, no, I forgot this. Will, I imagine you want the scrap wood from your logs, don't you? We forgot to load that."

His customer grunted and answered with a belligerent tone in his voice, "'Course I do. It belongs to me, don't it? I'm payin' for it, ain't I? I want every inch of what's comin' to me."

Samuel nodded to Solomon and Jake, "Would you two load that scrap onto Mr. Granger's trailer?"

"Sure, Pa. I'm a lot warmer when I'm movin'," Jake said good-naturedly. When he and Sol started stacking armloads of the wood and heading out the door, Samuel made a point of saying loudly, "Thanks, you two," before turning back to Will.

The man opened his coat and reached into the large front pocket of his bibbed overalls to pull out a worn leather pouch. He cleared his throat. "Let's see, what did I owe y'all? Twenty dollars, right?"

Just at that moment, Jake rushed back inside the mill, quickly sliding the large doors shut and latching them. "Solomon said he'd stay with the wagon, Pa, and anchor a few more ropes to secure the load." He turned to Will Granger and added, "Then he'll ready the horses for your drive home."

Samuel ignored his son while he glanced quickly toward Lee, then back to Will. "Will, we agreed on Thursday that the charge would be thirty-five dollars."

Will Granger's face became as dark as a storm cloud. He waved one huge square fist in Samuel Gilmer's face. "Tarnation!" he bellowed. "You know I can't pay that kinda money for a pile of logs! Y'all said twenty dollars, and twenty dollars is all I'm payin'!"

Samuel didn't flinch. Locking eyes with his customer, he said in a calm voice to his son, "Jake, I really appreciate your help this afternoon. I want you to go up to the dam and shut off the water going to the flume. Afterwards, when you walk up our hill, grab some more firewood off the porch for your Ma, so she can keep the stove and fireplace burnin' bright. Make sure our home is warm and that your Mama has enough wood to finish cooking dinner. Then you can stay indoors there and warm yourself."

The boy took a quick glance at his father's face and eyes, nodded silently, and left quickly through the side door. As he was closing it from the outside, Jake cast a quick accusatory glance toward the giant of a man threatening his father. As Jake trudged toward the dam through snow now reaching halfway up his boots, he kicked at a mound of snow, puzzling why their neighbor was so ornery and speculating about how his Pa and grandfather would handle him.

Samuel struggled to maintain his composure as he continued eyeing the man. "Look, Will, we're neighbors, and I certainly want peace between us. This ain't about trying to cheat you, and you know it. It's a matter of honoring a contract. If you aren't able to pay all of it right now, I'm sure we—"

Will struck his fist on a nearby shelf. "I don't reckon the price we agreed on was that high. Since I don't see anything in writin'—"

Lee had been standing silently through the transaction with his hands in his pockets, chewing on a toothpick-size sliver of wood, but seething in anger. He had waited as long as he could, hoping Samuel could handle the situation himself, but now the elderly gentleman took a step toward Will Granger. His voice was calm, but his eyes flashed sparks.

"Now, see here, Will Granger. I've listened to as much as I can take. Nothin' in writin'? Well, it just so happens that I'm wearing the same overalls today that I had on Thursday. Samuel is now the owner and operator of this sawmill, but I still have a business mind. I also have a pretty good memory. I've tried to teach Samuel about the importance of keepin' good ledgers and puttin' things down in writing, but Sam gets so busy with the operation of the mill that he sometimes forgets. Let's just see what might be in my pocket…"

Lee Hanner fished around in the large center pocket of his overalls and pulled out several slips of paper. "You see, Will, I always keep a pencil in here for keepin' track of measurements and doin' calculations. I also write down every transaction that comes through this mill every day that I'm helpin' Samuel." As Lee unfolded the scraps of paper that he had stored in his pocket, he mumbled a word or two before he smiled. He held the paper at arm's length and announced triumphantly, "Ah! Here it is. Will, tell me if this here is your signature on this contract for sawin' your pine logs."

Will snatched the scrap of paper. After reading it, his face grew even redder—with fury and embarrassment, Samuel guessed, nodding slightly in thanks to his father-in-law. "You've been hidin' that, to make me look bad!" the man shouted. He pulled a roll of bills and a handful of coins out of his pouch, slapped the money on the tool bench, then stalked out the door. The wind slammed it shut before he could have the satisfaction of doing the same thing.

"Tarnation!" Samuel exhaled, peering out the snow-lined window to watch Will climb onto his wagon seat, slap the reins, and roar "Go!" to his horses. Samuel watched until the wagon reached the main road, which was by now nearly invisible under the snow. The wagon disappeared slowly as the horses labored up the hill and toward the Granger farm, leaving behind narrow wheel tracks and two sets of hoof prints that were rapidly filled in by drifting snow.

"Lee, we don't get paid enough to put up with that." He sighed, turning from the window at last. "How did you happen to have that paper in your pocket? I don't remember Will signin' anything."

His father-in-law shook his head at Samuel, but grinned proudly. "That's because you were outside helping Will's sharecroppers roll those big logs off the wagon, Samuel. You worked up the estimate while the logs were still on the wagon, writin' down how many total boards we could get from those three logs, and you left the paper on the tool bench just before going outside to help them unload. I explained the bill to Will, and then I asked him to sign the paper if he agreed."

Samuel looked sheepish. Lee paused, then added quietly, "That's just good business practice, son. Especially with people you think might argue with you when the job is done."

"I'll remember from now on," Samuel said.

"But Will actually got a bargain after all, despite all his belly-achin'." It seemed Lee wasn't done with his lessons. He continued, "By the way, Samuel, you were off on your estimate. Will actually got five more boards than you charged him for." Lee started laughing then and slapped his son-in-law on the back. "Let's leave the cleanin' up until Monday. I'm about to freeze in here. This sawdust can wait another two days. Let's get home and hug that wood stove."

After checking to make certain that the coals in the little cast-iron stove were now tiny cinders and safe, Samuel handed Lee Hanner the cane that always stood ready in the saw mill, to give the elderly man more support as he made his way homeward.

Lee Hanner regarded his son-in-law as he gratefully took the cane. "Samuel Gilmer, I want you to know I'm right proud of the miller you turned out to be and the man you've become. When I first took you on as an apprentice years back, I had my doubts. You were pretty arrogant and a bit slow to learn. On top of that, you started keepin' company with my daughter, Anna. I didn't take to that at all, but Helen told me, 'Give that boy a chance. There's a lot of good in him. A woman sees deeper.' I watched as you two fell in love. Not only were we partners in business, but you moved in with us as family. After Helen died—that's two years ago—I've been seein' so many more of your good qualities. 'Course, it's been seventeen years now since y'all married. Anna must be a good influence on you, Sam!"

Samuel Gilmer grinned at his wise father-in-law, "Yes sir, I reckon she is!" He threw his shoulder against the door with all his might and they both dipped their heads as they entered into the wintery blast.

Sam closed and latched the door to the saw mill. Arm in arm, the two men trudged up the hill to the white, two-story country farmhouse Lee's Pa had built sixty years earlier. The sight of the smoke rising from two chimneys and the lantern light that brightened the first-floor windows promised hope and warmth to the tired, chilled men. Lee stumbled several times, but Samuel kept his hand under his father-in-law's arm all through the difficult, slippery climb, until at last they reached the first step of the porch that stretched along the entire rear of the house.

Catching his breath with an effort, Lee Hanner grabbed the baluster and pulled himself up onto the porch steps. Following close behind him in case Lee stumbled, was Samuel. On the porch, Lee exhaled thankfully.

"Now, I have to figure how to get this old boots off."

Samuel gestured to a rough-hewn bench that stood beside the back door. "Here, Lee, sit down. I'll pull your boots off." After some painful groaning, Lee was out of his boots. In his stocking feet, he quickly pulled the latch on the kitchen door and walked into the fragrant room, right up to the wood stove.

Then Samuel pulled off his own boots. His toes were so cold that they ached and his stockings were damp, but he remained on the porch a moment longer, surveying the back yard as if seeing it for the first time. The winds and snow flurries were dying down, making the landscape look almost foreign to him. This world was blanketed in a lush white blanket—like a bridal veil, he told himself, surprised at the thought. The air was hushed, almost reverent.

The saw mill, which had seen strife earlier, reposed dark and quiet down the hill to the right; just the peak and the roof of the mill were visible from this point. The log-and-clapboard barn—which Lee maintained was older than the farmhouse—lay straight down a very gentle incline. Wooden gates, wooden fences, and wire fences radiated out from the barn, all of them lined with white coats. A short distance out from the porch and to the left stood a massive white oak tree, which hosted a swing that was swaying gently, offering a ride to its passengers: six inches of fluffy snowflakes. Just beyond the giant oak and slightly to the left the chicken house roosted on the hillside. Samuel imagined the flock of hens huddled on their nests, their heads buried in their feathery breasts.

For as far as Samuel could see, pastures spread out and stretched from the edge of Beaver Creek (temporarily buried under snow at the foot of the hill behind the barn) to the rolling hills beyond. For a moment, his eyes misted in appreciation of his blessings and the scene of such peace and beauty that belonged to his family.

But then Samuel shivered and remembered his wet, stocking feet and the cold. Picking up two pairs of boots, he opened the door and stepped across the threshold, into the warmth of his home.

Heavenly smells of fresh soup and greens on the wood stove and cornbread in the oven raced to Samuel's nose. Lee Hanner was standing to the side of the stove, rubbing his blue-veined hands together over the warmth. Samuel walked up to his wife, a blue-eyed beauty who had just celebrated her thirty-sixth birthday, wrapped his arms around her from behind, and kissed her behind her ear. She squealed before turning and smiling up into her husband's eyes. Then she patted her auburn hair, which had been gathered up into a "Psyche knot".

42

"Eeeek! You are Eskimo cold, Samuel Gilmer. Especially that nose of yours," she protested, laughing as Samuel teased her by pressing his frozen nose onto her warm cheek. She giggled and her cheeks flushed as she turned her attention to the soup, pouring it into a large tureen.

Meanwhile, Lee Hanner was grabbed from behind by the small, eager little arms of his youngest granddaughter, six-year-old Lillie. "Pap-paw!" Lillie exclaimed excitedly. "I'm so glad you're home now. Are you warming up? Mama made your favorite soup—smoked ham and peas—to warm up your insides. I mixed the cornbread and put the skillet in the oven all by myself. Mama let me."

Samuel tiptoed up behind his youngest daughter, who was chattering away joyfully to her grandfather and her mother, and swooped her into his arms, dancing her around the middle of the kitchen floor, swinging her so quickly that the girl's thick, long red braids almost wrapped around them both. "How's the smallest and most energetic little girl at Tucker Schoolhouse?" he teased. "I imagine you'll be almost as good a cook as your Mama any day now." As he set Lillie down again on the kitchen floor, he grinned at his wife.

Molly, their sixteen-year-old daughter, returned to the kitchen after carrying the greens and the cornbread to the dining room table. Tall, with thick blond hair and deep blue eyes, she always moved with her head held high, mindful of her good posture. Molly smiled at the men who had just come inside. "Hi, Pap-Paw. Hi, Papa. I saw Mr. Granger leaving with a wagon load of boards. He certainly must have been tickled and impressed that you worked in this weather to have his lumber cut on time."

"Daughter-of-mine, do not give me indigestion before we even start eating," groaned Samuel. He carried the large white tureen of soup to the table just as Jake appeared, announcing "I'm hungrier than a bear cub."

When everyone was seated, the family members held hands and said a blessing over the food.

"I have a story to tell you, Papa," young Lillie said as soon as "Amen" had been uttered. "Let me tell you what happened when I went to the chicken house to gather the eggs." Most of the hens were already off their nests, she explained, adding, "But one must have been sleeping soundly because when I started to peek underneath her, the hen squawked so loud it hurt my ears! And then she started flapping her wings as hard as the winds were flapping outside. She slapped me in the face! Then the ruckus upset the other hens, who started flap, flap, flapping their wings and clucking louder than anything you've ever heard. Feathers flew all over the coop. It looked like the time Jake had a pillow fight with Molly. I told that old hen, 'Now see what you started! You got so many feathers flyin' around in here I could make a new pillow!'"

Lee Hanner guffawed and slapped his thigh. "Oh, how could anyone ever have a bad day if they've been around Lillie Gilmer! You're such a joy, sweetheart!"

Laughter and conversation made every family meal time as happy as Anna's cooking was delicious. Sam described how tirelessly Jake had worked at the saw mill. "Like a man twice his age," he said proudly. "We couldn't have finished without Jake's help. He worked as hard as I've seen any grown man work, and he follows directions like a soldier." Jake's cheeks flushed red, and he beamed with pleasure.

After finishing two slices of pie after the meal, Lee Hanner backed his chair from the table and declared, "My thanks to you three beautiful women. Having food that delicious makes working most of the day in the cold almost worthwhile. Well, I'm full, and my whole body is aching tonight. I figure where I need to be right now is in my bed and snuggled under an extra quilt. Good night, everyone."

"I wonder how many people will be able to make it to Alamance Church tomorrow morning," Molly mused out loud as she glanced out the window into the darkness. "I'm supposed to be leading the children's Sunday School lesson."

"Don't worry, Molly," chirped Lillie. "If nobody else comes, you can teach me!"

Molly grinned and returned to the table for her share of pie. When dessert ended, the three children cleared the dishes off the table. Molly washed, Lillie dried, and Jake put the dishes away because Lillie was too short to reach the cabinets.

"It's about time you three followed Pap-paw's example and headed to bed," Anna suggested.

The three children hugged their parents and started for the stairs to the attic, where they slept. Jake grabbed another quilt from the linen closet to put on his bed. Molly pulled a quilt made by their "Mam-maw" Hanner over Lillie and kissed her good night. Then she spread another of her grandmother's quilts on her own bed before undressing and sliding under the mound of covers.

"A fine meal, as always, Anna," Samuel murmured, piling more logs on the fire in the fireplace. He pushed the screen in front of it to prevent any sparks from popping out while Anna slid a few more sticks of wood into the cast-iron cook stove. Both fires sent heat up through their respective flues; each chimney flue went through one of the two bedrooms upstairs on their way up and over the roof, providing a source of some warmth for the attic rooms where the children slept.

"It's been a long, cold day," Samuel said softly, plopping onto the settee in front of the fireplace and patting the seat next to him.

"It has, indeed," Anna said, joining him there. Together, they sat in silence, enjoying the comfort of the softly crackling flames, lost in their own thoughts.

Without warning, Samuel stood and took his wife's hand. Wordlessly, Anna followed her husband into the mud room off the kitchen. Wrapped up in their coats, they slipped their feet into boots and stepped onto the back porch. The snow had stopped and the beams from of a nearly-full moon made the snow glisten and sparkle. The clear sky burst with a full canopy of stars. There were no other lights to dull their majesty. *"The heavens declare the glory of God,"* Anna marveled softly, breaking the silence.

Samuel nodded. Moments later, he added, "I see that Dan has gone 'way back into the corner of his dog house," pointing to the small structure beside the chicken house; it was barely visible across the fresh-laid snow. "That's sure to mean that the weather is going to stay really cold. I'm glad I added more straw for him yesterday."

Anna squeezed her husband's hand. "I'm so sorry that Will made things difficult this afternoon for you and Pa. I don't think he's an evil person." When Samuel didn't answer, she continued. "I think something must have hurt him badly to have made him so angry." Again, Samuel stood, silent, by her side. "And just think how lonely he must be in that little house," Anna said, wrapping her arms around her husband's waist. "I think Will Granger needs love the way seeds need water and soil. I'll bet that's what is missing in his life."

"I'm glad it's not missing in my life," Samuel said, kissing his wife soundly. Afterwards, Anna leaned against her husband as he wrapped his arms around her shoulders and whispered, "Well, I sure know what I need right now, Mrs. Gilmer."

"Oh?" she asked, looking slyly at her husband.

"Yep. I need to get back in this house and warm myself over the stove again. I'm an Eskimo once more," he announced as he leaned down to rub his red nose against Anna's ear.

Her startled squeal awakened Dan. The beagle opened one eye just long enough to see who had interrupted his sleep. Then he yawned, stretched, and burrowed deep into his warm bed of straw before resuming his slumbers.

Little Mill on Beaver Creek

CHAPTER TWO: *RESCUE AND RECONCILIATION*
Monday morning, February 24, 1913

Samuel and Lee were finishing the last sip of their morning coffee as the sun burst above the horizon, shining brightly. The temperature, Samuel remarked, had passed the freezing mark—and was now hovering around thirty-nine degrees.

"The snow will surely start melting," Lee announced, smiling. "Yes, sir! Soon as that high pressure system came through yesterday and the cold damp air went on its way, the misery eased from my hip. I feel like I can make that big hill just fine today and do a good day's work."

To the rural students in Guilford County, North Carolina, this day would bring a treat: no school, since ice still clung to the major roads and measured more than the regulatory six inches. Jake and Lillie were ecstatic at the news, planning all sorts of outdoor adventures.

A sudden knock at the back door startled the two men. They opened the door to find Josiah Forsyth and his ten-year-old son Billy standing on the back porch. Behind them, their mules were hitched to a wagon that had been pulled to a stop under the white oak. "Mornin', Josiah and Billy," Samuel said, extending his hand. "Y'all come on in.

Jake told me you'd appear this mornin', that you need oats and clover hay to tide your cow over until this harsh winter weather ends."

As the new neighbors quickly removed their boots and crossed the threshold, Lee shook Josiah's hand and studied the man who had moved his family into an empty homestead up the hill a quarter-mile west of the mill just after Christmas.

"Mornin'!" Anna Gilmer bustled into the warm kitchen and hurried over to the stove, to offer Josiah a cup of hot coffee before the men returned to the outdoors. But before she could lift the pot, Josiah raised his hand and shook his head politely. "Thanks Ma'am, but my wife had a nice pot of coffee ready when I came in the kitchen after milkin' the cow this mornin'. Thank you kindly for the offer!" He quickly followed Lee and Samuel back out onto the porch. When their boots were laced, the men headed straight to the barn.

"Josiah, why don't you untie the mules from the tree and lead them down the path to the barn with us?" Samuel suggested. "With Jake and Billy helpin' us, we'll have that hay loaded in no time. Mr. Hanner will keep track of the number of bales. I don't want him liftin' anything."

At that moment, a very small girl with long red braids emerged from the nearby chicken house, carrying a large basket her mother had woven. She turned to her father and grandfather with a big grin on her face. "Papa! I found eight eggs this mornin' after I fed the chickens and gave them water!" Her green eyes danced as she turned toward Josiah Forsyth and Billy. "Mornin', Billy. Mornin', Mister. You sure have some nice mules." Lillie patted one of them on the muzzle with her free hand.

Josiah laughed, "Well, thanks, little miss! Samuel, who is this delightful lady with such lovely red hair and freckles on her nose?"

Samuel smiled proudly as he put his hand on his daughter's shoulder. "This is our youngest child, Lillie. She loves feeding the hens, and she's named all of them." He turned back to Lillie, "Thank you, sweetheart. Be careful carrying those eggs up the steps."

Out in the barn, Jake whistled as he fed and milked the cows; he had already given oats to the horses and opened the door so they could go out into the snowy pasture. His last task was to open the barn door, but at that moment Samuel surprised him by pushing the doors open from the outside.

"Didn't mean to scare you, Jake," said Samuel. "Go ahead and let the cows out, and then we'll all load up hay bales for Mr. Forsyth."

Jake nodded to his Pa, said "Howdy" to Mr. Forsyth, and then grinned at Billy. They sat close to each other at Tucker School, and in the short months since the Christmas break, had become good friends.

The hay-loading went quickly. Then Josiah asked, "I know you're going to go clean up in the saw mill. Billy and I have never seen a water-powered saw mill up close. Do you mind if we come along?"

"Sure!" Samuel brushed wisps of hay off his hands. "You can leave the mules and the wagon here." He talked as they all walked the short distance from the barn to the mill. "Hanners' Mill is a half-century old now, built by Lee's grandfather. This man taught me everything I know about sawing lumber. I learn new things from him nearly every day."

They were nearing the large bend of Beaver Creek. To their left was a dam ten feet high. They paused for Samuel to explain, "As you can see, Beaver Creek is not a very deep or fast-moving stream. Sometimes during a dry summer, the water level drops to nearly a trickle, so we need a dam to create a pond until that water is needed. Lee's grandpa came home from the War of Northern Aggression and the first thing he did was dig out the biggest boulders he could find and mortar them together. He did his work so expertly that after six decades, we haven't had a leak.

Samuel pointed to the top of the dam. "That spillway releases excess water when the level behind the dam gets too high. On this side, you see a flume coming off a few feet below the top of the dam." He pointed to a wooden structure that looked like a small bridge with closed-in sides. "A metal door at this end of the flume seals it, keeping the water out. When we use the water wheel, we go to the top of the dam and turn the iron wheel. That starts water flowing through the flume. A damper at the end near the wheel will divert the water out over the little spillway and back into the creek below."

He grinned at his son. "That's where Jake comes in handy. When we're ready for the wheel to start turning, Jake pushes a lever inside the mill, flipping that steel damper at the top and forcing the water over the top of the mill wheel, which then starts to turn."

Josiah nodded. Billy elbowed his friend. When they reached the mill, Samuel easily opened the same door that blizzard-force winds had battered on Saturday afternoon. As the boys followed him into the mill, Jake grinned at his friend. Billy, he knew, loved anything mechanical. "Can you show me how to saw a log, sir?" Billy asked eagerly.

Lee chuckled at the boy's enthusiasm. "Well, we don't have a log ready to saw today, but we can start up the blade and the log carriage and show you how it works. Some other day, come home from school with Jake when the wheel is turnin' and we'll be pleased to show you."

While Lee and Samuel began cleaning the log carriage and the blade, Josiah, Billy, and Jake grabbed a broom and helped clear the mill of the debris left on Saturday. "Jake, why don't you and Billy walk to the dam and turn the valve to start water flowing this way?" Samuel suggested when their work was done.

The boys raced each other up the path, and Jake showed Billy how to turn the big steel handle. Water rushed through the wooden flume and up to the mill building. Billy shouted with excitement. "You've got one fine toy here, Jake."

When the boys returned to the sweet-smelling darkness of the mill and the sound of the water rushing over the wheel, they could feel the floor vibrating, thanks to the gears underneath. Jake's grandfather said, 'Well, we have nothin' better to do today, so why not show our neighbors how this mill works?" He nodded to his son-in-law.

Samuel explained, "The big wheel turns a horizontal gear on the main shaft, turning another gear, which makes the large flywheel turn. Belts and gears move this large vertical saw blade. To move this log carriage, the gear turns—you'll hear a clicking as that pin moves from one notch to the next, gradually moving the log carriage toward this blade, which saws through the log up and down. First thing we have to do is 'square up' the log, removing all the bark and making the edges straight on four sides so we can   width and length."

Samuel pointed to the blade. "The spaces between the teeth allow sawdust to be carried away, so it won't bind the blade or cause it to break. When we do this, we get a big sawdust pile, as you already saw. We'll sharpen the blade after every large order."

Billy's eyes brightened. "Mr. Gilmer, sir, before we go, could I see underneath, where the flywheel and the gears and the belts work?"

Samuel hesitated. "Billy, you certainly can, but not today. The hill drops suddenly around the other side of the crick and the snow hasn't melted. Those rocks are slick, so heading down there today isn't safe.

53

ERRATA, page 55, line 19. Please add, after "can" : …"…begin to saw the lumber. Then, we set the gauge to make all our lumber exactly the same…"

But if you cross over the bridge and come around that side, you'll see something. Mind you, stay on top of the hill. I don't want anyone falling down that embankment. Jake, why don't you boys shut off the water while you're there?"

Billy grinned. "Thank you, sir. The boys ran out the door together.

Josiah turned to Samuel, pulling his leather pouch out of his pocket. "I don't want to forget to pay you for the hay, Samuel. I'll be planting oats and clover come spring, but I sure appreciate this help for now." Josiah paid Samuel and then held his hand out to Lee. "I'm obliged to you for takin' the time with my boy."

Lee shook Josiah's hand. "Pleased to. Y'all be sure to stop in here again."

Josiah and Samuel walked out together and started up the snow-covered hill, following small boot tracks to the bridge. They crossed the bridge and then glimpsed the two boys on the side of the hill that faced the mill wheel. Billy was in front, pointing to something under the mill and asking Jake a question as he crept down the steep bank.

"Billy, you gotta stop! Come on back!" Jake shouted, his heart leaping into his throat. At the same time, Samuel rushed to the hill, ordering, "Billy! Stop right there! There are rocks under that snow. You'll slip!"

His warning came too late. Billy's foot slid out from under him, sending the boy careening downward on his backside. Jake reached out to grab his friend's hand as Billy fell backward, but he missed. As Billy slid down the hill, his arms flailed, desperately trying to find anything to slow his fall. He flipped over to snag a tree root, thinking he would be safe, but the root snapped. Billy rolled once again and screamed as he plunged over the rocky edge.

"Billy!" hollered Jake.

The two young fathers raced full-speed around the bank, gasping when they saw the boy disappear over the edge and down toward sharp granite rocks. Quickly but cautiously, they grasped trees on the edge of the cliff and neared the edge. Peering down, they could just make out the boy's figure, motionless on a rock and dirt outcropping not much wider than his body. A thick root from a huge chestnut oak had prevented Billy from bouncing off this rock and continuing his terrifying plunge,

Samuel whirled and yelled for Jake. "Run to the mill and grab a thick ten-foot rope. Hurry!" Jake's feet slipped on the snowy surface as he raced up the hill toward the wood bridge. When he came down the other side, toward the old mill, he screamed, "Pap-Paw! Get the big rope!"

Lee Hanner had heard the commotion and was already at the side door looking toward the road. He made record time to the brackets on the wall where the assortment of ropes hung, and snatched the thickest rope. By the time Jake was at the door, Lee was ready to hand the rope to him. Jake gasped as he spun around to return to the accident scene. Lee rounded the corner and started up the hill, shouting, "What's happened? How can I help?"

By the time Samuel saw his father-in-law's face, he had formed a plan. "Lee, get four medium ropes and the brown tarp with grommets. Now!" Lee nodded, waved his hand to show he understood, and hobbled as fast as he could back down the hill, with Jake following behind him. By the time Jake got there, Lee had the ropes and the tarp and was heading out the door.

"Jake, what happened?" Lee asked as Jake bent nearly in two, gasping for air. "I know something is serious."

"Billy fell off the side of the far bank and landed on a rock half-way down. He hasn't moved, so it must mean he's hurt bad. Pa or Mr. Forsyth is going down to tie the tarp around Billy to pull him back up." Jake took off like a rabbit chased by a wolf.

Lee Hanner leaned against the side of his mill, bowed his head and prayed out loud, "Gracious Father, hear us. A little boy is hurt bad and needs your help. We know you are with us. Help these men to get to Billy, and help them get Billy safely back up. Please heal all his injuries. In Christ's Holy Name, Amen." Lee suddenly felt weak in his legs and his stomach churned. In all the years of Hanners' Mill, no child had ever been injured.

Back at the scene, the men were arguing about the plans. "It's my mill and I've been down there before. I should go," Samuel insisted.

"He's my boy and I'm smaller than you," Josiah countered. "I'll be easier to lower down the hill. You look like you've got the muscles to make sure I don't follow Billy's path."

They hurried to secure the ropes through both grommets at either end of the tarp. "This'll act like a sling to pull Billy to the top," Samuel explained to his son. Josiah tied the thick rope around his waist and knotted it firmly. He draped the ropes of the tarp around his shoulders, letting the tarp hang down his back. The other end of the thick, strong rope was tied in a secure knot around the trunk of the chestnut oak.

Samuel Gilmer grasped the rope firmly in his hands and planted his feet squarely, careful to stay above the slippery rocks. He began easing Josiah Forsyth slowly and gently over the edge and down to the narrow ledge where Billy lay, neither moving nor responding.

Meanwhile, Lee Hanner hurried to the bridge, hoping to flag down anyone coming by. Another strong man would be needed to help haul the man and boy back up the slippery slope.

Following Josiah's shouted directions, Samuel lowered the man inch by inch Josiah used his feet to maneuver from one slippery rock to the next on his way down, rather than dangling in a free-fall. "Slowly now. I'm moving over to the left now," he said, his voice firm and calm. "Slower. Slower…I'm grabbing the trunk of that tree. Okay. My feet are on the rock beside Billy, but I don't have much room to turn. I'm keeping the rope around me."

Moments later, he gave Samuel a status report. "Billy's left arm is bent behind him and his right arm is thrown over the tree root. He's lying face-up on the rock. His eyes are closed. His left leg is bent, and the right leg is hanging off the edge of the rock."

Josiah paused, and Samuel imagined him bending over his son to check for injuries. A moment later, Josiah's voice reached Samuel's ears. "He's breathing. There's a pulse. Billy, Billy, can you hear me, son?" Straining his ears, Samuel couldn't hear any response from the boy, but Josiah continued talking. "Billy, I'm here. I'm going to slide this tarp under you, and we're going to get you back up to the top. Here we go…"

From the tugs Samuel felt on the rope, he could tell that Josiah wasn't wasting any time securing the boy on the tarp. It wasn't long before he heard his neighbor call, "He's moaning. He's coming around."

Then, "Billy, don't move, son. I know you're hurt. I'm sliding this around you so they can lift you up."

Samuel felt a jerk on the rope and heard Josiah call, "Okay, he's in the tarp. He's conscious now. Start pulling. Slowly…Slowly…"

Samuel knew that Josiah was trying to prevent Billy's body from banging against the rocks and hillside any more than necessary. Time seemed to stand still as Samuel strained to pull his load back and up the hill. "That's good," Josiah called from below. "Four more feet to go…Three more feet…Be sure to keep pulling once you get him over the top—we don't want him sliding back. Two more feet….All right, start looking for the tarp now."

With a mighty heave backwards, Samuel managed to yank the tarp and its cargo over the hilltop. "Have you got him?" Josiah called.

Samuel yelled, "All right! We have him!" As Jake rushed to his friend, Samuel doubled over, gasping for air. When he stood, he could see his father-in-law in the distance, flagging down a neighbor who had arrived on horseback. The two men hurried to the hilltop.

"Stand firm. Help is on its way," Jake shouted to Billy's father. Minutes later, he announced, "Mr. Johnson is here now, and he brought his horse."

"Jake, tell Mr. Forsyth not to move, just to keep holdin' onto that tree. We'll get him soon," Samuel ordered.

Michael Johnson slid from the back of his horse, grabbed the reins, and raced his horse to the top of the hill. When the horse arrived, Samuel kept the end of the rope tied to the tree, but also looped it around the horn of the saddle. As Michael Johnson kept the horse steady, Samuel hurried to kneel beside Jake, to see his friend Billy.

Jake had managed to tug the tarp and his friend from the edge of the incline, and he surveyed the boy anxiously. Billy was shivering, bleeding, blinking at him, and frequently wincing in pain. Jake took off his coat and wrapped it around Billy's chest and shoulders, hoping to keep him warm. "I'm here, Billy," he said, patting him awkwardly on his shoulder. "Pa and Mr. Johnson will be pullin' your Dad up the hill right now. Don't move. You're hurt."

After Samuel threw off his coat and wrapped that, too, around the boy, he called down the hill, "Josiah, are you ready? We have a strong horse and we're commencin' to pull you up now. You can let go of the tree." He nodded to Michael Johnson, and shouted, "Here we go!"

Reins in hand, the neighbor stood close to the head of his horse and urged him to move. "Come on, Black Jack, pull. Easy, boy. Come on. Step up now!" The horse nickered, seeming to be surprised by the extra weight he was called upon to pull. But, obediently, he bent his shoulders to the task and started walking, one step at a time, up the hill. Samuel kept close watch on the knot of the rope. It held steady.

Slowly, slowly, Josiah Forsyth rose up that sheer cliff. There weren't many places he could place his hands or feet to make the ascent easier, but he struggled to make sure he didn't crash into a rock as he dangled in the air. Higher and higher he was lifted. Finally, he could reach out and grasp clumps of the slick, wet grass at the top of the hill. The horse continued slowly pulling him to safety.

"Yahoo! We made it!" the men whooped when they saw their neighbor's hands appear over the top.

"Don't grab those rocks in front of you, Josiah—they're the ones that made Billy slip," Samuel ordered. "Let us haul you a little farther. All right, you should be able to see us in a moment."

Almost immediately, Josiah was pulled above the crest of the hill, and he found himself on his knees on the ground. But his rescuers didn't stop the tension on the rope or relax until he was pulled beyond the steep drop and could wrap an arm around the trunk of a small maple. On what seemed wobbly knees, he stood up.

"I can't thank you enough for rescuing my boy and me," he gasped as he quickly untied the rope around his middle and hurried over to his son's side.

"Glad to see you're okay," Michael Johnson asked. "Is there anything else I can do? Do you need me any longer? I'll put you and the boy on Black Jack's back, if that would help."

"No, but thanks," Josiah said. "Sam and I can tote Billy somewhere safe. I need to examine him first before he's moved."

With a good-natured wave of his hand and a nod at Samuel, Michael Johnson mounted his horse again and continued on his way. Lee Hanner limped back over the bridge at a pace that amazed his son-in-law and grandson, then disappeared from view.

Kneeling in the snow by Billy's side, Josiah Forsyth handed Jake back his coat and commanded, "Jake, I need you to hold Billy's head just as steady as you can, in case he has a fractured cervical vertebrae. I'll do a quick examination here before we move him. Then, before he catches an inflammation of the lungs, we'll need to get him home and examine him more thoroughly."

When the Gilmers remained silent, he noticed they were looking puzzled. "I guess Billy didn't tell any of you that I'm a doctor?" he asked.

The Gilmers shook their heads and Josiah continued, "I thought I'd get the farm in working order before I hang out my shingle and set up my practice here. We've been fixing that big house we bought so I can see my patients in the front parlor and my work won't interfere with the family. I've ordered the equipment I'll need, but it won't be here until the middle of March." He bent over Billy with a grim look on his face. "Looks like my son is my very first patient."

As he checked Billy, Samuel and Jake listened to his questions. "Can you tell me your name? Who am I? Do you know what happened to you?"

Billy winced as his father felt the bones in his cheeks, all around his neck, and then the back of his head. However, when he caught his breath, he was able to answer. "Pa, you know my name is William Jefferson Forsyth. I wanted to see where that axle of the mill wheel was connected to the flywheel. I went down too far, my feet went out from under me, and I slid down the bank. I went over the edge. I hit my head and arm hard when I landed on that rock. That's all I remember."

At that moment, his father's probing fingers caused him to shout, "Ow! Right there above my wrist really hurts, Pa."

His father nodded, but continued to probe his body for other trouble spots. "I'll bet it does, son. At least one of the bones in your forearm is broken. You have a big knot on the back of your head, but luckily that's the hardest part of your skull. I don't think your neck is broken."

He turned to Samuel when he completed his investigations. "If you can spare Jake, I'd be grateful if he could ride home with us and help keep Billy's head and neck straight until I can examine him better."

"Of course," Samuel said.

The doctor took a clean handkerchief out of his pocket and gently patted a gash behind Billy's ear and one on the back of his head, both of them bleeding sluggishly. He frowned at his son. "You'll need some stitches, that's for sure."

"I'll do anything you need me to do, Mr. Forsyth," Jake said, feeling more grownup already. Glancing away, he saw his grandfather driving the Forsyth wagon in their direction. "It won't be long before you're headin' home now, Billy," he said, trying to reassure his friend.

When Lee pulled the mules close to the boy lying face-up in the tarp on the ground, Josiah Forsyth thanked the family for their help before giving his next order. "If we keep Billy on the tarp and we all carefully lift him on the hay near the rear of the wagon, he'll be cushioned. Jake can hold his head steady all the way home." He turned to his son and said firmly, "Billy, as we lift you, and then on the wagon, you must lie absolutely still. Do NOT try to sit up until I tell you. Understand?"

Billy locked eyes with his father, "Dad, I couldn't, anyway. My leg and arm hurt bad." He winced in pain.

Awkwardly, Jake followed behind his friend and the tarp, holding Billy's head as the men lifted the boy, still wrapped in the tarp, up into the wagon. Dr. Forsyth rearranged the hay to support Billy's neck properly and then nodded to Jake. Jake hopped onto the rear of the wagon, situated himself behind Billy, and put his hands on either side of Billy's head before Dr. Forsyth placed the rear gate of the wagon in position.

He swung onto the wagon seat quickly and looked down at his anxious neighbors. "Sorry for the fuss and bother, Samuel, Lee. We surely didn't intend to embroil you in an adventure this morning." Then he clicked his tongue. With surprising gentleness, his mules took off, pulling the wagon along the main road to the Forsyth home, which was not far in the distance. Dr. Forsyth spoke man-to-man to the boys during that slow, bumpy ride.

"I want to thank you for your help, Jake Gilmer, and the help your Pa and Grandpa gave us this day. But you boys need to think about what happened and learn a lesson. We all heard your Pa tell you boys to stay away from the edge of that creek bank because of all the slippery rocks hidden under the snow. I know you were excited about being together. And I know how much Billy loves machinery. Jake, I imagine you understood the dangers and you would never have gone up there if Billy hadn't begged you. But, Jake, part of growing up is obeying authority, listening to and following instructions, and taking responsibility for your actions. A true friend says no when the occasion warrants a warning. And, Billy, a true friend listens. It's hard to do, but you needed to do that. Now you boys have seen what happens when you don't heed your folks. All we can do is pray that Billy's injuries are fixable and he can quickly recover."

Dr. Forsyth seemed to shiver before he added, "Think for a moment, boys: if Billy had continued to tumble down that hill to the rocks below, this would have been a tragedy. We're more fortunate than you realize right now."

He paused, perhaps debating about whether the lesson had registered with the boys. "I imagine you both need a good friend," he added. "Let's make sure from now on that you share good times together. No more accidents! Understood?"

"Understood," Jake said fervently.

"Understood," Billy echoed.

Jake glanced down at his friend, frightened and ashamed. He grinned weakly into Billy's eyes, determined to remain strong for his friend. He could tell Billy was in pain and trying not to show it, but each time they rode over a bump in the road, the boy groaned.

To Jake, the mules seemed to be going much too slowly. He thought they would never reach the Forsyth home. But, eventually, Dr. Forsyth turned the mules into his farmyard and up to the front door.

Billy's father hopped down from the wagon seat and quickly came around to the back of the wagon. Only when Jake got ready to hop down from the wagon did he let go of Billy's head. Dr. Forsyth and Jake gently slid Billy and the tarp off the bales of hay and carried him up to the porch. By the time they reached the top step, the door opened and June Forsyth stepped out. "Josiah, why did you park the wagon here and not," she began. Then, when she saw her son, she added, "Oh, dear God! Billy! What happened?"

"June, I need you to run back and make sure that my examination table is clear and my medical kit is open. I'll need soap, bandages, neck brace, sutures, antiseptic, and a tea kettle full of boiling water" her husband said. "Our son took a terrible fall down the steep bank beside the mill. I don't know how badly he's hurt."

Though she turned pale, Mrs. Forsyth swung into action. After holding the door open for the men and their burden, she disappeared down the hall. "Fortunately for me, my wife is a nurse," Josiah Forsyth told Jake as they maneuvered past drywall, stacks of lumber, and tools on their way to what would soon become the examination room. Billy's mother lit lanterns as she entered the room and briskly began gathering the required medical equipment.

They followed her quickly and carefully. Mrs. Fletcher found a neck brace in one of the drawers of a medical cabinet and gently wrapped it around Billy's neck as soon as her son was safely on the table. Jake watched Dr. Forsyth cut his son's clothing off. He glanced at Jake, still standing in the door of the examining room. "Thanks for your help, Jake. You should go now."

Jake nodded. "I'll let himself out, sir." He folded the tarp and tucked it under his arm, then turned to his friend, who was lying white-faced and silent on the examining table. "I hope you feel better real soon, Billy," he added.

Jake left the house feeling the weight of the world on his shoulders. For the first time in his life, the world seemed dark and forbidding, and Jake felt lost and helpless.

During Jake's absence, Samuel returned home to relate the events of the morning to Anna. "I seem to have lost my appetite," he told his wife, refusing her offer of an early lunch. Then he returned to the saw mill to help his father-in-law, knowing that Lee had been distressed by the morning's events. When Samuel opened the barn door, he found Lee storing the ropes after lubricating the log carriage. "Anything to stay busy," Lee grunted when he saw who entered the mill. Wordlessly, Samuel organized his tools on the workbench. After nearly two hours had passed and there was no sign of Jake, Samuel returned home and found Anna kneading bread near the stove.

"Honey, have you seen Jake?" he asked her, without his usual light-hearted banter. "I ain't seen hide nor hair of him. We need to have a serious talk."

Anna nodded. "Jake opened the door about twenty minutes ago to let me know he was back. He said he didn't want to eat, that he was going out to the barn." She touched her husband's arm. "Samuel, he's devastated. Please choose your words carefully."

Samuel grunted and turned to walk away. But then he stopped. He looked back at Anna again, his expression softened. "All right, Anna. I will."

As Samuel Gilmer started across the back yard toward the barn, the snow was melting quickly. The temperature was still rising, he noted.

By the time he reached the barn and opened the door quietly, he was calmer, though he still planned to talk sternly to Jake before levying some corporal punishment.

At first, Samuel didn't hear anything. But then the sounds of soft sobs and nose-blowing reached his ears. "Jake?" he called. "Where are you, son?"

Another loud sniff could be heard before Samuel saw Jake's tear-stained face appear at the open door of the cattle stall at the rear of the barn. Jake had a pitchfork in his hand, Samuel noticed. The boy's overalls were dirty and his face was streaked with tears, dirt, swipe marks from his hand, and a few pieces of straw and manure. "I'm in here, Pa."

"What in the world are you doin' in there, Jake?"

"Muckin' out the cow stall. I figured it needed to be done, and I needed to do somethin' like that right now." When Samuel looked behind Jake, he discovered that the wooden wheelbarrow Jake had wheeled to the stall was more than half-full of old straw and manure. The large back door of the barn was open, and Samuel noticed another pile in the manure wagon outside the gate. Jake had been hard at work digging and tossing, sobbing and blowing and wiping, his father realized.

Samuel looked at Jake's red eyes and his slouched and beaten-down demeanor. The father's heart ached. He spoke softly, "Son, I had come down here to rake you over the coals and then whip your behind. Now I'm lookin' at you and I realize that there's no punishment I could give you right now that's worse than what you're givin' yourself. Come over here. Sit beside me."

Samuel dropped onto a long bench just inside the barn door and patted the bench. Jake propped the pitchfork against the wall and shuffled slowly toward his father. Head drooping and looking miserable, he plopped down beside his father.

"Jake, it was a great mornin' to start off, and we had a nice visit with the Forsyths," began Samuel. "Then Billy wanted to go up that hill and see gears and belts and shafts of the mill. I told y'all why I was worried, but you went up there anyway. I know you yelled for Billy to back up, and I know he didn't listen to you. But Jake, you should have stopped the boy from goin' up there in the first place. You knew there'd be other days when y'all could see the millworks without puttin' yourselves in danger."

The boy bent his head, as if studying the muck on his boots. His father continued, "You, Molly, and Lillie have come from the bottom of the dam and followed the creek around to the mill many times—when the wheel isn't turning, of course. You've touched that wheel and watched me fix things underneath. But we always did things safely and we talked about why safety was important. Billy's curiosity and your lack of judgment got him hurt bad, Jake. I don't need to tell you what would have happened if the Lord hadn't intervened and stopped Billy's fall."

Samuel sighed, putting an arm around his son's shoulder as he saw huge tears starting down Jake's cheeks. "Son, I see how tall and strong you are, how hard a worker you are, and sometimes I'm guilty of thinking of you as a young adult. Jake, I know you're only ten years old and you still have a lot to learn. I forget sometimes how energetic and foolish I was at ten years old. Now you understand why I need you to follow directions carefully, for your own safety and the safety of others. Don't you?"

He waited for Jake to nod. "I understand that you want to do grown-up things right now, not later. Many times you make the right choice, and I'm right proud of what you have done. Other times, like today, you're still that little boy who isn't grown up yet."

Jake buried his face in his father's shoulder. "I know, son," Samuel said, trying to soothe his boy. "Right now you're feelin' guilty and you're worried about your friend. If workin' hard out here is helpin' you feel better, then do it. But remember one thing: your Ma and I love you. Nothin' will ever change that." Samuel cleared his throat and said in a louder voice, "Well, what's done is done. You'll learn from your mistakes, won't you?"

When Jake nodded, Samuel added, "I'm disappointed in you right now, but you are still my son, and I know you'll make me proud."

Jake embraced his Pa, sobbing like he might never stop. "Oh, Pa, I'm so sorry! We sure weren't thinkin' of danger, just adventure. But it was so scary seein' him go over the side." Jake described the trip to the Forsyths' home and what the doctor had said to him. "I don't know if Billy is going to be okay or not. I've been here prayin' that God will make him all better, and to please forgive me."

"God always forgives, son. It's us humans who have to forgive ourselves sometimes," Samuel said, patting his son on the back.

"I don't know if Billy will ever want to talk to me again!" Jake mumbled. "I think his Dad hates me. Oh, Pa, I wish this had never happened!"

"Jake, why don't we go to the Forsyths' house tonight? Mama said she's fixin' ham and beans and biscuits for them. You can apologize to them all and see Billy for yourself. At least you'll know how badly he was hurt. We'll ask if there's somethin' you can do to help them."

"You mean it, Pa? I sure would feel better." Jake started to wipe his eyes again with the back of his hand.

"Uh, wait a minute" Samuel said, pulling out a clean handkerchief from his pocket and handing it to his son. "Here...and yes, we really are goin' to take some food over. But do me one favor before you get in our wagon and sit close to your Mama, Jake."

Jake looked up at him. "What, Pa?"

"Clean yourself up, boy! Cleanliness is next to godliness—and we need more of both. I'm talkin' warm water and soap. And leave them clothes and boots out on the porch!" Samuel tapped Jake's knee. "Stay here and work if you wish, but come in soon, to clean up and eat something."

Jake watched his father leave, feeling as if there might just be sunshine in his world again one day. He finished cleaning out the stalls, then tossed down three bales of straw from the hayloft and spread it around the floors of each stall.

That evening as the sun started sinking over the horizon, Samuel, Anna, and Jake climbed aboard their wagon. Samuel shook the reins and clicked his tongue. "Let's go, SueJean!" Several baskets of hot food rested in baskets in the back of the wagon, where Jake sat. He was nearly drooling from the aroma of country ham, green beans with corn, baked apples and hot biscuits. Jake directed them to the Forsyth farm, which his parents had known by its previous name, the Patillo Farm. When the wagon reached the farmyard, Samuel pulled the reins and parked in front of the house. Before he could jump off the wagon seat, June Forsyth opened the kitchen door. She looked puzzled until she saw Jake seated behind Anna. Her face brightened. "How nice of y'all to visit! Come right on in."

As the Gilmers carried the baskets of food, June Forsyth ushered them into her kitchen. "What a surprise! And the food smells delicious. I must admit that I didn't have much time to cook, with my patient in the other room. Thank you! But you didn't need to do this."

"I figured you'd be right busy taking care of Billy," said Anna, "plus, I've been meanin' to visit and introduce myself for some time now. This is a neighborly greeting."

"I'm so glad to meet neighbors! Please, sit down,'" June invited, apologizing for the carpentry clutter in the hallway. Then she smiled at Jake. "I'm sure you want to see Billy. My husband is with him right now, putting a splint on his arm." When she noticed the Gilmers casting glances around the house, she explained, "The front parlor will be Josiah's waiting room. Next to it is a smaller parlor, which will be his office. We'll turn that closet into the storage room for patient records. We'll let Billy sleep on the couch in here for now so he doesn't have to walk up the stairs—the last thing we need is for him to fall and injure any other body part."

She ushered the Gilmers into the new examintion room. "Here we are. Josiah, Anna and Samuel brought over a meal for us, and it smells very tasty. I think Jake wants to see how Billy is feeling now."

Dr. Forsyth was just finishing up with his patient. "Hi! I hope you'll forgive me for not shaking your hands just now. Billy definitely has a broken left radius, and even though I couldn't feel a break in the ulna, I've splinted the arm. It was a clean break, I'm thankful to say."

"Was his neck broken?" Jake asked, fear etched onto his face.

"No, and the left leg is badly sprained, but not broken," the doctor reported. "But he won't be able to bear weight on it for at least a week. He'll be able to use a crutch with his good arm tomorrow, though."

When he saw Jake surveying the bandages, he added, "The knot on the back of his head is exactly that—a knot. I'm happy to report that there was only a slight concussion. He has his share of cuts and bruises. I put stitches in his cheek and on the back of his head. Fortunately, his spleen is fine. His ribs are badly bruised, but I couldn't find any that were broken."

"It's a miracle he didn't do worse," Mrs. Forsyth said under her breath. Anna nodded in agreement.

"I hope you'll still think this scamp is a miracle once he doesn't need his crutches any longer," Dr. Forsyth said dryly, grinning at his wife.

As soon as his father finished with the splint, Billy struggled to sit up. Although his cheek and eye were swollen and purple and had a bandage on his head and his ear, he still managed a thin smile.

Jake, who had not spoken, stepped shyly around Anna Gilmer. He gulped, then looked first at June Forsyth before walking up to Billy. "I want to apologize, Billy. I'm just as sorry as I can be that all this happened. It's all my fault. We should have stayed in the mill and waited to explore the machinery when the weather was warm and dry enough to wade around from the creek."

Jake gulped and added, "I was so scared when you slipped and went down that hill and I couldn't catch you! I don't have any excuse, Billy. I'm just plumb sorry. After all this, I don't know whether you'll ever want to talk to me again. But I hope you will."

Billy protested, "No, Jake, it was my fault, and I told Ma and Pa that. I'm the one who kept on going down the hill when you told me to stop. You're still my friend, Jake."

"Let's leave the boys alone to visit, and I'll put the tea kettle on the stove in the kitchen," June Forsyth suggested, ushering the Gilmers out of the room.

Billy waited until their footsteps echoed down the hallway before whispering, "Listen! I've got to tell you that there was an angel watchin' out for me this morning!"

When Jake looked startled, he added, "I was fallin' fast, never more scared in my life. Then, all of a sudden, I felt somethin' like peace. I started to slow as I fell, and I felt something—hands, maybe, around me and underneath me. You saw how small that rock was where I landed"?"

Jake nodded.

"I think an angel pushed me back onto that rock and turned my head around so I'd land on the back of my head, not my face. That big ol' root stopped me from rollin' off."

Jake's eyes widened as Billy finished his story. "How did that get there?" Billy didn't wait for his friend to answer. "I'm telling you, Jake, I was held and protected today. Someone—or something—saved my life!"

Jake's eyes were as round as a dinner plate, but before he could say anything, Dr. Forsyth came back into the room with a triangle of cloth, which he fashioned into a sling for the arm. "I'm sure that if Mr. Gladstone can get to school in the morning, Tucker School will be open," he told the boys. "I've written a note saying that Billy has been in an accident and will miss at least one week of school. Jake, would you take this note to your teacher? Tell him I'll stop by after school tomorrow and get Billy's books."

"You don't have to, Pa," Billy protested.

"You'll have plenty of time on your hands to keep up with your schoolwork—and then some," Josiah Forsyth said. "Since you won't be able to handle your chores for some time now, we'll find new ways to fill your days."

Jake grinned. "I'd be glad to deliver the note, Dr. Forsyth. An' I'll be glad to bring his books and write down the assignments."

After the Gilmers shared a pot of tea with the Forsyths, Samuel called to Jake. "We need to get home now and let these folks eat." He held his hand out to Josiah. "Thank you for the good news. I know you'll take good care of that patient of yours. We're so grateful that Billy is going to be all right. I believe in miracles, and I believe we've seen one today."

Before he left, Jake gently squeezed Billy's right hand, "I sure am glad to see you with your eyes open, Billy. We've both had a rough day— but yours has definitely been worse. Seein' you sittin' up now has made all the bad go away."

Billy's brown eyes twinkled. "I want a tour of the bottom of the mill from the creek side next time, okay?" The room was filled with laughter as Jake put his coat on.

After Samuel handed Anna up into the wagon, she leaned across her husband and told June Forsyth, "We feel so blessed that we'll be having a doctor in our community, Mrs. Forsyth. We've needed one out here for a long time."

"Oh, please call me June! Josiah graduated from the University of North Carolina in Chapel Hill," June Forsyth said proudly. "When he finished there, he moved to Greensboro to finish his medical training at St. Leo's Hospital. That's where we met. I was a nurse there. Josiah is lookin' forward to servin' this community a long time."

She put her hand on Jake's shoulder as he followed his parents to the wagon. "And, Jake, don't you worry. Billy is going to be all right.

He's so smart and he so loves machinery, but he has been known to charge into things without stoppin' to think." She shook her head before adding, "You're welcome here anytime. Billy might be a little bored until he is up and about again. How will we keep him from chasing you on one leg while using a crutch under his good arm?" She winked at Jake, who giggled.

That night as Jake got ready to climb into bed, he changed his mind. He knelt in prayer, "Oh Lord, I'm not the best prayin' person. Sometimes I do a quick thank you before I fall asleep, and sometimes I forget to pray at all. But right now, I just want to thank you for helpin' my friend Billy today. You spared his life, and it looks like Billy will heal from all the hurts he got today. Thank you! I'll be able to have more fun times with Billy. Thank you, too, for the good talk I had with Pa. Please help me to become the kind of man he is. Help me think next time before I do somethin'. This growin' up is a hard thing, but I have to remember that you are always with me. Bless my family that I love. Amen!"

CHAPTER THREE: *TROUBLE AT SCHOOL*
March 25, 1913

DIIINNNGG DONNNGGG!

Promptly at ten minutes before eight o'clock, Mr. R. M. Gladstone walked outside the Tucker School building to ring the school bell, warning student stragglers that the time was near for school to begin.

On that rare warm day in late March, Mr. R. M. Gladstone had arrived at the school on Williams Dairy Road promptly at seven o'clock. He unhitched his horse from the wagon and put both in the shanty behind the school. He knew he had precisely fifty minutes to prepare for the day: loading the stove with firewood and lighting the tinder on cold mornings, trimming lamp wicks, doing a quick sweep of the floors, winding the clock on the wall, and writing the young students' subtraction problems on half the blackboard, followed by the long-division and fraction problems for the older students on the other half. With an eye on the clock, he collected the oldest students' slates and wrote out their geometry proofs.

Mr. Gladstone liked routine and order. A middle-aged man with a thin gray mustache and thinning gray hair, he always started the school day with the Pledge of Allegiance to the flag and a prayer, followed by mathematics, since he knew that earlier in the day, "the pupils' minds are still sharp and fresh." The arithmetic lessons were followed by lessons in grammar. These were followed by reading and spelling for the three different age levels. Afternoon was the time when he taught science and history and assigned the students' homework.

As he completed his preparations for the day, twenty-seven boys and girls chattered or played tag in the school yard, determined to make the most of their free time before the signal from their teacher to enter the one-room schoolhouse. Rain had pounded Piedmont North Carolina the previous night. This land was famous for its dense red soil and notorious for producing serious potholes on the road leading to Tucker School. Most students were carefully avoiding the craters and the splashes that would cover their clothes with red clay. They knew they would be wearing those same clothes a few more times before their mamas would have the opportunity to scrub them on their washboards.

All the children carried their lunches in small pails, and some also brought a favorite toy to play with during lunch break. Jake and his best friend Tom could be counted upon to arrive with small cloth bags filled with marbles. Lillie Gilmer had carefully wrapped the cloth doll named Susie that her Mam-maw Hanner had made for her two Christmases earlier. Lillie cherished that doll, since it was the last gift Mam-maw had been able to make with her painful and gnarled hands before she contracted pneumonia. She died just weeks after finishing Lillie's gift. Susie was wrapped in a baby quilt that Mam-maw had sewn for Lillie when she waited for her to be born.

Promptly at eight o'clock, Mr. Gladstone emerged onto the school's little porch once again, and rang the bell for the second time. All talking and laughing ceased. One by one, the children filed past Mr.

Gladstone, who greeted them before they stored their lunch pails in the cloakroom and settled into their assigned seats.

The youngest students sat in the front of the classroom, on the left side in two rows, with four in each row. That's where Lillie could be found. The smallest in her class, she sat up front, her feet dangling. By the end of the year, she hoped, her feet would touch the floor. Across the aisle sat the older pupils in three rows, with three in each row. The wood stove radiated heat from in the middle of the school room and served as a dividing line between the younger pupils and the teen-aged pupils, who worked at their own blackboard on the school's back wall. At this time, ten desks were arranged back here, although the big boys would begin to disappear from the classroom as soon as planting season started.

Molly Gilmer was now sixteen years old, which meant she was in her final year at Tucker School. She was spending a lot of time pondering what she would do when she left the school for the last time. After learning the basics in history, science, mathematics, reading, grammar, and spelling, Tucker School students were issued a certificate from Guilford County, signifying that they had achieved a reasonable education and they were employable in the city. Every year, several graduates from this school would pursue professional careers. With their parents' approval and support, they would apply to schools of higher education, either Normal Schools, or colleges. Now and then a young woman chose to attend a nursing school in one of the state's hospitals. But, Mr. Gladstone realized that no matter how smart they were, most pupils in rural areas never went beyond the classes offered in one-room schools. They remained close to the place where they were born and raised. The girls would marry young men they met in the school, the community, or in church, and most of these young men would follow in the footsteps of their fathers, becoming tobacco farmers, dairy farmers, blacksmiths, store owners, carpenters, or millers.

In the rural areas of North Carolina, teachers had to be flexible with their school schedules and attendance during the seasons when crops had to be planted and harvested, and hay was ready for baling. This meant that Mr. Gladstone made the best possible use of his time with his students.

After the next week, school would be dismissed for a two-week spring recess, so the young people could help with the planting of fields and gardens. Still, although he was a compassionate man and a good teacher, Mr. Gladstone expected all his students, at all ages and ability levels, to do their very best in school, arriving with completed homework and the alertness required to respond with correct answers when called upon. He was what parents called "no-nonsense" in his approach to his pupils' behavior during class and on the school grounds.

On this particular March day, the youngest students were learning about subtraction. They had been given five problems to work on for the previous night's homework. When the lesson began, Lillie slumped into her chair, so her toes could actually touch the floor. "I don't understand what Mr. Gladstone said in class about this, Molly," she had cried in frustration the night before, when Molly was helping Ma with supper and Lillie was struggling with her homework at the kitchen table.

"I'll help you as soon as I get the cornbread in the oven," Molly had promised. And then she worked for more than an hour with Lillie to teach her a simpler way than the one Mr. Gladstone had demonstrated. "There, do you understand now?" she asked. "There can be different ways to accomplish the same thing." Lillie nodded and hugged her sister after she finished her work.

On this particular morning, Mr. Gladstone walked up to the blackboard and pointed to the first problem he had written there. It did not look like one of the problems he had assigned last night, and Lillie's heart started beating fast. She was puzzled and alarmed—especially when the teacher called, "Lillie Gilmer, I'd like for you to come work this problem."

Hesitantly, Lillie walked very slowly to the blackboard and took the chalk from the teacher's hand before facing the problem:

$32 - 18 =\_\_$

Lillie wrinkled her brow and studied the equation. When she glanced at Mr. Gladstone, he asked impatiently, "Young lady, did you do your homework last night?"

"Yes, sir, I did. And I thought I understood it. But now that you're starin' at me, I've forgotten how I did it."

A snort and a giggle erupted from the second row. Joyce Ann Carter had been heard to tell a friend that she "strongly disliked that Lillie Gilmer." She sought any opportunity to criticize her. Mr. Gladstone gave Joyce Ann a withering look. He cleared his throat. "Lillie, this is very similar to the homework that you did last night."

A hand waved from the back of the room, and Molly's calming and respectful voice asked, "Mr. Gladstone, may I have a word with Lillie? I'm sure she can do this problem."

Just hearing her sister's voice calmed Lillie's nerves.

"Well, this is highly unusual, Miss Gilmer but I will give you one minute." Molly nodded, smiled, and walked to the front of the room. She bent down to Lillie's height as she pointed to the problem with her left hand and whispered in Lillie's ear. Lillie nodded so emphatically that her red braids danced. Then she turned once again to the blackboard.

"Mr. Gladstone, I'm sure I can do this now. I just need to regroup the numbers. Let me rewrite this." She talked as she wrote, "That is three 10's and two 1's, take away one 10 and eight 1's. First, I'm supposed to take 8 away from 2. But I can't do that. So now this is like running low on sugar, and running over to my neighbor's house to borrow some."

Mr. Gladstone loosened his grip on the wood pointer he always held in his hand, and he actually managed a tiny—and rare—smile as Lillie continued her explanation. "So when I run over to my neighbor on the left to borrow from her three 10's, she says, 'Of course,' and gives me some. She now has 10 less, and I have 10 more. Her 3 tens have become 2 tens, and my 2 one's have become 12. I can take 8 away from 12, and that leaves me with 4. I go over to my 10's column and take the 1 away from the 2 that are left. That becomes 1 ten. My answer is now 1 ten and 4 ones, or…14."

Before the teacher could nod his approval, Lillie added, "I should recheck this answer by adding up again from the bottom to the top. 14 + 18. Give me just a moment here, please. Well, look: that adds up to be 32." Lillie handed the chalk back to Mr. Gladstone with a big grin on her face and returned to her seat.

"Well done, Lillie Gilmer." Mr. Gladstone turned to the rest of the class as Lillie's face flushed pink with pleasure. A few of her young classmates clapped, but in the row behind Lillie's desk, Joyce Ann Carter's face was flushed too, but with fury. She grunted, "Show-off!" as she bent over her own work again. When Lillie heard her, the smile disappeared from her face.

"Now, students, work on the other ten problems on the board without talking," Mr. Gladstone ordered, and he moved to the other side of the room, asking an eleven-year-old to come forward and work a long division problem. When he successfully arrived at the answer, Mr. Gladstone called on John McDonald to come forward and work a fraction problem. At the back of the room, the older students were working on their algebra and geometry proofs.

The rest of the morning passed uneventfully. Mathematics was followed by a grammar lesson on prepositions for all the pupils under the age of twelve. The teacher smiled when he propped an easel in the front of the classroom and placed on it a drawing of a large oak tree with a small hole in the trunk of the tree, just below the first branch. From behind his back, Mr. Gladstone produced a cardboard figure of a squirrel in a walking pose standing on two legs, with a bushy tail held straight up. The students laughed.

"Little squirrel is here to demonstrate some of our most commonly used prepositions," Mr. Gladstone said with a hint of a smile on his face. "Children, I am going to give you one example of a preposition, and then I want you to raise your hand when you think of more. All right? Here goes one preposition." He moved the cardboard squirrel through the air toward the tree. "The squirrel can walk *to* the tree. The preposition, of course, is *to*. Now I want you to help me think of other prepositions."

Hands popped up all over the classroom. Billy's idea was "He can climb *up* the tree."

Sylvia suggested, "There's a hole in that tree. The squirrel can climb *in* or *into* the tree."

George was also creative. "Squirrels like to dig. He could dig *under* the tree."

Other observations were: *around, from, on, away, out,* and *behind.* There was a pause, as the students continued thinking. Steve Sizemore's hand popped up. "Oh, Mr. Gladstone, a hawk dived down and grabbed our squirrel and flew him off to his nest. He carried the squirrel *over* the tree." Laughter and applause greeted that answer.

Mr. Gladstone smiled, "Yes, and you used another preposition in that sentence. A hawk carried him off *to* his nest. *To* is a preposition." He looked pleased as he said, "Fine job, students. Any time you're wondering whether a word is a preposition or not, try this squirrel-and-tree test." He pulled out his pocket watch and glanced around the room. "The morning has flown! It appears that lunchtime has arrived. Listen for the bell in one hour, and have a good lunch now."

As Molly prepared to leave the room, the teacher called out, "Molly Gilmer, after you eat your lunch, would you please come to my desk?"

As quickly and soundlessly as they could, the twenty-seven students rushed for lunch pails, jump ropes, and marbles, then scattered around the school grounds, to talk, walk, or play games in the field close to the school. "Let's eat fast and play tag!" Lillie suggested to three little girls. Skipping past bigger girls who were jump-roping, they found a dry and grassy spot where they could giggle and chatter while opening their pails to reveal sandwiches, apples, and wedges of pie and cookies. Before they had a chance to sit and eat, however, Joyce Ann Carver planted herself directly in front of Lillie.

"I'll bet Mr. Gladstone is gonna rake Molly over the coals for interruptin' him and givin' you the answer to that problem," she said. "Maybe he'll kick her out of school."

Lillie studied the taller girl with a calm look on her face. "Molly didn't do anything wrong, and you know it. She saw I was nervous. She just wanted to calm me and remind me about what she taught me last night. She sure didn't give me the answer. After I remembered what she taught me, I could do that problem on my own."

Joyce Ann moved aside to let Lillie's friends pass, then she grabbed Lillie's long red braids. Quick as a flash, Joyce Ann had knotted them behind Lillie's head. "If I had that carrot hair, I sure wouldn't show it off. I'd hide it under a bonnet. It's strange. And those freckles? Ewww." She marched off triumphantly.

Lillie shouted back, "My Mama says that my hair looks like a sunset!"

"Hold still, Lillie," Sylvia said. "I'm working on your hair. Honestly, that Joyce Ann is in a mighty horrid bad mood today. I wish she'd just go home. Even better, I wish she'd move far, far away. Stop wiggling, Lillie!" Finally, she announced with satisfaction, "There. I've got it." Then she ran her hand down one long braid. "I sure wish I had your hair, Lillie. It's such a special color. I look at mine and all I see is the color of straw. I think Joyce Ann is just mighty jealous."

"I'm hungry. Let's eat." Lillie plunked down on the patch of dry grass and her friends joined her.

As soon as the last cookie and pie wedge disappeared, the little girls reached deep into their lunch pails and pulled out their dolls. All of them had been made by someone in their families, and each doll was wrapped snugly in her own blanket. Before they could play for long, however, Joyce Ann again interrupted them, taunting, "You're just silly little babies." Before anyone could respond, Joyce Ann rushed over to Lillie and snatched her doll out of her hands. "Silly little babies! Silly little babies!" she shouted, holding the doll so high that Lillie couldn't reach her.

"You give Susie back right now, Joyce Ann," Lillie shouted, stamping her foot. "My Mam-maw Hanner made her for me and sewed that dress. I haven't done anything to you. Stop being such a bully."

Lillie's friends were also up on their feet, begging Joyce Ann to return the doll to Lillie and go away. Other children heard the shouting and stopped what they were doing to see what was going on. Encouraged by the attention, Joyce Ann danced in a circle, holding the doll high and chanting, "Maybe I will, or maybe I won't. Maybe I'll take this ugly ol' thing home with me."

"No, you won't!" Lillie shouted, stamping her foot again.

Joyce Ann sneered, "You acted all smart and prissy this morning, and you think you're so great. I'll bet you've got another doll at home and you won't miss this ugly old thing at all."

Lillie's voice sounded more desperate, which was probably just what Joyce Ann wanted, Lillie's friends realized. "Joyce Ann, she's my only doll. I've taken right good care of her," Lillie pleaded. "I love her. Please, please, give her back."

That's when Jake saw the commotion. He sprinted over to the girls from the ball field as Joyce Ann backed down the school's dirt drive, sneering, "Oh? Good care, huh? It doesn't look like it now." She tore the pretty blue gingham dress off Susie, pulling so hard that the doll's left cloth arm was torn. Lillie screamed when she saw the arm dangling by only a thread.

Joyce Ann swung the doll in the air, and everyone around her gasped. Lillie was stunned—but just for a moment. She felt her cheeks blaze in rage. Jake said later, "Lillie's Scotch-Irish temper boiled like a tea kettle left too long on the stove." Certainly, she felt angrier and more betrayed than she had ever felt in her six short years.

It didn't matter to Lillie that she was facing a girl eight inches taller and probably forty pounds heavier. The outrage she felt and the look in Joyce Ann's eyes were more than Lillie could stand. She balled up her fists and darted full-speed at the older girl, driving her right shoulder into Joyce Ann's solar plexus.

Lillie's sudden charge caught Joyce Ann completely off guard, and she was knocked backwards, landing in a big puddle of the reddest North Carolina mud.

Fortunately for Lillie's doll, an older boy nearby who had been intending to referee the situation caught Susie as the doll flew through the air. At the same moment, Jake arrived on the scene. He screeched to a stop over the very disheveled, very muddy, very humiliated Joyce Ann Carter. His fists clenched. "I ain't never hit a girl, but if you ever, ever touch my sister, Joyce Ann Carter, you'll be sorry you got out of bed!"

At that moment, Mr. Gladstone, closely followed by Molly Gilmer, ran out of the school house. His face beet red, the teacher waded through the crowd of children. "What is the meaning of this outrage?" he demanded to know. He glanced down at the dark-haired girl sitting in a puddle of red water and mud, then he glared at Jake. "Jake Gilmer, did you push Miss Carter into the mud? Answer me truthfully, young man."

Sputtering, Joyce Ann was now on her feet, wiping red dirt from her face. "No. Lillie Gilmer shoved me, Mr. Gladstone."

R. M. Gladstone whirled to face Lillie Gilmer, still flushed in the face, standing there without a word. His eyes were huge in shock. "Lillie, is this true? Is that possible?"

"Yes, I shoved her, Mr. Gladstone," Lillie said softly, staring at the ground. Then as she recalled all the indignities she had suffered that morning, Lillie looked up at her teacher, speaking in a stronger voice. "I didn't know she was going to fall. I didn't know she was going to land in that mud." Tears filled her eyes and she pointed to Susie, held in the big boy's hands. "Look what Joyce Ann did to Susie! She was bullying me all during lunch and I didn't do anything. She tied my braids in a knot and made fun of my hair, and I didn't do anything. But then she came over and laughed at us playing with our dolls. She grabbed my Susie, and when I asked her over and over to give her back, polite as I could be, she ripped Susie's beautiful dress and tore off an arm. That was more than I could stand!"

The young man who had protective custody of the doll handed her to Mr. Gladstone, who studied it carefully. "All that Lillie said is true, Mr. Gladstone!" Lillie's three friends echoed. Meanwhile, Molly stood behind her little sister and put both hands on her shoulders. Lillie's cheeks were red and blotchy. Jake shoved his hands in his pockets, looking miserable. Joyce Ann kept her head down, not letting anyone see her face. Silence filled the school yard as everyone waited to hear the teacher's verdict.

"All right. All you other students may play quietly out here until I come back. Lillie, Joyce Ann, and Jake, come inside with me."

The three children trooped behind their teacher to his desk, where he took out a pen and writing paper. Without a word, he commenced writing. None of the children dared say a word, and not one dared to look anyone in the eye.

"Joyce Ann, you started this morning with an unchristian attitude. You were mean-spirited towards Lillie when she was doing the subtraction problem. But that wasn't enough. Your bullying behavior on the playground was inexcusable. But, even worse, you badly damaged this girl's property. You will be suspended from school for the rest of this week. But, be warned: you will be responsible for everything I am teaching this week and all the homework."

The girl opened her mouth to protest, but the teacher held up a warning hand, "That is not all. You will write a letter of apology to Lillie and bring it back to school. I will read it to the entire class before you give it to Lille, so it had better be sincere and written with correct spelling and grammar."

He handed a sheet of paper to the girl. "This note will explain to your parents what has happened. They must sign the note and you must bring it back to me when you return to school." When Joyce Ann tried again to protest, he ordered, "Silence, please. Get your things and go home." Joyce Ann accepted the note meekly and hurried out of the classroom, keeping her head lowered. Outside, the other students watched in silence as she started down the muddy dirt road. No one said a word to Joyce Ann, and no one made a move toward her. Stone-faced, silent, and miserable, Joyce Ann Carter rushed to the corner and disappeared from sight.

Mr. Gladstone's tone was much softer with Lillie. He took a moment to write another note, and cleared his throat. "Lillie Gilmer, I am surprised that you would behave like that. You are usually such a sweet girl. I have never before seen you lose your temper. Still, the situation was extraordinary. It's not easy to face someone who is constantly bullying you, and I can fully understand how you would become distraught at what happened to your doll."

Lillie tried to defend herself, but the teacher silenced her as he had silenced Joyce Ann. "You must understand, Lillie, that fighting on school grounds is not tolerated. I know you are six years old, but that is no excuse. Miss Lillie Gilmer, one must control one's emotions at all time in society. You cannot push anyone into a mud puddle when you're a grownup, and you cannot do it as a child."

He held out a sheet of paper to Lillie, as he had done to Joyce Ann. "We all must be good neighbors, even when other students aren't treating us like good neighbors, Lillie. So, to that effect, I am suspending you for the rest of today and all of tomorrow."

He explained that he was sending a note home to her parents and that Molly would to bring home her assignments. Then he added, "You must write a note of apology to Joyce Ann, due when you get back here in two days."

"I don't think that's fair, sir," Jake protested. The teacher held up his hand, silencing Lillie's brother. But Mr. Gilmer didn't take his eyes off the little girl.

"Lillie," he warned, "I want you to be very careful what you say to your classmate in this note. Tell her how you should have handled this situation. You must use your best spelling and grammar, and you must give it to me to read and approve before I give it to Miss Carter. I will not read it aloud to the class. Do you understand?"

"Yes, sir." Lillie stammered, holding her head down. Both Jake and Mr. Gladstone could see tears dripping from her cheeks. The teacher sighed when he put the note in her hand. "Lillie, we all learn by making mistakes. I hope that your doll can satisfactorily be repaired. Now walk directly home."

But Lillie waited to hear her brother's verdict. "Jake Gilmer," Mr. Gladstone said. "I have a younger sister myself. If I saw an older, taller, larger person—boy or girl—bullying my sister the way Joyce Ann was bullying Lillie, I probably would have reacted exactly the same way you did just now. Young man, I understand that you did not touch Joyce Ann. I also have no doubt that if Joyce Ann had hopped up ready to retaliate against Lillie, you would have done something you might later regret. Jake, you're a good brother and you did pretty well by just announcing your intentions of potential violence instead of acting on your emotions."

Jake waited for the other shoe to drop, knowing what the teacher would say. "I am sending you home now with your sister, to allow you to calm down and talk with your parents. You are expected to be back here in school tomorrow morning. Is that clear?"

Jake managed a little smile. "Oh, yes it is, sir."

Mr. Gladstone shook Jake's hand. "Go on home now. And, young man, you are right to protect your sisters. Just keep in mind that at all times and in all places, handle anger constructively, not destructively. Never bring a fight to the school, for instance."

"Yes, sir."

The two Gilmer children started for the door. Jake gave Lillie his handkerchief, and she managed to wipe off the tears before they walked outside and faced the other children. Their schoolmates watched curiously as the brother and sister passed by, heading toward home. They were quickly joined by Molly, who took Lillie's hand as they walked together.

"Molly?" Lillie whispered, clutching her poor bedraggled doll. "Why are you going home? You weren't in my fight."

Molly smiled and hugged her sister. "No, I wasn't—though that doesn't mean I wouldn't have liked to tell that Joyce Ann a thing or two. I have something to share with Mama and Papa." She refused to tell them anything, no matter how hard they pleaded. She just gave them a wink and a smile.

"Oh, Lillie, let me see poor Susie." Molly reached for her sister's cherished possession, remembering how important a doll had been to her when she was Lillie's age. She carefully studied the rips and tears and Joyce Ann's muddy fingerprints, then she frowned before she handed Susie back to her little sister. "Lillie, I am pretty sure that I can repair Susie and make her almost as good as new. She lost a bit of stuffing and her beautiful dress was torn at the shoulder, but I know I can re-stuff Susie and sew her arm back on without anyone ever knowing something had happened. And if I make two new seams in that dress and add a button or another decoration to hide the uneven tear, I think Susie will be as good as new."

"Oh, Molly, I love you! You're the best sister I could ever have." Tears welled in Lillie's eyes.

"Goodness! Did something happen at school? Is everyone all right?" Anna exclaimed, stepping onto the porch when she saw her children arriving home hours before school usually ended. Samuel was just finishing his lunch, and he joined Anna on the porch.

"It's a long story," Molly warned.

"And not a good one," Jake muttered.

The two younger children handed their parents the letters Mr. Gladstone had written and then took turns telling their parents about their difficulties that day. When Jake finished his story, Anna spoke. "Oh, Lillie, I am so terribly sorry about what happened. You kept trying to make peace—and I'm proud of you for ignoring her insult about your hair. Bullying is such a hard thing to deal with. Even though the Bible says, *Turn the other cheek,* we don't want to encourage anyone to abuse us or someone we love."

"Maybe you shouldn't take Susie to school again, Lillie," Samuel suggested, pulling his little girl onto his lap. "Molly says she can fix her like new again, and I think Susie would prefer to stay in her nice, warm home when you're at school."

He put his hand on Jake's shoulder. "Son, I'm proud of you. It's important to stand up for your family. That's all I have to say about what happened today."

Samuel then stood Lillie on her feet and looked directly into her eyes, "Lillie, we shouldn't take the law into our own hands. I know there was nothing you could do to keep Joyce Ann from doing what she did today, but we don't shove people when they act in a mean way. Think for a moment, Lillie: that girl could have hit her head on a rock or tree stump when she fell, hurting herself badly. You wouldn't want that, Lillie."

The little girl hung her head and mumbled, "I guess this is one of those times when I'm 'posed to remember that sticks and stones can break bones—but words *can* hurt me, Papa!"

"I know, Ladybug. But whenever that happens, remember all the fine words that can make us feel good about ourselves. There, now, give me a big hug. I see Mama has a glass of milk and hot cookies for you. Think about what you aim to write to Joyce Ann, and let Mama and me hear it." He added, "By the way, I'm really proud of how you solved that math problem." He smiled at Molly. "You had a fine teacher last night."

Molly stood and faced her parents. "Now it's my turn. I also have a note from Mr. Gladstone." Molly carefully pulled an official-looking letter out of her pocket and handed it to Samuel. Anna rose from the table and leaned over her husband's shoulder. As they read, smiles crossed their faces. Then both reached out to embrace their firstborn.

"A recommendation to attend North Carolina State Normal and Industrial School in Greensboro!" Anna said breathlessly. "Mr. Gladstone thinks you should go to college and become a teacher. Oh, sweetheart, that's what I have been wishing for you since the day you first headed off to school." She held Molly close.

Molly admitted, "This is what I've been dreaming about for so long. And Mr. Gladstone said he had no doubt I could do all the work and make a fine teacher."

Samuel grinned at his wife. "Think of it, Anna! Our daughter, a future teacher. I'd say this news is a fine ending to a difficult day."

Anna wiped the mist from her eyes. "However, we have some time before we'll be sendin' Molly off to Greensboro, and we all have chores to do between now and then." She hugged Molly one more time. "Jake, this stove is eatin' firewood today—it needs a few loads from the woodshed to get us through dinner. Molly, I think this news calls for a celebration cake—and you can choose the recipe. Lillie, the chickens have been calling your name, waitin' for their feed."

The children scattered and Samuel returned to the mill. After Lillie carried the pail of cracked corn to the chicken house, she poured the corn into their food trough and poured out her heart to the hens. She related the tale of her confrontation with Joyce Ann Carter. Though the clucking hens didn't offer any suggestions about what she should have done to handle Joyce Ann's bullying, they were good listeners.

That night, after the youngsters were in bed, Samuel and Anna snuggled on the couch, talking softly. Samuel looked at his wife with a mischievous grin. "We were thinkin' about letting our youngest take dancin' lessons. I guess we missed her calling. I think we should sign Lillie up for football or wrestlin'." Anna pretended to be shocked, but ended by kissing her wisecracking husband soundly.

Little Mill on Beaver Creek

CHAPTER FOUR: *WHAT HAPPENED TO THEM, PAP-PAW?*
March 29, 1913

In the Gilmers' corner of North Carolina, the second half of March is traditionally the time when gardens are planted and fields are sown with wheat, corn, and oats. Farmers spend the winter's long, dark evenings studying the *Farmer's Almanac,* hoping to determine the exact date when the last frost will occur. Planting can commence shortly thereafter.

Planting time in rural areas was critical to everyone's livelihood and survival—whether they were farmers, millers, or shopkeepers. Vegetables from the summer and fall gardens had to sustain a family through the cold winter months and into late spring, when gardeners could begin to harvest greens and spring crops. Farmers sowed oats, wheat, and corn in freshly plowed fields to feed not only people, but also their cattle, sheep, goats, horses, mules, and donkeys during the winter months.

When the grains were harvested, farmers carted their crop of oats to grist mills, where they were ground into oatmeal and oat flour. After the wheat was threshed, it was finely ground into flour used for baking, and the bran that was left behind after the milling process was fed to the animals. Both humans and animals enjoyed corn, but different kinds.

Families picked corn from their gardens on hot summer days and happily devoured the ears. Field corn stayed on their stalks until the ears became firm and dry; at that point, farmers and their families harvested the ears and dropped them into large bags. Later, they would shell the ears using hand-cranked corn-shelling machines. Some of the shelled corn would be stored away to be used as seed for the next year's crop, but most of the shelled corn would be placed in bags once again and then hauled in wagons to the grist mill. Millers finely ground some of it into corn meal and other bags of corn would be less finely ground, producing stone-ground grits, a staple widely enjoyed throughout the South. The corn stalks were chopped and stored in silos or buried in a pit in the ground, where it was allowed to ferment. The result was called silage, which provided food for cattle in the winter.

Important byproducts of wheat and oats are the hay and straw made from the stems of the grains. Dried oat and wheat stalks were bound tightly and stored in barns until winter, when they would be fed to the farm animals. When warm and clean, straw was also excellent bedding for all farm livestock—much preferable for animals than having them sleep on damp, cold ground. A lot of manure winds up on the floor of a barn, as Jake well knew, since mucking the stables was one of his least favorite chores. He quickly learned that when manure falls onto straw instead of on the barn floor, the stalls are much easier to clean. In the spring, he forked the mixture into a manure-spreader, a machine that SueJean pulled around a pasture. The Gilmers used this straw-manure mixture as a natural fertilizer for their crops.

Neighboring farmers teamed up during planting time, helping each other prepare and plant all the fields. First, each farmer plowed his own fields, using horses or mules to break up the hard soil. This took some time—often several days, if the fields were large—unless the farmer had several horses or mules, several plows, and another man or strong sons to help with the labor. Plowing was hard, dirty, tiring work.

Because he was large and strong for his age, Jake was allowed to start plowing by the time he turned nine years old. After the fields were plowed, Samuel hitched his horses—or, more often, his mules—to the disc harrow to break up hard clods of soil. This machine had several sharp round cutting blades suspended underneath a heavy platform and hitched to the same mules or horses. It actually made little furrows in the now-soft earth so the seeds would have a good place to germinate and grow.

Once the plowing and harrowing were finished, the Gilmer children (and once or twice, Anna, too) walked the fields, picking up stones that had come to the surface during the winter frosts and plowing. They tossed them in piles beside the field.

Then it was time for planting. Lee Hanner and his son-in-law—and, often a farm hand or neighbor—would team up and operate the seed drill. One man (usually the owner of the field) drove the horses or mules that were hitched to the seed drill. This machine ran on large wheels. It looked like a long, wide box with a series of plow points underneath it, the smaller point behind. Farmers filled the box with seeds, and as the plow points dug furrows into the soft earth, seeds dropped through the points into the furrows. The points had tubes running into the seed box.

As the mules pulled the seed drill, the sharper point dug a little furrow in the front, then seeds slid down the tubes from the box and dropped to the ground. The smaller metal object behind the seed points was angled slightly. This pushed dirt over the seeds to cover them. While Samuel operated the seed drill, Jake followed behind, to make certain that the seeds were flowing out the chutes from the seed box and onto the ground. Jake kept watch on the seeds remaining in the seed box, so he could tell his father when it was time to stop and refill the box with more seeds. This machine—which helped revolutionize farming techniques during Lee Hanners' lifetime—could plant as many as twelve rows, evenly spaced, at the same time.

"I don't like doing this," Lillie said soon after she turned five, when she was sent to the fields with Jake to clear away the rocks, limbs, and small roots. "I don't like to get dirty!" she insisted. Jake just groaned. Later, her grandfather put her on his knee and explained, "I know, Lillie. That's a dull, dirty, tedious job. But it's a very important job. This makes sure our tiny little seeds find a home in the soil and grow into big and healthy plants."

"Well, I guess I can do it if it's an important job," Lillie said. When Anna overheard Lillie bragging to her doll Susie about the importance of her "grown-up job," she smiled.

This planting season, Lillie was a year older and had a sense of adventure. Jake had aroused her curiosity when he explained that picking up rocks and other debris from the plowed ground could also lead to archeological discoveries. Within the first hour of work in the fields, Jake found two treasures in the earth: an Indian arrowhead and the head of an ancient axe. "Look, Lillie," he said, running to his little sister. "This is the best part of this chore. We need to keep our eyes peeled for Indian treasures."

"Treasures?" Lillie repeated in a whisper of awe, reaching out to feel the tiny chip marks on the arrowhead Jake found.

"Here, put this in the pocket of your apron," Jake suggested, handing her the arrowhead. "I'll keep the axe head because it's heavier and sharper. We'll have a contest to see who can find the most and the best. Pa keeps a collection on one of the crossbeams in our barn."

"I found another arrowhead!" Lillie called out, waving her arms to Jake moments later. When he came running, they brushed the dirt off to find an ordinary pointed rock.

"Sorry, Lillie. That's just a rock shaped something like an arrowhead," her brother said. "Keep looking."

"Hoeing isn't as dirty as clearing the rocks, but it hurts my hands," Lillie complained several weeks later, when the seedlings began to appear and the time came to hoe the weeds out from among the family's fledgling crops. Her brother had given her a small rake, which his Grandfather Gilmer had made for Samuel and his brothers years earlier. Lillie looked ruefully at the blisters on the palms of her little pink hands. "I don't like doing this!"

"Don't worry. When you're bigger, you'll probably get to work in the kitchen, baking cookies and pies and eating them instead of doing this," Jake said, in an effort to console her. "We can still find arrowheads, remember. Let's have another contest to see who finds the best ones." Lillie agreed enthusiastically. To her eyes, every rock shaped anything like a triangle was an Indian arrowhead. After washing their finds in a pail, too often Lillie discovered that many of her treasures were ordinary rocks. And they would soon be dropped into a tire rut in the road or in a washed-away area.

She squealed excitedly one day when Jake announced, "Look, Lillie! This morning we've found twelve arrowheads—and all of them are tip-top." Instead of leaving them in the barn, where they would be stored, Lillie gathered them in a little berry basket to show her grandfather.

"You shouldn't bother Pap-paw," Jake protested, though he was secretly pleased at his sister's excitement.

"Pap-paw always has all the time in the world to listen to me," Lillie said, running down the hill toward the mill, keeping a protective hand over the archeological discoveries. Jake glanced at the barn, where the stables needed his attention. But he shrugged his shoulders and followed his sister to the mill.

They found their grandfather had finished cleaning sawdust off the log carriage and was beginning to lubricate the saws. When Jake opened the door for Lillie, Lee Hanner was examining the saw blades to see if they needed to be sharpened or replaced.

"Pap-paw, look at what we found today!" Lillie squealed. "I know some are Indian arrowheads, but do you know what the other things are?"

Lee Hanner stopped his work, smiled at Lillie, winked at Jake, and carried an old wooden chair to the door of the mill. "I need to let the bright sun shine on these important treasures if I'm to appreciate them," he said. He studied each one carefully. "Here's an arrowhead, and another, and another...Oh, this one is particularly fine," he told his grandchildren. They crowded closer to look. "See? The arrow point is made from white quartz," Pap-paw marveled. "More often, around here, the Indians made them out of slate."

Next, he picked out a long, thin stone with chips evenly cut into the sides. "This still has sharp edges," he marveled. "Now this is a well-made tool."

"I think we have a spearhead," Jake said, showing another of his treasures. His grandfather nodded.

"And look at these, Pap-paw!" Lillie pointed to two treasures similarly shaped. "Are they axes? Or tomahawks?" The grandfather and grandchildren studied the shapes: short and fat. "I'd like to think they're axes—for cutting trees on this very land," Lee Hanner told the children. "Look at the notches here. These heads were tied firmly onto sticks, using leather rawhide straps. Someday we should find a good stick and a good strap and see how well this axe works."

"That's a great idea!" Jake said. "I wouldn't mind chopping wood so much if I could use a real Indian axe."

"You may live to regret those words, but we'll see," his grandfather said with a grin. He picked up another field treasure. "Now, here's something I haven't seen in some time."

"What is it, Pap-paw? Lillie asked.

"See this smooth, long rock?" He held the artifact in his hand. "It's made of granite, not quartz or slate like the other tools. This is used for sharpening things. Like us, Indians had to keep their tools very, very sharp—especially the edges of the arrowheads and spearheads, if they wanted to hunt deer and bear and birds successfully." He hefted the rock in his hand. "See how heavy it is? Granite is especially strong, so this stone won't easily break."

He laid all the field treasures in a row on the floor at their feet. "These are tools. But they're also works of art," he told the children. "The Indians were very patient and precise when they chipped away at rocks, forming them into the tools they needed. They used other very sharp rocks for the job—and they worked very, very hard at it. Each of these tools took a long, long time to make."

"Pap-paw, I found this thing and I don't know what it is." Lillie presented a rock that fit perfectly into her hand. It was apparent that someone had shaped it very carefully and deliberately. "One side is flat like a pancake," she said, "but the other side is rounded. And the edges are thin and very sharp. Be careful when you hold it!"

Lee Hanner smiled as he studied this tool. "Sweetie, you've found a hide scraper. The Indians didn't let anything go to waste. They skinned the animals they hunted—deer, beavers, muskrats and bears— after they drained the blood. Afterwards, they stretched the hides out over a smooth dry log, or they laid them across a clean flat surface, or they laced them onto a wooden drying rack with the fur side turned away from the sunshine. Then they used this scraping tool, pushing down hard, making a sawing motion back and forth."

Lee demonstrated, holding the tool and moving it through the air. "The Indians—I believe it was usually the women and girls—worked patiently to get the fat and flesh off that skin and make it perfectly clean. If they didn't remove every last bit of the flesh, the hide wouldn't tan properly. As you can imagine, this took a very long time."

"They must have known what you taught us, Pap-paw: if you do something important, you should do it well," Jake suggested. Lee looked pleased. Then he continued his story. "The Indians ate the meat of the animals, used the sinews for strings on their bows, and used the animal hides for many, many things. They covered the doors and windows of their homes with hides. They sewed them into moccasins and clothing. Bear skins were especially good to wear or sleep under during the winter.

The Indians made leather bags from the skins, so they could carry things on their backs or on horses. And they used the skins for the costumes they wore during the special ceremonies they held around campfires."

Lee Hanner glanced at Jake, who was already becoming proficient at shooting. "Always remember, Jake, an Indian never killed an animal for sport. If they had to kill an animal for food, they knelt beside the body and apologized to the animal for taking its life. They made sure to use every part of that animal. Nothing was wasted. Indians lived off the land and knew they owed their lives to the creatures and the soil. They respected all living things. That's a lesson we need to remember."

"Why are there so many of these Indian tools here on our land, Pap-paw?" asked Jake. "Why do we find them every time we dig in our fields?"

"That's a good question, Jake," his grandfather said, standing and stretching. "On this very spot, where we're standing, a very large Indian settlement once stood. The Indians lived here for thousands of years—until about two hundred years ago. We love our farm, and so did they. It was as fine a place for them to live as it is for us. They planted crops in the same spot near the creek where we planted corn last year. This land offered them plenty of food to eat, plenty of water to drink from our fresh springs, and plenty of fish to catch in our creek and lake."

"What did they like to eat, Pap-paw?" Jake asked.

"They grew lots of the same vegetables we eat: squash, pumpkins, and beans. Those Indians were smart. They taught white men to plant corn by putting a fish in the hole under the seeds because the fish becomes a good fertilizer. And they planted bean seeds in the same mound, so the bean vines could climb up the corn stalks."

"Did they like fishing as much as I do, Pap-paw?" Jake asked, peering through the mill's window at the icy creek water.

"They must have," Lee said. "Judging by some shell mounds I dug up on the river banks when I was a boy, they liked little river clams and crawfish to eat. Also turtles and frogs. The weather here wasn't too bad in the winter because the ice and snow only come two or three months every year. Our Indians didn't have to endure the long winters northern tribes faced. When the temperatures dropped below freezing, they were ready, thanks to those deer hide clothes and the warm fur coats they made."

Lee paused and smiled at his grandchildren before asking, "Can you guess what animals they trapped?"

"Beavers and rabbits," Lillie said.

"Raccoons. Muskrats. Foxes," Jake added. "Those are all the animals people around here trap."

Their grandfather nodded, but grinned and said, "They also caught groundhogs and minks."

"What were their houses like, Pap-paw?" Lillie asked.

"Our land was covered in trees, and they used some of those trees to build their huts. They bent strong wooden poles to make a kind of dome, then they covered the poles with hides and slabs of bark. Perhaps they even used some of those big rocks on the creek bank to build shelters for themselves or stables for their horses. They wouldn't have had cows until later, when settlers brought them from Europe, but the Indians did have buffalo around here—and buffalo provided a lot of meat, sinews, grease, and big hides."

"Buffalo?" Jake exclaimed. "I didn't know buffalo lived around here. I thought they lived out West. How did Indians kill such big animals when they didn't have guns?"

Lee affectionately ruffled the boy's hair. "All the braves worked as a team. Hunting big animals took many arrows and spears. And remember, as time passed, Indians began using iron and steel instead of stone. Steel is much sharper. But I'm sure in the early days, many a buffalo and bear were brought down with their flint tools and ingenuity."

He decided to ask a question of his own. "Can you think of other foods the Indians ate?"

When the children were silent for a moment, he hinted, "Think Thanksgiving."

"Turkeys?" Lillie suggested.

Lee nodded. "And geese, pheasants, ducks, and doves. Some they shot and some they trapped. They knew every plant and how it could be used for food or medicine. They picked dandelion greens, sorrel, and other greens that grew on these hills. They found mushrooms in the woods—they knew which ones were safe and which ones to avoid. They snacked on acorns, hickory nuts, and berries. When they got sick, their medicine men used the moss, tree bark, plants, and berries found in the fields and woods to treat them."

"Wow! This must have been a busy place hundreds of years ago," Jake said.

"Yup. The Indians worked here, lived here, sang and danced here. Their children played here on the same spots where you play. And sometimes they fought with other tribes or with white people. Although they left our land long, long ago, they left us many of our place names and some treasures we still find in fields and along stream banks."

"Those Indians really had a great life here. What happened to them, Pap-paw?" Lillie asked. "Why did they leave our land?"

Lee Hanner sighed. "The settlers from Europe didn't treat them very well, Lillie. They brought European sicknesses that killed many Indians. Some of them are sicknesses we get, like measles, mumps, and chicken pox. Many Indians died of smallpox—luckily, doctors can give us vaccines for that awful sickness nowadays. In many cases, white men forced Indians to move away from their traditional hunting grounds and river banks. And white men hunted too many of the animals for sport, so there wasn't enough food for the tribes to keep living here."

He paused and added, "Remind me to show you the Indian graves behind Alamance Presbyterian Church. We don't know how those people died, but it could've been from the illnesses they caught from white men."

"I thought white men were the good guys," Jake protested.

"I hate to tell you otherwise, but we weren't. Not always, anyway," his grandfather said. He spoke about the laws white settlers passed that forced the Indians farther and farther west, away from the lands where their ancestors had lived for many centuries. He told them about the Trail of Tears, when most of the Cherokee Indians living on or near the Smokey Mountains were forced to move to reservations in Oklahoma. "On the long trek there, many Cherokee died—from exhaustion, starvation, thirst, sickness, and grief," Lee said.

The children looked horrified. "This isn't a happy story, but it's one you need to understand," the grandfather told the children. "Many times when the Indians fought back, the white people killed them—and they had guns. At first, the Indians did not. Guns kill people faster than spears and tomahawks. In the colonial days, settlers and Indians fought terrifying wars. Both sides burned settlements and killed people mercilessly.

"And that ain't all," Lee continued, wondering if Anna would thank him for giving her children nightmares. "White men have slaughtered nearly all the buffalo that some tribes relied upon for food and clothing. I've heard that settlers and fancy rich men from the cities massacred thousands of buffalo at a time, either to get them off the land so they could plant crops, or just for sport. When the buffalo disappeared, so did the way of life for many tribes, and the Indians had to move."

"Mr. Gladstone told us about John Smith and Pocahontas up in Virginia, and about an Indian brave named Squanto who helped the Pilgrims in Massachusetts, but that's all I knew about Indians," Jake said.

Lee nodded. "The Indians believed that all things from the earth were gifts from the Great Spirit—this would be the being we call God. They thanked the Great Spirit for what they had. They knew that when people care for the land they live on, and when they live in peace with all the creatures on the land, the Great Spirit will care for him and give them all they need."

Lee Hanner sighed and rose from the chair, speaking soberly, "Young 'uns, keep these Indian tools and protect them. Someday, they may no longer be found. Show them to your own children and explain to them about the people who once walked where we walk, who lived right here where we live. Tell them that these Indians loved this land—maybe even more than we do."

Little Mill on Beaver Creek

CHAPTER FIVE: *"I THINK I TOOK A WRONG TURN"*
April 19, 1913

Jake finished his morning chores in double-quick time on a fine Saturday morning in April because he wanted to go rabbit hunting.

"Be careful!" Anna Gilmer urged.

"Bring us home some dinner," Samuel added with a grin.

Jake quickly put on his hunting vest, dropped five shotgun shells into the ammunition pocket, slapped his hat on his head, and reached for the Winchester Model 1897 twelve-gauge pump-action shotgun he had inherited from his father. As he grabbed a handful of Molly's cookies and started for the door, his mother cautioned him. "Don't be too long, Jake. And remember what your Pa taught you: before you cross a fence, lay that gun down on the ground on the other side, and only then climb the fence."

"I'll remember, Mom," Jake said. He whistled to Dan, the family beagle, who raced up to the boy, wagging his tail enthusiastically. Jake bent and patted his head. "Good boy. You wanna go huntin', Dan? Wanna chase a rabbit?" Dan bayed in agreement, jumping up with his front paws on Jake's thighs. Dan's liquid brown eyes danced with total devotion to his young master and excitement about the hunt.

The boy and the dog passed by the barn, crossed Beaver Creek at a spot where the cold rushing water was narrow, and started up the hill towards the woods. Warm spring sunshine beamed down on them. The quail were calling to each other across the field. Bees were hard at work humming over the batch of spring clover. Without warning, a startled rabbit jumped up from the grass, bounding toward the cover of an evergreen. Dan raced in pursuit immediately, baying joyously as he ran.

Jake opened the chamber on the side of the barrel and inserted two shells. He pulled back on the pump mechanism underneath to load a shell into the firing chamber. By the time he was ready to get a bead on the rabbit, it had disappeared, with the dog in hot pursuit. Jake dashed after them both, but realized they were heading too close to the horse out in the field for him to get a good shot. Jake lowered his gun.

"Shucks," he muttered as he put on the safety before running after the hound. All Jake could see at that moment was the white tip of Dan's tail waving like a flag. Into the shadows of the trees they all ran. Jake heard Dan baying again. The beagle must have picked up the rabbit's scent once again. Through the underbrush, Jake glimpsed Dan's tail up ahead, to the right. "Good boy, Dan! Stay on him."

Careful to not trip on briar vines and tree roots, Jake dodged through the woods. He paused and flipped off the safety when Dan chased a rabbit in his direction and out through a clearing. Jake stopped, jerked the shotgun to his shoulder, aimed just in front of the fleeing rabbit, then squeezed the trigger. He took care to shoot before Dan got too close to the rabbit.

"BOOM!" The Winchester kicked back against Jake's shoulder and the rabbit fell to the ground. "Wow! I got him." Jake called to Dan, running over to see his prize. "Good job, Dan. Good chasing. Look at this guy. He's big." He picked the rabbit up by the ears. "Sure 'nough, you'll get some rabbit innards tonight, Dan."

Jake's mouth watered as he pictured his mother stewing the meat with spices and gravy—after she cleaned all the shot pellets out of him. Jake put the safety back on his gun and decided to return home right away. But when he glimpsed something red and white darting through the briars, he shoved the rabbit into his vest pocket and set off in pursuit.

"Can that be the red fox that attacked our chickens?" the boy wondered aloud as he ran. The Gilmer family had lost three of their best laying hens since Christmas—but only on the especially cold nights when Dan slept in the barn instead of near the coop. Two neighbors had also reported losing two or three chickens just in the past month. Although several farmers had gone out hunting for the marauding fox, so far no one had been able to bring him down. "He's cunning," Samuel had told his family several nights after hearing a commotion in the henhouse and grabbing his gun. Every time he returned empty-handed. "He always manages to slip away just as I get my finger on the trigger."

"Ha, I've got you now, Red. No more chickens for y'all." Jake put the strap of the shotgun over his head once more and hurried deeper into the woods, following the path he thought the fox had taken. Dan caught the scent under a briar bush and started baying, his tail waving excitedly. But moments later, Dan stopped abruptly and sniffed the ground, walking in circles. He, too, had lost the scent.

Jake wasn't willing to give up yet, however. He followed a bend in the creek, then headed up a hill and deeper into the woods. When he reached a large rock on the bank where the stream bends sharply, he failed to notice an iron post beside the stone. "Have I ever been here?" he puzzled aloud. Then he shrugged. "I need to find that fox. Dad will be proud and surprised, and all the neighbors will be glad the chicken thief is gone." He promised himself, however, that if he didn't see the fox in a few minutes, he'd give up and go home.

But he didn't really think that was necessary. Dan was still circling back where he had last smelled the fox, and Dan had a famous sense of smell—and sport. Right now, his tail was wagging slowly and he was whining in confusion, but he remained at that spot. Jake pulled back on the pump mechanism of his gun, ejecting the used cartridge.

The woods were very dense here, with little light reaching the ground. The only landmark that looked familiar to Jake was the creek. A sudden noise up ahead caused the boy to look around the scenery sharply. "This is a bit spooky," he muttered.

Up the hill about twenty yards on the other side of the stream, he could glimpse a small wooden lean-to, with three sides and a rusting tin roof. Peering cautiously through the briar thicket, he saw that the roof had a crooked chimney on top and smoke was drifting lazily upward. Jake's curiosity was roused. He wondered if this was a temporary campsite for another hunter. "Surely no one lives here?" he asked himself.

He unshouldered his shotgun and picked his way through the briars for a better look. A round stone base supported walls of stones that continued upward. They were mortared together, Jake guessed, with creek mud. "Is that a type of fire pit?" he murmured. He noticed a pile of what appeared to be fresh-cut firewood higher up the hill. He sniffed the air. A fire was glowing under a steel pot that had an upside-down funnel on top. The machinery was made of copper, but it had turned green in color. A coil of copper tubing came out of that funnel and descended into the top of an oak barrel.

The contraption was intriguing, and Jake studied it, forgetting about the fox and even forgetting about Dan for a moment. A large tube emerged from the top of the barrel, going into the top of another barrel just down the slope of the hill. A short copper pipe stuck out from this barrel, and as Jake inched closer, he could see liquid draining out of that tube into an earthenware demi-john. Jake crouched. He didn't want to cross the creek and get too close to this strange campsite, but he was all-fired curious about what this could possibly be.

His nose wrinkled. "Ewww. That smells funny," he said softly. "I don't like this." He decided it was time to find Dan and go home.

He had been squatting long enough that his knees had grown stiff. Grunting, he stood. And stared straight into the barrel of a shotgun.

"What're y'all doin' here?" growled the man at the end of the shotgun. It took Jake a shocked moment before he recognized the owner of the shotgun.

Will Granger.

Jake hardly recognized the man. The few times when he had seen him, Will Granger had looked scruffy and rough, but now his body and his clothes were filthy. His beard had grown long and unkempt, and his eyes were bloodshot. Unconsciously, Jake sniffed again and wrinkled his nose. The man smelled like the liquid coming out of that contraption. But what was even more worrisome was the fact that Will was obviously not happy to have someone looking at his campsite. He kept his shotgun pointed at young Jake.

Jake took a step backwards, tripped on a root, and landed on his back on the ground. He could fell himself trembling, but tried not to let the man see his fear. "Mr. Granger, sir, it's me, Jake Gilmer. I'm sorry if

I'm trespassin'. I think I took a wrong turn. When I shot this here rabbit, the shot scared up a red fox, and I was tryin' to track it."

When the man didn't respond and didn't lower his shotgun, Jake continued, "I lost the trail and I wound up here. I'm just huntin', sir. Look, I'm layin' my shotgun down." Jake very slowly and carefully placed his shotgun on the ground.

The man grunted, finally lowering his own gun. He spat tobacco juice at Jake's feet. "Boy, didn't you see that iron rod in the ground beside the big rock back yonder at the turn of the creek?"

"No, sir," Jake said, looking puzzled.

"That means you're trespassin'. You're a kid, and I know you and your Pa. But that don't mean I welcome you nosin' around this here property ever again. You hear me, boy?"

Jake slowly raised himself off the ground. "Yes, sir, Mr. Granger. I won't come up here again, I promise. I'm sorry if you thought I was nosy. I just wondered about that peculiar-lookin' camping shelter. And then I wondered what that strange-looking contraption is."

"Never you mind what that is," Will snarled. "Go on home now, 'fore I change my mind and use this gun after all."

Jake immediately started hightailing it home through the underbrush, but he didn't get far before Will Granger hollered, "Hold up, there, boy! You won't get no more rabbits for your Mama if you don't have your gun."

Jake turned sheepishly and retraced his steps. As he bent to retrieve his gun, he kept his eyes on the shotgun in Will Granger's hand. "Th-thank you, sir," he stuttered. He could hear Dan thrashing through the undergrowth, heading in his direction.

Will Granger grunted, but looked a mite less fierce. "Here comes your dog, boy. Now, GIT!"

As Jake took off sprinting once again, the man shouted after him, "Hey! You didn't see nothin' up here, neither! Understan'?"

Jake ran as far and as fast as he could before a stitch in his side forced him to stop and catch his breath. As soon as he could fill his lungs with air, he was off again. He had never been so glad to see his own pasture. By the time he made his way up the hill toward the barn, his chest was burning as he gasped for air. He barely made it onto the porch of his home before he collapsed.

"Jake, whatever is the matter?" Anna demanded an answer as soon as she pushed open the porch screen and walked out onto the porch.

"Got...you...a...rabbit," the boy managed to gasp.

"Jake, honey, are you all right? You look as if you'd seen a ghost! You didn't get hurt out there, did you?" His mother bent over him, searching for some sign of injury. Dan jumped onto the porch and licked the boy's face, as if he were equally concerned.

"No, I—I'm not hurt," Jake stammered.

"You sure?" Anna continued to study her son, but when he shook his head and Dan turned to lick him, she thanked both of them for the rabbit, promising to clean it immediately. "Dan, looks like you and your master have done a fine job trackin' that rabbit." Then she turned her attention back to Jake once more.

Jake shook his head as if answering her silent question. "No, ma'am, I'm all right. Just got a bit lost, that's all. That's why I'm late."

Anna nodded, patted her son on the shoulder, and didn't ask any more questions.

Late that afternoon, Jake joined Samuel in the barn in time for milking the cows, after passing Lillie, who had already fed the hens and was securing them in their house, and Molly, who was bringing in the laundry. The father and son worked together silently. Jake finished milking his cow before he decided to share his experience with his father. Hesitantly, he looked over at Samuel, who was sitting on the stool beside the second cow, still milking her. Jake slowly walked over until he stood beside his father.

"Pa, something happened after I shot that rabbit this afternoon. I can't tell you everything, but I've got to tell somebody."

Samuel Gilmer glanced quickly at his son. "Go ahead."

Jake sighed. "I was droppin' that rabbit into my vest pocket when I glimpsed a big red fox sneakin' behind the briar bushes just ahead of me. Dan caught his scent and started after him. That fox ran into the woods up the hill, and I lost him, but Dan kept goin' 'round and 'round in circles, whinin' because he lost the critter's scent. I decided to see if I could find the fox on my own."

He took a deep breath, afraid to meet his father's piercing gaze. "Well, I went up into the woods and around the sharp bend in the creek— the one where a big rock sits up on the hill. Then I went down into a little holler where the bushes are really thick."

When he took a long time to choose his words, Samuel asked quietly, "And then what happened, son?

Jake looked at the barn floor. "I was gonna turn an' come back to find Dan—I really was. But I saw a peculiar-lookin' shelter in the thicket on the other side of the creek. And smoke was comin' out of a little chimney, so I was curious about who might be there. I stayed on the other side of the creek and I didn't go there, but I squatted down to study it. I couldn't make sense out of what I was seein'. But finally my knees got really stiff and I stood up."

"And?" Samuel prompted.

"Well, Mr. Granger was there. He looked…he looked…well, rough like. And he was mighty angry with me. I was so scared that I fell hind-end first."

The two barn cats, a gray tabby and an old yellow cat, named Puss and Boots, sauntered up to Samuel right then, meowing. "Hi, there," Samuel said, pulling a small bowl off the stall shelf. He held the bowl under the cow's teats and squirted the cats' dinner into the bowl, which he handed silently to Jake.

Automatically, Jake put the bowl on the floor just outside the stall and patted the cats' heads as they walked over with tails held high. Samuel said not a word as he finished milking Elsa, but Jake could tell his father hadn't forgotten about the conversation.

Finally, Samuel spoke. Softly. "Jake, did Will Granger have a gun?"

"Pa, he told me not to say nothin'. I ain't supposed to say *nothin'*. He yelled that I was trespassin'."

When Samuel continued to stare at his son, Jake looked down at his boots and admitted, "Yes, sir, he had a gun."

When he saw no change in expression on his father's face, he spoke in a rush, "I 'pologized and ever'thing. I tried to explain why I had gone up there, and I promised I wouldn't do it again."

"And then what happened?"

"Mr. Granger told me to git. Fast. And don't come back."

Samuel's face registered his anger. "I'm real sorry for being up there, Pa!" Jake added hastily. "If he comes here and tells you that I've been snoopin' around and trespassin', I wanted you to know it was an accident."

Samuel stood, picked up the pail of milk and the stool, and looked into Jake's eyes. "Jake, you were wrong to be on Mr. Granger's property. That surely was trespassin', son. I believe you when you say it was accidental, but, you see, Mr. Granger was so angry because he was doing somethin' wrong."

When Jake looked puzzled, Samuel said, "You're pretty tall now, Jake, and since you were squattin' down, he probably mistook you for a thief or a revenuer."

"Revenuer?" Jake repeated. He'd heard that word before. "You mean that was a *still* he had up there?"

Samuel nodded. "He had that gun to protect himself, and that makes what he was doin' even more wrong. But the fact that he pointed that gun at you is what has me riled up."

"Did you know that he was makin' moonshine, Pa?"

"I wasn't sure, but I know enough about Will Granger to guess what he was doin' in that holler. And, from what you told me, I don't think Mr. Granger was in any condition at that moment to think clearly. That's why he was so mean."

Samuel grasped his son's shoulder tightly and spoke firmly. "Jake, I want you to stay away from Will's land, but I don't want you to worry about this anymore. Thank you for tellin' me, son. Now, let's tote this milk to the spring house." He patted Jake on the shoulder and released him before they left the barn.

The cows continued eating their hay. They could be trusted to keep a secret.

That night, after the children went to bed, Samuel and Anna bundled up in coats and sat on the porch swing. It swayed back and forth as they held hands and listened to the frogs croaking down in the creek. Off in the distance, an owl hooted and whippoorwills sang a goodnight song.

"Honey, was Jake actin' a little strange when he got back from huntin' this afternoon?" Samuel asked, his voice sounding casual.

Anna studied her husband's face. "As a matter of fact, he was a mite pale, and seriously out of breath. He said he was all right, that he had just been lost for a while."

Samuel nodded. "Yes, he did get lost. After he killed that rabbit we ate for dinner, he saw a red fox and decided to try to find it himself since Dan had lost the trail."

Anna looked inquiringly into her husband's face when he paused in the course of his story. Eventually, he continued, "Jake wandered up a hill and into Will Granger's woods. He stumbled upon Will's still, Anna. He hid on this side of the creek, wonderin' what it was he was lookin' at, and Will Granger found him. Will was drunk and saw a young man with a hat studyin' the still. He must have assumed he was a revenuer. Or someone there to steal whiskey. Will pulled his gun on Jake, Anna."

She gasped. "Merciful heavens! Oh, Samuel, he could have shot our son!"

Samuel pulled her close. "But, he didn't, Anna. Jake is fine. He just learned a hard lesson today. I'm gonna wait for a good time to talk with Will. Now we know why no one has seen him in more'n a week. He's been up there makin' 'shine and drinkin' heavy."

"Is it safe to confront him?" she asked anxiously.

"I'll certainly wait for him to sober up first," Samuel assured her. "He may not even remember everything that happened with Jake. I've thought about it and decided I'm not gonna talk with the sheriff about the still. But I do think I should talk to Will about how dangerous this situation could have become."

"Why'd would someone with a nice farm turn to moonshinin'?" Anna asked, sounding exasperated.

Samuel shook his head. "You said it yourself, Anna. Something must have happened in the past to make Will this way. Maybe he needs a friend about now. Maybe he needs to listen to someone, instead of shuttin' himself away from people."

"You're right, of course," Anna said slowly. "I believe he needs to know that someone cares about him. We are all our brother's keeper; let's look for an opportunity to be that for Will."

CHAPTER SIX: *A LONG AND SERIOUS DISCUSSION*
April 30, 1913

Wagon brakes squealing, Will Granger pulled beside the mill. Riding beside him on an old brown horse was Solomon, one of the sharecroppers living on Granger land. "I've come with more logs. I need twelve-foot lengths," Will Granger grunted at Lee Hanner in greeting. Then he pointed to Solomon. "He'll help roll these logs off the trailer." Two very large logs weighed down the wagon, with two smaller logs, probably from the top of the same poplar tree, resting beside them.

"Hi, neighbor," Samuel said, emerging from the mill, wiping his hands on a rag. "I haven't seen you since that big blizzard when you picked up your pine boards."

Will didn't look at Samuel when he answered, "No, I've been...busy." He cleared his throat and appeared to gaze at a point beyond Samuel's left shoulder when he added, "Anyway, I'm right sorry about the way I yelled at y'all back in February. I had no right to talk like that. I should've written that price down, to start with."

He cleared his throat again. "Well, enough about that. I've been watchin' this poplar tree for some time. It was leanin' over my house, and it was as dead as could be. My men and I managed to cut it down so it wouldn't land on my house or barn."

Samuel walked to the wagon to inspect the logs. He nodded. "They're in good shape. No sign of rot. They'll make fine boards."

"I don't need any more lumber right now," Will said, "but I'll pay you for cuttin' it and storin' it."

Samuel pulled out his tape measure. Will Granger held one end at the top of the longest log while Samuel pulled it down to the bottom end. After he measured the diameter of each log, he pulled out a small notebook and the stub of a pencil from his overalls pocket. He propped the notebook on the back of the wagon as he did some calculating. When he sensed Will Granger watching him, he grinned. "And to think I used to cry when I did arithmetic homework in early grades. It was hard for me then, and I hated doing it. I never dreamed I would be usin' all those mathematical skills every day of my adult life."

His listener nodded, but said nothing, and Samuel returned to his calculations. "All right, Will, I've worked up an estimate for turnin' these fine logs into lumber, but why don't I just keep that in my files? Business is quiet right now, so this is a perfect time for work on these logs. I'll store them here for up to six months. If you use the lumber yourself, I'll charge you for my work at that time. If, after six months if you don't come back for the boards, I'll sell the lumber to someone who needs it and give you a percentage of my profit. How does that sound?"

His neighbor nodded and stretched out his hand. Then the men set to work. Propping sturdy planks against the rear of the trailer, they looped chains around the logs and rolled them off the wagon slowly. Then they chose sides of each of the logs, lifted them, and lugged them inside the building. As soon as they were done, Will shook Solomon's hand. "Much obliged, Sol. I 'preciate your help." The tall quiet man nodded, climbed back on his horse, and rode away.

"Would you like some water from our well? It's tasty and cold, if you don't mind a short walk up a short hill," Samuel suggested.

Will nodded, "A drink of cold water would be welcome." They drank from the well near the house, and then Samuel said, "Will, before you drive your wagon back home, why don't you sit with me on the porch and visit a spell?"

Will Granger looked uncomfortable, but to Samuel's surprise, he agreed. As they settled onto chairs, Samuel began the speech he had rehearsed for two weeks. "Will, I ain't gonna meddle in your personal life, but somethin' happened recently on a Saturday afternoon that has me concerned. My boy Jake went rabbit huntin' and wound up by mistake on your property. He didn't tell me much. Said he'd promised to keep his mouth shut. But I can guess what he saw."

Will Granger spat a stream of tobacco juice, narrowly missing the porch step. But he continued to listen to Samuel.

"Will, what you do on your property is absolutely your business. But when you point a gun at a ten-year-old boy, well, that changes things."

Will had been looking down as Samuel talked, but at the last sentence, he jerked his head toward Samuel, "I did *what* with my gun?"

"You pointed it at my son."

The man wiped his brow with a grimy handkerchief. "Samuel, I swear to you, I know I had my gun with me when I saw someone comin' up the hill with a gun. Didn't know who it was, so I hid and watched him squattin' down, starin' at the...uh, my still... You can't blame me for thinkin' he was a thief or the law."

"Maybe not, but you were lookin' at a ten-year-old, no matter how big he is for his age," Samuel said, keeping his voice light and friendly.

Will Granger cleared his throat. "Sam, I was drunker than I've ever been in my life. I don't 'member what I said or did. A week there without eatin' or sleepin' while I kept brewin' up that 'shine made me sicker than I've ever been. My mind wasn't right."

"Is that a good excuse, Will?" Samuel asked, his voice still friendly.

"Well, a man has a right to privacy on his own land. I 'member yellin' at a boy and tellin' him he was trespassin'. I 'member orderin' him off my property. But I don't 'member pointin' my gun at him."

He buried his face in his hands. "Oh, God! Samuel, I wanted to scare him off, sure, but if I really pointed a gun at Jake, I'm just as sorry as I can be. I like the boy. You folks've been real nice to me. To think about what coulda happened if my finger had jerked on the trigger—and I that shaky from the booze and anger." Samuel could see anguish on the man's face. "Forgive me. That'll never, ever happen again. I know I've gotta break up the still and get out of brewin' that likker. Maybe this is the shock I need to stop drinkin' once and for all."

"I'm a teetotaler myself," Samuel said casually, putting his hands behind his head and leaning back on his chair.

"Well, the likker makes me feel sick, makes me shaky, and turns me into an angry old man," Will Granger said, resting his elbows on his knees and holding his face in his hands. Look at me. I'm jes' thirty-three years of age, and I feel like I'm a hundred. I know that when I drink to forget my sorrows, I only make things worse."

He stood suddenly and walked to the porch railing, staring off into the distance. "You're my witness, Sam. I'm swearin' off moonshine for good. I ain't gonna cook it no more. I ain't gonna sell it no more. And I'd be obliged if you'd keep a watch on me to hold me 'countable."

"What if we agree that if and when you get a hank'rin' to drink, you come over here?" Samuel suggested. "I've got plenty of work around this place, and I'll share it with you, to keep you busy and around people. I'll even promise some of Anna's good cookin'. And when you're ready, you can talk."

Samuel Gilmer held out his hand when Will nodded. He stood and grasped the outstretched hand. "Will, Anna and I will always welcome you here," Samuel told him. "In fact, we've been concerned about you livin' and workin' alone all the time. We surely don't want to see you sick or in jail."

"Will you 'pologize to Jake for me?" Will asked gruffly.

"Jake knows you weren't yourself that day," Samuel said, shrugging his shoulders. "He's heard about how dangerous moonshine can be. I'm thankful that's the first time he's seen it up close. He told me the smell made him gag, so I'm hopeful this will be the last time he goes close to a still. He'd value your friendship, Will."

The neighbors walked in silence back to Will's wagon. Will Granger climbed onto the seat and picked up the reins. "Samuel, someday I want to do somethin' nice for that boy." He cleared his throat and gazed into the distance. "You have a fine family. You're a lucky man, havin' a lovin' wife and three young 'uns. I wish I did. Count your blessings." Will's voice caught in sudden emotion, but he cleared his throat and nodded, "I'll be seein' you, Samuel. I'm obliged to y'all."

CHAPTER SEVEN: *A VERY SAD DAY*
June 14, 1913

"Sure does feel good to have a long stretch of summertime," Jake announced at breakfast, yawning with satisfaction the day after the Tucker School's spring commencement. A moment later, Lillie appeared in the kitchen, rubbing her eyes with the back of her hand.

"You may find you're busier than you ever were durin' the school year, son," Samuel announced, reaching for one last piece of toast before rising from the table. "Your Pap-paw and I're deliverin' a load of red oak floorin' lumber two miles away to young George Preston and his bride, who're buildin' a fine new home. That means we have extra chores for you today."

As the youngest children hastily washed their faces and hands, Anna arranged a dozen Mason jars on the table, then returned to the stove to stir a bubbling kettle of applesauce. "I'm just about ready to preserve these early June apples," she announced. "You two missed Molly. She's already eaten and churned butter. Your father saddled SueJean for her, and she's gone to deliver some bread, eggs, and butter to Mrs. Wiley on Alamance Church Road."

Anna checked the temperature of the wood stove before delivering two plates of flapjacks and bacon that had been warming on the back of the stove to the newcomers sitting at the table. "Jake, I'm almost out of firewood for the stove. I'd appreciate it if you'd take the cart and the axe out back to the woodpile and split enough wood for a two-day supply. Lillie can go with you and help you load the wood into the cart as you split it."

The children had lingered over their meal before heading down the path to the edge of the woods. They paused along the way to admire the sweet-smelling early summer morning and listen to a Carolina wren chattering noisily in the ancient oak tree. As Jake pushed the wooden cart holding the wedge and axe, Lillie skipped ahead, singing Stephen Foster's "Oh! Susanna," which her class had performed the last day of school. Tail wagging happily, Dan trotted beside the cart.

Near the woodshed, an opening in the stand of trees allowed a beam of warm sunlight illuminate the path. Jake noticed how it made Lillie's red braids shine like new copper. "Lillie," Jake bragged, using his grown-up voice, "I'm gonna surprise Mama with a three-day supply of firewood because I'm a lot stronger than I was last summer. I feel nearly grown up today." Lillie giggled, glancing back at him. Jake continued, "Let's make Mama happy and—"

His thoughts were interrupted by frantic barking. Dan darted past Lillie. He seemed to deliberately shove against her, almost like he was pushing her back from something. With a startled exclamation, Lillie fell backward, just missing the moving cart. Jake swerved to avoid her, then dropped the handles.

"What's the problem, Dan?" he asked, watching the beagle stop abruptly on the trail and growl, head down. Dan looked absolutely menacing as he focused intently on something in front of the children. When the dog didn't respond, Jake yelled, "Dan, what are you—?"

And then he saw it. A copperhead.

"Lillie!" he ordered, sounding as frantic as the dog. "Get behind me. COPPERHEAD!"

Dan leapt forward, lunging at the snake that had been sunning himself on a stump. Then the dog jumped back and lunged again while Lillie scrambled to her feet and took quick steps backward. Faster than a flash of lightning, Jake grabbed the axe from the cart and ran forward as Dan continued to growl and bark and leap at the now-coiled reptile whose slumbers had been disturbed.

Jake gave the snake a wide berth, intending to approach him from behind his head. But his plans went awry. Just as Jake raised the axe, the snake struck the dog, sinking his fangs into the side of Dan's neck. Dan gave a heart-rending yelp as the snake held on for a second or two before releasing its grip on the dog. Blood was dripping from Dan's neck when he fell to the ground.

"NO!" Jake screamed, swinging the axe with all the power of his might, his fear, and his anguish. He lobbed off the head of the copperhead as Lillie screamed. Jake immediately dropped the axe, and both children ran to kneel beside their beloved beagle.

Dan struggled to get back onto his feet, but he was no longer barking. His warm brown eyes flickered from one child to the other, as if to ask, "Did I do all right?" Then he collapsed onto the ground.

Jake's eyes filled with tears as he cradled the limp dog in his arms. "Oh, Dan, I'm so sorry. I'm so sorry, boy," he repeated again and again. He struggled to rise from the ground while holding Dan close to his chest. "Come on, Lillie." His voice shook. "Let's get Dan home."

Despite the incline, the boy carried Dan at a slow trot as Lillie raced ahead, crying and yelling "Papa! Mama! Pap-paw! Come quick!"

Anna rushed onto the porch, drying her hands on her apron. "Lillie! Whatever is wrong, honey?" she called as she hurried down the porch steps to meet her daughter. Lillie grabbed onto one of her mother's hands and started pulling her toward Jake. "Hurry, Mama," she sobbed. "Dan got bit by a bad snake."

Anna dropped Lillie's hand and raced across the back yard just as Jake emerged from the woods carrying his beloved dog. When Anna reached his side, Jake stopped to gasp for air, and Anna scooped the poor, limp beagle into her own arms. "Come, son," she said softly. Together they made the sad journey to the back porch, which Dan had left so eagerly just minutes earlier. Anna placed Dan on the braided mat at the door and knelt to examine him.

Hearing the commotion, Samuel Gilmer ran from the barn and Lee Hanner limped from the garden. They reached the porch in time to see Dan have a convulsive seizure. "Oh, mercy, the poison has spread all over his poor body," Anna gasped. Dan's family gathered in a half-circle around their dog, watching with agonized faces as Dan twitched painfully and drooled profusely. The only part of his body he could move independently was his tail, and the tip swayed gently, as if waving goodbye.

Samuel knelt beside the dog, immediately seeing the two fang holes on Dan's swollen neck. "Dan was bit by a young, very angry copperhead," he told his children. "That snake unloaded all its venom into a major blood vessel. There's nothin' we can do now but comfort our friend here." Samuel looked up at Jake. "What happened?"

While they spoke, Anna grabbed her abandoned dish towel, ran to the well, pulled the lid back, and lowered the bucket. She carried the cool, fresh water to the porch, drenched the dishtowel in it, then wrung out the cloth. Kneeling on the other side of the dog, she wiped his wound and gently wiped around his mouth and face, to clear away the drool and vomit.

Meanwhile, Jake described Dan's bravery. "I just know Dan purposely pushed Lillie so's he could save her from steppin' right on that snake, Pa," the boy said, his eyes fixed on his beloved beagle. "We didn't see him until Dan started barking and growling. The snake was the color of the leaves and the dead limbs on the ground, you see. Dan jumped in front of Lillie to stop her, and I know he fought that snake to give me time to grab the axe and get over there to help. He didn't even run away to save himself, Pa." Jake paused and gasped, "Can't you do anything to help him? Please!"

Lee and Samuel shook their heads simultaneously. "I'm so sorry, Jake," Samuel said, resting his hand on his son's shoulder. "There's no cure for a copperhead bite like this." Lillie sobbed softly as they all watched the light start to leave the dog's eyes. Once more, Dan struggled to breathe. Then, with one last gesture from the white tip of his tail, he gazed deeply into Jake's eyes, sighed, and closed his eyes.

"Dan can't be dead. Don't let him die, Pa!" Lillie cried. Her mother gathered her little girl close and rocked her back and forth, tears running down her own cheeks.

Jake turned away for a moment, trying to not show his feelings, but when his Pap-paw came over to him and reached out, Jake buried his face on his grandfather's chest. "It ain't right, Pap-paw." Jake's voice shook. "Dan was my dog, and I was supposed to protect him. I didn't move fast enough. I tried—really I did—but I didn't move fast enough!"

Samuel wiped his own tears away, blew his nose, and rose to his feet. "I thank God that Dan was there today. Our beagle saved my little girl's life." He reached for his daughter, swung her into his arms, and held her close. "We're all going to miss Dan terribly. But we know he served a higher purpose today."

"He's a hero, Jake." Lee Hanner added.

"Let's find a good spot to bury our dog," Samuel suggested. "Jake, you and I can dig him a fittin' grave."

"And then we'll gather and honor him," Anna added. "Molly should be back from Mrs. Wiley's place in a short time."

"Come, Jake," Samuel said gently, resting his hand on the boy's shoulder as he bent over his dog, stroking his head gently. "Can you help me find a good place?"

Samuel turned to Lee. "If you get the shovel, I'll move Dan off the porch." Gently he lifted the dog, mat and all, and carried him to the shade of a tree.

Together, Jake, Samuel, and Lee selected a spot on the edge of the field that could be seen from the house. "This is where Dan used to find rabbits nibbling on clover early in the morning. This was one of Dan's favorite places to hunt," the boy said.

Lee nodded, "After we're finished, we'll plant some of your Mam-maw's favorite flowers right over him."

Inside the house, Anna poured a kettle full of hot water into a bowl, lathered her hands with lye soap, and scrubbed them. "Your turn, Lillie," she said. She looked down at her daughter. "Oh, Lillie, you're trembling. Baby, are you sure you're all right? Are you sure you didn't get bit by that copperhead too?"

Lillie shook her head. "No, Mama, but I've never been that scared! Everything happened so fast. I think if Dan hadn't been keeping the snake busy, it might've bit Jake, too."

Anna held her daughter very tightly. "We are so very grateful for Dan."

As the men dug the hole, Jake disappeared into the house, returning with a pine box that he had built with his grandfather's help nearly two years earlier. Until now, it had held his toys. "Pa, I reckon this is the right size for Dan."

Samuel smiled. "I'm proud of you, son. That's a mighty fine resting place for Dan. Your Mama told me to put that braided mat in the grave with him. We'll lay it in the box first, and Dan'll have something soft to lay on."

"Remember how he loved to curl up on the mat by the stove?" Jake said, his eyes misting again.

Lee cleared his throat. "I think the hole is big enough. I see Molly comin' up the hill. Why don't you go get your Mama and Lillie, and tell Molly what happened?"

As Jake turned to go, Samuel arranged Anna's apron, the dish towel, and the braided mat in the bottom of that box, then gently placed the dog's lifeless body on top. Dan was lying on something soft, with the scents of the people who loved him.

Samuel strode to the barn and helped Molly pull the saddle off SueJean as Jake broke the sad news to his sister. She wept as she walked hand-in-hand with her Pa to see Dan lying there in the box. Lillie and her Mama were coming out the door when Lillie cried, "Wait. I gotta get something." The child ran back inside the house and up to her room. In just a moment, she came running out with her baby quilt neatly folded. "I want to give this to Dan."

Anna hugged her daughter. "Oh, sweetheart, that's so nice of you. But you always sleep with this on your pillow."

Lillie stroked the blanket. "I am going to be seven years old in July. I'm old enough now to sleep without it. Dan deserves it." When the mother and daughter reached the grave, Lillie dropped to her knees beside the little wood casket, unfolded the blanket, and stretched it over Dan. She bent and kissed the top of his head, and then pulled the blanket over his head. "Isn't that what they do with people before they shut the casket, Mama?" she asked. When Anna nodded, Lillie whispered, "Rest in peace, Dan. You're the bravest dog ever."

The family stood in silence a moment. Then Samuel cleared his throat. "Jesus said *Greater love hath no one than this: that he lay down his life for his friend.* Our dog, Dan, did just that this morning. He saw danger for the children that he loved so much, and he knew he had to protect them. Dan's bravery surely saved the lives of our Lillie and Jake, and for that, all of us are grateful. We thank God for all the good times we had with Dan over the last seven years." He fell silent.

Molly spoke. "You know Dan had one terrible fear, and that was thunderstorms. I remember one afternoon during a thunderstorm when I couldn't find either Lillie or Dan, who had been playing together on the porch. I started searching, and I found Dan underneath Mama and Papa's bed. And there beside him, on that floor, was Lillie, holding onto this same little quilt. She told me that she was keeping Dan from being scared." Everyone laughed.

Then Anna spoke. "I will always remember that confrontation Dan had with the skunk that was intendin' to make a home under the smokehouse. I think I had to use ten Mason jars full of tomato juice to get that smell out of him." Despite their tears, her family shook with laughter. "You know how that dog hated a bath? That's why I didn't invite him into the house often. But on that occasion, he knew he needed tomatoes, soap, and water. He held still until I was finished and rinsed him. I think he couldn't stand the way he smelled, either."

Jake's tribute began after he swallowed convulsively several times. "I had lots of fun huntin' rabbits with Dan. I loved to hear him baying as he ran and I loved watching that white tip of his tail wavin' like a flag behind him. Thanks to Dan, I brought home some fine rabbits for Mama's kettle. Dan never did get that fox he wanted, but at least the fox didn't attack chickens when Dan slept near the chicken house."

Jake and Samuel gently lowered the box into the hole, then filled the hole with the red Carolina clay. Jake walked around to mash the soil down on the grave, and then this father rolled a granite rock onto the spot, to mark the grave. Lee spoke for the first time. "I'll build a trellis here and plant a red trumpet vine," he promised. "My wife loved them so much, and the hummingbirds'll be all over it."

The Gilmers nodded, solemn once again. Before returning to the house, the men removed their hats and everyone sang a verse of "What a Friend We Have in Jesus".

That night, after Lee Hanner excused himself and headed to bed, Anna and Samuel sat on the porch swing, swaying gently. Nearby, Molly was knitting, and Jake and Lillie were playing checkers. Lillie looked up. "Papa, do you think animals go to heaven when they die?"

Samuel smiled. "Well, the Bible does mention that the wolf will dwell with the lamb, the leopard will lie down with the goat, the calf and lion will live together, and a little child shall lead them. I'm not sure about all animals bein' up there, but I'm certain, sure as I'm sittin' here, that a dog as brave and good as Dan is up there right now, chasing rabbits, running through soft green grass, and drinking out of clear brooks. Yes, Lillie dear, I can tell you that Jesus is pettin' that sweet dog on the head, scratchin' his ears, and smilin' before sendin' Dan off to run and play with the other dogs. We'll see Dan again, Lillie. You can be sure of that."

CHAPTER EIGHT: *FIRE!*
July 8, 1913

"Whew! After such a hot and humid July day, this cool breeze sure is welcome." Anna stopped shelling butter beans long enough to flap her apron at her face before returning to work. She and Molly had finished the evening dishes and were shelling beans overflowing two big peach baskets Jake had delivered to the porch. Now and then they watched Lillie skipping around the yard chasing June bugs and dragonflies. "I'm anxious for the first fireflies of the night to appear, Mama," Lillie said happily. Moments later, she stopped in her tracks abruptly.

"Mama, it smells like smoke. Like someone's burnin' somethin'," Lillie said, sniffing the air. Anna and Molly stood and scanned the landscape. "It's comin' from the woods up the hill!" Molly exclaimed, pointing.

Anna hurried to the edge of the porch and shaded her eyes with her hand, to block the sun on its slow slide down to the horizon. "I can't see anything because of the thick trees," she declared.

"Look! Two horses are comin' up our road!" Lillie said, pointing.

Thundering hooves were kicking up a cloud of dust as they galloped up the hill with riders the Gilmers didn't immediately recognize until their neighbor, Joe Smithson reined his horse to a halt in front of the porch. "Beg pardon, Mrs. Gilmer." He hurriedly tipped his hat. "It's Will Granger's place. We think the smoke and flames are comin' from one of his dryin' barns. We're gonna see if there's anything we can do." They raced off.

At that moment, Samuel and Jake could be seen hurrying up from the barn, each carrying a pail of fresh milk. Samuel thrust his pail into his son's hands. "Take these to the spring house, Jake." As he headed to the pasture where SueJean was grazing, he called to his wife. "I'm goin' up there, Anna." The family watched him jump on the back of the horse and gallop toward his neighbor's tobacco barns.

Samuel arrived just in time to witness the roof of Will Granger's oldest and largest drying barn collapsing in a heap, feeding the bonfire with dry wood and probably as many as one hundred racks of North Carolina flue-cured tobacco, tobacco that would have been ready for market in a week or two, Samuel knew. He joined the bucket brigade that snaked from Beaver Creek to the barn. Neighbors scooping buckets of water from the creek and passing them down the line to men who threw the water onto the burning wreck of a building.

"This barn is a total loss, but we need to prevent embers from spreading to another barn!' Samuel shouted. Will Granger looked nearly frantic, dipping bucket after bucket of water from the creek and passing it quickly to the next man in line. Little boys stationed at the other end were grabbing empty buckets and racing back to where Mr. Granger scooped water.

"It's gone. It's lost." Will Granger was covered in soot, sweat pouring in rivers of mud down his face and neck. "All my hard work!" he cried helplessly. In less than an hour, the largest of his four barns, packed full of tobacco leaves hanging there to dry and cure, was now reduced to smoldering ashes.

Will's barns had wood-burning drying fireplaces on two sides of the building. Though the foundation of the smoldering building was made of stone, as were the fireplaces, the grates at the front of those furnaces that kept hot coals in place must have rusted through, one of the firefighters suggested.

"Will had planned to tear down this barn after this crop went to market, so's he could build a new one," Joe Smithson told Samuel as the fire brigade shifted to wet down the adjacent barn. "All it would've taken was one piece of red-hot wood to roll out onto the ground, and if a rack of nearly-dry leaves fell on top of the coal, it could ignite a fire that would quickly spread if there was anything on the ground nearby." The firefighters coughed and choked on the overpowering and acrid fumes, fighting to contain the fire.

When the neighbors finally realized that the adjacent barn was safe, they ended the bucket brigade and gathered in clusters, watching Will Granger with sympathetic glances, knowing that the disaster could have been theirs as easily as his. One by one, they patted Will on the back as he collapsed onto a stump, gasping for air.

"I'm so sorry, Will."

"Bad break, Will."

As Will Granger's closest neighbor climbed onto his horse, Samuel heard him mutter to a friend, "Even a man as ornery as Will Granger doesn't deserve this. His livelihood just went up in smoke."

Samuel, James Thacker, Dave Forbis, and Mike Johnson helped Will onto his feet, and the five men walked over to Will's well shelter. James Thacker took the cover off the well and lowered the bucket into the clean, cold water. He served dipper after dipper to the hot, thirsty men before giving himself a swallow.

Will dropped onto a nearby log and covered his face with his hands. "I jes' checked both barns before supper tonight. The leaves were nearly ready for market. Maybe one rack fell when I closed the door, because the wind had kicked up at that moment. Must've been a few hot coals on the ground in front of the fireplace grates is all I can guess. By the time I washed my supper dishes and came back onto the porch, flames were flickerin' through the cracks in the door."

He rubbed his face again. It was as black as the ashes of the barn, Samuel noticed. Mr. Johnson said quietly, "That old, dry wood and all those dry leaves—the barn went up like paper in a wood stove."

Will Granger groaned, "It's gone! Completely gone. I have one more barn full of tobacco and two that are ready to be loaded, but this is half of my crop." His voice broke. "What am I gonna do?" The huge man sat there, head in his hands, with sweat and tears rolling down his cheeks. His companions collapsed on the ground beside Will, remaining silent for several minutes. In time, Will gasped, drank several more dippers of water, and then poured water over his head and into his hands, to wash the soot and grime from his face. He looked from one man to another, and sighed.

"How can I thank y'all for comin' over here and helpin' me? My other tobacco barns, my house, my barn, and the cows and horses are fine, thanks to y'all." His sigh seemed to come from deep within his soul.

"How are you set, Will?" Samuel asked quietly.

"With the tobacco I have left in the fields, I'll have just enough room in the other barns after I empty out one next week and take those racks to the auction. Somehow I'll need to replace the barn that burned tonight—but I'll be mighty short of cash this year. I lost half my crop." He shook his head. "Funny thing is: I was planning to take that old barn down late this summer, after it was empty and build a new one with the sale of that tobacco. I already have one piece of corrugated sheet metal for the roof of a new barn stored it in my smokehouse."

"Good," James said. "There's nothin' wrong with that stone foundation and the two rows of logs at the bottom. You've got the foundation and the roof ready to go."

"I planned to use sealed kerosene heaters in the new barn," Will said, staring morosely at the smoking cinders. "I just don't know how and when I'll get 'er done. I have bills comin' in that this tobacco money was earmarked for. I just don't know where that money'll come from now…" Will's voice trailed off again.

Samuel spoke. "You know, Will, I have a whole stack of sturdy poplar lumber stored in my shed that came from your tree. I won't charge you for makin' those boards. Things were quiet during the week I sawed them. And those logs produced more lumber than I estimated. You have enough in that stack to build the entire tobacco barn, even beams for the tier-poles."

Will Granger stared at him, speechless, as Samuel continued, "Lee, Jake, and I will load the lumber on my wagon, and we'll haul it over for you."

James Thacker added, "We can get neighbors to donate a day. We'll all work together to help you rebuild that barn."

"I have some sturdy poles that could be the corners of the building and more if you need supports," Mike Johnson added. "Heck, I own the general store. I have the nails, brackets, hinges, ropes, pulleys, and tar for protectin' that roof. I'll haul everything you need over tomorrow."

David Forbis offered left-over corrugated metal roofing stored in his shed. "I'd thought about replacing the roofs on my smokehouse and well house, but they'll do for another year," he said. "Ought to be enough to finish the roofing for that tobacco barn—and I've got several pairs of metal shears that can do the job." He looked at his neighbors. "Why don't we agree to meet here early Saturday?"

Will Granger's mouth dropped open. "Why would y'all do that for me? I've done nothin' nice for any of y'all. If anything, I've growled, yelled, and grunted at you. I ain't been neighborly. To say the least." Perhaps to mask the emotions racing across his face, Will stood and walked to the porch. He reached for a kerosene lantern and lit the wick. "Sorry, folks," he muttered. "Night is fallin', and you're still here helping me. I sure don't know why."

"Why are we helping you?" Samuel repeated. "We're all neighbors here, Will. We all go to church somewhere, and we're taught that we're supposed to love our neighbor. The good book reminds us, *It is more blessed to give than it is to receive.*" The men nodded solemnly.

Michael Johnson pulled out his pocket watch and held it close to the lamplight. "Yes, we help our neighbors. I'm sorry that we don't know you very well, Will. Too often we get busy with our own business, and too often we jump to conclusions instead of givin' each other the chance everyone deserves. You work hard, Will. We all know that. You're here alone except for those sharecroppers, and right now you can use some help. You'll get it."

He stood and slapped his hat against his leg, to rid it of cinders before he added, "If you want to thank us later, jes' do somethin' kind and generous for someone else in need." He moved toward his horse.

"I've gotta go home now, wash up, and get some sleep. I'll be over here tomorrow around noontime with those supplies."

James and Samuel watched Mike and David ride away, then they took turns shaking Will's hand. "It's been a tough day for you, Will," Samuel said. Clean up, eat somethin', and get some good rest. We'll haul that lumber over here tomorrow. Weather permittin', a team of men will get the new barn up for you very soon. There're good people in this community. We all help one another. Don't you worry any more tonight."

True to their word, neighbors delivered the necessary building supplies to Will Granger's farm over the next few days. Will and the two sharecroppers' families who lived on his land cleared away all the debris as soon as the ashes cooled. When Mike Johnson delivered the support poles and concrete mix, Will and his sharecroppers dug the necessary holes and used a plumb bob to ensure that the poles would stand perfectly perpendicular. Then they mixed and poured concrete around the poles. Two days later, the concrete was solid and ready to support the new construction. The foundation was ready by Saturday morning.

As Samuel had pointed out, the tobacco barn's rock foundation and the lower two rows of solid oak logs were intact and ready to support another tobacco-drying barn. Will had just finished eating a dry biscuit, grits, and bacon and was finishing the last swallow of his coffee early Saturday morning when he saw six wagons loaded with men, teenage boys, ladders, ropes, and a vast assortment of tools coming across his field.

"I am astounded that y'all took time from your own crops to come help a stranger—and a gruff one at that," he said, shaking his visitors' hands, some of whom had been recruited by James Thacker, Mike. Johnson, and Samuel.

Working without blueprints, they simply asked Will Granger where he wanted the door and the ventilation window, which would be opened and closed to control the heat and humidity during the drying process. And then they began their work. The most important part of the barn would be the support poles and the roof trusses that span the inside of the building, one man explained to his son. "Tier-beams allow men to climb up high to maximize space inside the barn. They also support the racks of tobacco leaves as they cure in the dry heat—but you know that."

As the walls were assembled, the rhythmic taps of hammers and ringing of saws rang out over this hill as neighbors helped their neighbor without any thought of reward. While the young and strongest men helped hoist the trusses with ropes and brute strength, others waited on ladders with hammers, screws, and nails to secure the walls in place.

As noon approached, their wives and daughters brought picnic baskets loaded with food to share for the noontime break. Baked chicken, sweet potatoes, collard and beet greens, johnnycakes, and pies were quickly consumed. The meals were filling, and the neighbors shared stories as they ate. As soon as the men were back at work, the women cleared the meal away, returning dishware and utensils to their baskets, then driving off in their surreys or on horseback.

It was no easy matter to cut the corrugated steel material for the roof. The job required tin snips and strong men with thick gloves. These men persisted, and by the middle of the afternoon, the roof was firmly in place. Tar was spread over the seams and all the nails to prevent leaks.

Because Will Granger dried his tobacco following the flue-cured method, one upper section of a wall had a shutter that could open with the use of pulleys and rope, thereby controlling the temperature as the heat cured the tobacco. Marshall Smith, a master carpenter, constructed the shutter out of extra scraps of wood. Then he covered the outside of the shutter with a piece of the corrugated steel. The shutter measured five feet long and three feet wide. When opened, it would allow heat and humidity from inside the building to escape. Mr. Smith tested the shutter to make sure it would open out to a forty-five-degree angle, although for most of the year, it would lie flat against the side of the building. Experienced tobacco farmers like Will Granger would know how to control this shutter for proper curing.

When they dried tobacco, Carolina farmers tied three leaves together at the stem, then hung them upside down from six-foot-long hardwood sticks. They knew that Granger's new barn had to be equipped to hang all these sticks in a way that would best utilize the space. While some men worked on the roof, others were working inside the barn, setting those cross-beams of sturdy poplar wood. Several layers of beams were suspended across the inside of the drying barn. The farmers positioned them properly to hold the six-foot-long tobacco sticks. The beams had to be strong enough to hold the weight of a man, because the farmer would climb from one beam to another to hang the tobacco racks, starting at the top and working his way down to the level below it, filling that row, and continuing down until the barn was completely full of tobacco.

Structural brackets anchored these beams into the walls. Some of the teenage boys were sent upward to test these out. "They're strong enough to do the job," one called, proud to have a job he could do well. Another secured the pulleys for the shutter's operation. The men had already threaded the ropes through the pulleys.

The curing process for North Carolina tobacco usually takes a week. The temperature inside the drying barn begins around 120 degrees and goes up as high as 180 degrees in a few days, when the furnaces are on. This removes the water from the tobacco leaves without allowing them to become so dry they turn brittle and shatter when touched. The delicate process requires skills that farmers gain by experience. In just a few days, a cured tobacco leaf will lose more than three-quarters of its weight—that equates to an acre of tobacco losing five tons of water by the time it's ready to sell at the auction market.

Just before dusk, when the cows started mooing, the main work on this new tobacco barn was completed. Marshall Smith was putting the finishing touches on the door, which he built out of the same poplar lumber as the barn. The door was no larger than a regular house door—which was traditional for a barn used for only a few weeks a year. Samuel helped Marshall hang the door with sturdy new hinges and a wooden latch to hold the door shut. Samuel studied Marshall's face, as Marshall picked up his tools. This man had a propensity for practical jokes.

"Marshall, you're grinnin' like a possum. What've you done"

Smith chuckled, "Jus' added some art work to that last door brace. Will won't see it till he opens the door. Don't want him to forget me."

Samuel took a peek. There was a crescent moon carefully carved out of the middle of that board, much like the shape on a privy door.

As the weary neighbors packed their wagons and hitched their horses for their homeward journeys, Will went to each one of the men, shaking their hands and thanking them over and over for their hard work and supplies they gave. "Someday I'll return this favor," he promised. "Y'all have taught me what it really means to be a good neighbor."

CHAPTER NINE: *WILL GRANGER'S GRIEF*
July 22, 1913

Sunday afternoons were reserved for rest and a handful of chores necessary to feed families and livestock. A few weeks after the construction of Will Granger's new tobacco barn, Samuel was sitting on the porch swing with Anna, enjoying a playful breeze after their Sunday dinner. The two younger children were playing in the creek, and Molly was visiting her best friend, celebrating her seventeenth birthday, when Samuel noticed a sound missing from his pasture.

"Say, Anna, have you heard Elsa's cow bell recently? I'm not hearin' but one cow right now."

Anna sat up straighter and peered into the pasture. "I can't say that I have, Sam. Both cows are usually movin' towards the barn by this time in the afternoon. Should someone go look for her, do you think?"

"I'm off. You sit still," Samuel said, patting his wife on her knee. He walked with a leisurely stride to the barn, where he found only one cow, Bessie, standing nearby. After a survey of the surrounding fields, he saddled SueJean and set off across the upper pasture. "SueJean," he said, grinning at the idea of holding a conversation with his horse, "I wonder if that sassy lady has found a hole in the fence somewhere and decided to take a stroll?"

The upper pasture bordered Will Granger's land. As Samuel started up the hill in that direction, he saw his neighbor in the distance with a wooden box at his feet—full of tools, Samuel speculated—working on a section of Samuel's fence at the spot where a dead pine tree had fallen and torn through the strands of wire. By the time Samuel reached the spot, Will had already moved the tree away from the fence and was nearly finished repairing the fence.

"Howdy, neighbor," Samuel said, jumping off SueJean and holding out his hand. "I didn't realize this fence had been damaged. The tree must've blown down in that rainstorm the other night. Thanks for repairin' it."

Will shrugged, "Well, since it was my tree that fell and tore the fence, 'course I should fix it, Sam." After shaking hands, he added, "Say, are you missin' a nice Jersey cow? Comes right up to people? She's what started all this work."

"I just happen to be missin' that very same cow," Samuel said.

Will grinned. "I was totin' my dishes to the sink after lunch when I looked out the window and saw a new cow in my pasture. I thought p'rhaps she might be yours. She walked over to me right neighborly, so I put her in a stall in my barn until I could find out how she got into my pasture."

Will cut the end of the last wire that had been repaired and reinforced. He tested all the strands before whistling to a tall black stallion who ambled toward his owner. "That should do it, Samuel," he said, climbing onto his horse's back. "Now, if you'll ride through that gate yonder, I'll meet you at my barn. You can say howdy to that cow of yours and lead her back home."

The men rode side by side up to the barn where Will kept his cow and horses, and there they dismounted. Will took the saddle off his horse and led him into his stall while Samuel tied SueJean to a tree beside the barn. Inside the barn, the men blinked as their eyes adjusted to the darkness. "Here she is," Will said, pointing to the cow. "Did you enjoy your visit, Elsa?" Samuel asked, patting his cow on the head. "Well, you look like you're pretty satisfied here. I notice that Will has already fed you your dinner, so I'll be takin' you home now." He grinned at his neighbor. "Much obliged, Will." But when he reached for Elsa's rope, Will suggested they get a drink of water and sit a moment. Samuel nodded, led Elsa into the late-afternoon sunshine, and wrapped her lead around the fence rail before following his host to his porch.

"I still can't believe how you and the other folks helped me out," Will Granger said quietly. "I know I didn't deserve that kindness, but I want you to know how grateful I am." He gestured to a bench, indicating that Samuel should sit on the porch. Samuel looked curiously at his host, who studied his boots for a moment before confessing, "I know everyone wonders why I seem so cussed mean. I think this's as good a time as any for an explanation, and since you seem to be makin' such an effort to be a good neighbor, I guess I should start by tellin' you."

Will Granger then drew a bucket of water from his well and delivered it to his guest on the porch. He reached the dipper deep into the bucket and handed it to Samuel. "Thanks," Samuel said, waiting patiently for the story to begin. Will sat on a simple wooden chair and sighed.

"You folks have only known me for a few years," he began. "I don't like sharin' my personal life with no one, Samuel, but now I feel I can tell you my story."

Samuel nodded.

Will Granger began his tale by explaining that he hailed from the McLeansville area. "That's where I grew up, where I went to church, and where I went to school. Had me a few girlfriends. One I even thought I loved—but I lost her through no fault of hers. I took her for granted, and I shouldn't have. I refused to go to church with her, and I shouldn't have. I told her that I believed in God, but jes' didn't feel comfortable in a church building, sittin' there and listenin' to a preacher."

He glanced at Samuel with a sheepish grin. "I have to keep movin', Sam. I'm no good at sittin'. I'm restless without somethin' to do. But then I met Suzanne." An expression of awe flitted over his face and he appeared to be looking far into the past. "What a beautiful, sweet girl," Will spoke in a voice so low he almost seemed to be speaking to himself. "She was nineteen. I was five years older. Since I already had a tobacco farm and a little house, her parents consented to our marryin'."

When he didn't continue his story for long moments, Samuel prompted him quietly. "I didn't know you were married, Will."

The man nodded. "Not only was she a wonderful wife, but she was a partner to me on the farm. Lord, you should have seen that little woman toppin' tobacco and tyin' it on sticks to go to the curing barn. And, smart? Readin' was always hard for me, but Suzanne would be able to understand and explain all those important papers we got from the government and from the bank. She was the love of my life. She was my best friend. She was the only friend I needed."

"You surprise me, Will," Samuel said. "You've been keepin' all this to yourself for a long time."

"You'll understand why when I get on with my story," Will said, pulling out a handkerchief and mopping his brow. "This ain't easy for a private man like me to talk about," he mumbled. Then he continued,

"Samuel, this woman was my life. I never thought I could be any happier, but then my sweet wife told me she was expectin'. I 'bout burst with joy and pride. Why, I just picked that little woman up and danced around the living room with her. She laughed, she was so happy."

"There's nothin' like that moment when the woman you love tells you that kind of news," Samuel agreed.

"We had dreams and hopes and made all the plans that you must've made with Anna." Again Will wiped his forehead with his handkerchief. "Well, five months went by and we were startin' to tell people our big news. But one morning, while she was cooking our breakfast, Suzanne doubled over and cried out with pain. There was blood all over the floor and her dress. Her face went white, and she looked like she'd faint."

Will described the scene, how he carried her to their bed, and she looked at him with sweat pouring down her face, pleading with him to get help. "I was scared to leave her, and scared not to go," he confessed. "We had a neighbor just a fourth-mile up the road, and I ran like the devil over there. He was out on his horse, and when he saw me, he galloped over. I told him about our emergency, and he said, "Hop on behind me, and I'll drop you off at your home and go fetch the doctor.' By the time Fred dropped me at our house, Suzanne had bled even more, and she was cryin', tellin' me the baby was comin'. She told me to boil water and get the clean strips from old sheets she had already prepared for childbirth. Before Fred returned with the doctor, the baby arrived," Will said.

Again, he sank his head into his hands. "I held my little boy so gentle-like. He was so very tiny. But all the parts were there; fingers and toes, little nose, and ears. He was blue and still, even when I cleared his mouth and breathed into him. He never did breathe on his own. All I could do was hold him tight and then put him in Suzanne's arms. She kissed him. We both cried."

He went on to tell Samuel that his wife bled to death while Fred hurried to town for help and Will was praying aloud, holding onto her hand. "I truly believed that God was going to heal her," he said. The look on his face convinced Samuel that Will was still puzzled by the end result. "When he came, the doctor said he didn't even know if he could've helped her if she was in a hospital." His voice caught. "My sweet Suzanne and our little boy both died that day. I buried my beautiful wife and our tiny son together. I named him William Granger, Junior."

Understanding his neighbor's anguish, Samuel put his hand on the man's shoulder for a brief and silent moment. Will continued, "That's when I lost my faith in God. I was lost and hopeless, and I had an ache in my chest that plagued me night and day. My heart felt broken in two, and I didn't care. Why should I be alive when someone as good and beautiful as Suzanne and our innocent baby didn't have a chance to live?"

He explained that he didn't know what to do with his pain and he couldn't blame anyone else except God. "Where was he when I desperately needed him?" Will asked rhetorically. "When I called out to God, he turned his back on us."

He sighed deeply. "So I gave away our things and moved away from our home. I never went back to church. I started drinkin' to try to forget the pain. Reckon I just got bitter toward life and toward everyone who dared to go on with their normal lives when my life was shattered."

The two men sat shoulder-to-shoulder in silence. Samuel Gilmer wiped his forehead with his handkerchief and loudly blew his nose. "Will, I just can't tell you how terribly sorry---"

Will interrupted, "And that's why I don't tell people my story. They start feelin' sorry for me. I don't need that."

Samuel lifted his hand to stop Will, "No, you didn't let me finish, Will. I said I am sorry about this. That's not condescending, and I'm not makin' light of your terrible loss. What happened to you was shocking, tragic, heart-breaking. I'm not surprised that it turned your life upside down and broke your spirit—I might've felt the same. I've never been in your situation, and I'm mighty thankful to God for that, but I understand how you would be angry at God and demand an explanation. You're not alone. Turn to the Book of Psalms and you'll hear King David asking the same questions. He shook his fist at God. He wanted to know why righteous people suffer while the wicked seem to prosper."

Samuel paused, then added quietly, "God never punishes us for wantin' answers, but often we just have faith to go on, trusting our Heavenly Father to make it right someday. Some people think that when they become a Christian, their lives will be easy. The truth is our lives are anything but easy. Jesus himself warned us *In this world you will have trouble. But, fear not, I have overcome the world.'* He does understand our pain, Will. I think He hurts right along with us..."

Samuel stood and walked to the edge of the porch, staring at the new barn without seeing it. "Some people skate through this life with relatively few scars," he acknowledged. "Others seem to be saddled with sorrow and problems every day of their lives. Will, I don't know what I would do if I were in your shoes, but I do know that I'd find a preacher to talk to. No matter what happens, we have choices to make about the way we live our lives. You can go on like you have been for six years, actin' hurt and angry and bitter—but you already know that only makes you more miserable. Or you can talk to God and ask, 'What is it you want me to do now?' You might not get a burning bush, but God talks in hints and whispers, and through other folks."

Will Granger looked at him with skeptical eyes. Samuel held his gaze. "I believe that God has a purpose for your life, and he is standin' right here beside you, anxious to help you find it. So am I, as a friend. I'll listen any time you want to talk."

Samuel looked down at his hands, to give his neighbor privacy to think about his words. When he faced him again, he was surprised to see the man sobbing. Samuel cleared his throat and put his hand on the man's shoulder again.

In a husky voice, Will thanked Samuel for his help with the tobacco barn, but especially for listening to what he had to say. He wiped his eyes as Samuel pretended to look elsewhere, and then admitted, "I don't like bein' angry at God and the world all the time. I'm tired of bein' bitter. Thanks, Samuel. Thanks for bein' a friend."

CHAPTER TEN: *LEE HANNER SAVES THE DAY*
August 3, 1913

As Molly was hanging laundry on the clothesline early on a hot summer day, two sassy hummingbirds buzzed back and forth by her face, attracted by her pink blouse and the red petunias hanging in a basket from the oak tree beside her. A male bluebird perched on top of the fence, boldly displaying his iridescent blue-and-orange coloring and his white under-belly. "You look like a fancy beau ready to go callin' on your sweetheart," she said, smiling. He darted away after a dragonfly.

Meanwhile, down at the mill, Samuel had hitched his horses to the wagon, which was loaded with lumber. He was heading down the road toward a customer's farm on Williams Dairy Road. Lee Hanner shaded his eyes for a moment, watching his son-in-law drive away before he returned to his chores: cleaning the floor of the mill and the carriage rail. He was reaching for some grease to lubricate the bearings for the rail carriage when he heard Molly scream. He rushed to the mill door with large, quick steps and saw Molly frantically running in his direction. As she nearly crashed into him, he grabbed her arms to steady her. Breathless, she managed to gasp out the words, "Coyote. Comin' toward the clothes line. He's sick, Pap-paw!"

Lee's granddaughter turned and pointed. Lee saw a mangy-looking gray coyote staggering and shaking his head before blindly crashing into a tree. The grandfather and granddaughter watched him shake his head again, looking dazed. A froth of saliva foamed down his muzzle as he approached the open yard where the clothesline stood. The coyote moved in the direction of the basket of wet clothes Molly had dropped in her haste.

"Sakes alive," Lee muttered. In one swift movement, he reached above the mill door for his long-barrel Springfield bolt-action rifle and walked outside, saying in a low voice. "You're right as rain, Molly. No self-respectin' coyote wanders near people in the middle of the mornin'. He's got rabies. You stay right here, hear me? I need to take care of this."

As Lee took a step in the animal's direction, the coyote paused to raise his head and sniff the air. Slowly he turned toward the barn. Lee spoke, more to himself than to Molly, "He's smellin' our chickens in the coop. I'm glad Lillie didn't let them out yet and Bessie's in the stable with her new calf."

"What—?"

"Stay where you are," Lee ordered again as he started up the hill.

Anna had paused while rolling out cookie dough to glance into the yard. When she saw the overturned laundry basket, she hurried onto the porch. "Molly? Is everything all right?" she called, looking around the yard before turning toward the mill.

"Anna! Get into the house. Now! And keep those young'uns beside you!" Lee commanded, pointing and adding, "Sick coyote. Molly's in the mill."

Anna saw the rifle in her father's hands and the coyote in her yard. She immediately ducked back inside the house, slammed the door, and called for Jake and Lilly. They clustered by the kitchen window in time to see Lee raise the butt of the rifle stock up to his right shoulder. Deliberately, he flipped up the bolt and pulled it back, to bring the bullet into the firing chamber. Then he pushed the bolt back down as the coyote staggered on his zigzag path, his head writhing on his shoulders. And then the animal slowly but deliberately began a trek toward the barn.

Lee guessed there was probably only one bullet in the firing chamber and one extra in the rifle, which hadn't been used since Samuel killed a deer back in March. That meant he had to get the perfect angle on his shot or he would miss the coyote's head or his heart. And he couldn't risk firing toward the house or the barn. He had to shoot before the coyote made another turn or rushed into the barn. Lee sighted quickly and carefully, then squeezed the trigger.

BOOM! The kick from the gun butt knocked Lee's arm back. Somewhere in the back of his mind a voice reminded him that he would have a bruise before the end of the day. But that was immaterial now. To his satisfaction, he watched as the coyote leapt into the air and then fell to the ground.

But was he dead?

Automatically, Lee pulled the bolt upwards and back one more time, loading the last bullet into the firing chamber. "Take no chances," he muttered, as though he was instructing Jake. Slowly he approached the beast.

When he saw no movement in the coyote's body, he bent over the corpse and discovered that the bullet had entered the coyote's temple in front of his right ear, which meant it had entered his fatally-infected brain. One shot had ended the creature's suffering.

Lee straightened and removed his hat, wiping the sweat from his brow. Only then did he notice his hands shaking.

Anna, Lillie, and Jake erupted onto the porch, and Molly hesitantly started her return to the yard. "Y'all stay away from this critter," Lee called sternly, holding up his hand. "He has rabies—and you could catch the ailment. There ain't no cure for rabies."

He nodded to his grandson. "Jake, I need two shovels, gloves, and some help digging a deep grave on the edge of the pasture."

Then he called to his daughter, "Anna, get me an old sheet or tablecloth you don't mind losin'. I'll throw it over this varmint. We've got to make sure nobody comes near. 'Specially Lillie."

Jake ran to the mill for the shovels and gloves. Molly walked as close as she dared to the still, stiff body lying on the ground and shuddered at its ravaged body before she went up on the porch and hugged her mother. Anna disappeared into the house, insisting that Lillie go with her.

"Wow, Pap-paw! That's one big ole coyote. Biggest I've ever laid eyes on," Jake exclaimed when he delivered the shovels and gloves to his grandfather. When Anna returned to the porch with an armful of cloth, Jake ran to retrieve it. Then the man and boy walked down into the pasture, knowing where a small gully in one corner would make digging easier. Field rocks had been piled near this site.

"Pap-paw, what was wrong with that coyote? What was he doin' here this time of day?" Jake asked.

"That coyote was sick with rabies, Jake," Lee explained, thrusting his shovel into the earth and pushing down on it with his booted foot.

"Rabies is spread when a sick animal bites a healthy one. And it always kills. You know that coyotes are night creatures who usually shy away from humans."

"The only ones I've seen up close have shiny coats and move quickly," Jake said.

"That's how Molly knew something was wrong. He was around humans in daylight and he couldn't move smoothly. When you see a critter foamin' at the mouth, that's a sure-fire sign of trouble. Of rabies. We need to dig this grave deep enough that other animals won't be able to smell the body and try to dig it up."

"What exactly is rabies, Pap-paw?" Jake was full of questions.

"A sickness that infects the brain. Whenever you see a dog or other critter drooling, vomiting, or their muscles jerking, beware of danger. When humans are bitten by a rabid animal, their necks stiffen, they say and do strange things, and in time they'll fall into a coma. When that happens, death isn't far behind." He paused and looked sternly at his grandson. "Do you understand why we have to be so careful?"

Jake nodded and worked silently as they dug deeper into the dirt and rocks. When they finished carving out a five-foot hole, Jake looked up at his grandfather. "Pap-paw, were you scared? That thing could've run over and bit you."

Lee answered with a grave face. "At the moment I shot him, Jake, I wasn't scared. But, after I saw him lying there dead, my hands started to shake. I started thinking about what might have happened if Molly hadn't seen him in time. Or if I missed and that coyote attacked our livestock, or (I'm still shaking about this) if he had bitten someone I love." He glanced up at the sky. "I guess the Lord was with me, because I didn't miss."

He ruffled the boy's hair. "C'mon, Jake, let's go home, wash up, and get some water. That took a lot out of me."

When Samuel drove the wagon into the yard, he immediately noticed the lump covered by a ragged tablecloth lying near the barn. He didn't take the time to unhitch the team from the wagon. He hopped right down, asking for an explanation. Lee explained what had happened. Samuel nodded, then went to the porch and called to his wife. When Anna walked onto the porch, he told her, "Anna, just as soon as we get that critter wrapped up and onto the trailer, I need for you to mix some strong lye soap with bleach in a pail. I'll pour it over that patch where the coyote fell." She nodded and hurried into the kitchen.

Samuel and Lee pulled on their gloves, gingerly wrapped the coyote's body in the tablecloth without touching it, then dragged their bundle to the wagon and swung it up onto the floorboards. In a matter of minutes, the coyote was unloaded and buried deep. The men covered the body with a carpet of stones, then filled the grave in with dirt, which Samuel tramped down before rolling more stones over the spot.

As they rode the wagon toward the barn, Samuel grinned mischievously. "I know for a fact that you haven't shot a gun since you killed that turkey for Thanksgiving two years ago. Nice shot."

Lee raised his brows and shook his head. "That was nothin' like shootin' a turkey."

CHAPTER ELEVEN: *CAUGHT IN THE ACT*
August 10, 1913

"Where's your Mama?" Samuel asked Molly when he arrived in the kitchen for breakfast, closely followed by Lee and Jake.

Molly delivered three plates loaded with country ham, grits, and biscuits to the three men. "She's out at the chicken coop, Papa. When I gathered the eggs this morning, I found feathers everywhere. We only have *four* hens left, Papa, so no eggs for breakfast this morning. Mama went to see what happened for herself."

Samuel frowned. "I know for a fact that you girls shut that latch last night after collecting the eggs. I counted six Dominique hens in the coop yesterday. How did that dadgum fox get in there?"

Before Molly could answer, Anna burst through the back door, wiping tears from her eyes. "Sam, he got in there again!" she announced. "There are feathers everywhere, and not one, but two, nice hens are missing."

"Not Vera?" her husband asked.

"Yes, Vera's gone!" Tears began to flow again. "That sweet Dominique hen followed me around the yard whenever I hung out clothes or checked the garden or walked to the barn. She was like my own special pet. I could rub her on her back---such soft feathers---and feed her mash right out of my hand. She was so much more than just a chicken!"

Anna sniffed and wiped her eyes, but when she heard Lillie's footsteps on the stairs, she warned, "I let Lillie sleep a little later this morning because I wanted to clean up the feathers before telling her that two more of her charges had disappeared."

"Lillie loves those hens," Molly added under her breath.

As soon as Lillie entered the kitchen, Anna tried to sound cheerful when she thanked Molly for making breakfast. "It looks wonderful. I just wish I felt like eating."

Before Lillie could ask about her mother's strange statement, Anna sat down and pulled her daughter onto her lap.

"Mama, why do you look upset?" Lillie asked, studying her mother's red eyes. "Is something wrong?"

"Dear, last night while we were sleepin', that fox broke into the hen house again," Anna said, hugging her daughter. "He carried off two more of our hens. I'm upset because he took our sweet Vera."

Lillie's buried her face in her Mama's apron. "Oh, noooo!" she wailed. "I'll miss her so much, Mama." When she had a moment to think, she dropped the apron and said anxiously, "I know I latched that door. How'd he get in there?"

Before anyone could speculate, she added, "That ole fox is so mean! Papa needs to get rid of him." But, with the optimism of youth, her anger died away and Lillie's face broke into a smile, "Maybe we can get some chicks and raise some more hens. Sylvia told me they have twelve new Dominique chicks that will be ready to leave their Mama soon. Maybe the Johnsons would let us have a few?"

Anna smiled without answering, then slid Lillie off her lap and served the little girl her breakfast.

"If I still had Dan, we'd go off and get that fox today," Jake said. "We came close once—sure wish I'd found the fox instead of Will Granger's ole…"

"We all miss Dan now," Samuel interjected quickly, before his son could blurt out the word "still." "Why don't you get the milkin' done, since you've polished off your plate?" Jake nodded and disappeared out the kitchen door.

After watching his wife gulp some very hot coffee, Samuel asked gently, "Feeling better?"

Anna nodded, waiting until Lillie finished eating and headed off to feed the four remaining hens. From the porch swing where Anna took another cup of coffee, she could hear her daughter ask each hen in turn about their welfare. "Are you nervous? Are you frightened? Let me pet each one of you. I'll be gentle." Lillie spoke in a comforting voice that sounded a lot like her mother's. Then she promised, "We'll take extra-good care to lock you ladies in there tonight."

After she fed the chickens an especially generous meal, Lillie opened the chicken house door, inviting the remaining hens into the yard to roam and search for bugs. Seeing her mother on the porch, she called out, "I'll go to the spring house for you, Mama." When Lillie delivered a crock containing milk from the previous night's milking, she asked if she could churn the day's butter.

"You're welcome to," Anna said. "Last night I washed, scalded, and dried the churn, so it's ready to go." She watched Lillie take off the lid and remove the dasher, then she poured a gallon of whole milk into the churn. "You're ready to go, Lillie," she said before returning to the kitchen.

Lillie settled down on her small ladder-back chair with the seat her grandfather had woven, inserted the dasher back into the churn, and secured the lid on top of the earthenware crockery. Slowly, then gaining speed, she moved the wooden dasher up and down, up and down, enjoying the smell indicating that more and more cream was slowly thickening into butter. "There's already chunks of cream floating on top," Lillie exclaimed with satisfaction minutes later, as she peered into the churn. She knew she wasn't strong enough to finish this chore, but it was fun to do her part while she watched the livestock grazing in the field beside the barn and listened to the quails calling *Bob-white!* and the Carolina wrens noisily singing their *teakettle-teakettle* song. She hummed a nameless tune as she churned.

As the mixture became thicker and the butter became more solid, Lillie found her work harder. Her arms began to ache as she continued to move the dasher up and down, so she was grateful when Molly appeared beside her. "Lillie, Mama wants you to go in and start washing the dishes while I take over the churning. She's going to finish her baking and then start the laundry."

Molly peeked into the churn. "You've done a fine job, Lillie— you haven't left me much to do today!" When her sister stood up and rubbed her arms, Molly added, "After you help me hang the laundry, we can put a blanket under the oak tree and play."

"Can we? That'll be fun! I'll work extra hard, Molly." The screen door slammed behind her as Lillie dashed into the kitchen to start the dishes.

"The water on our reliable old stove is already hot, Lady Bug," Samuel told her. I'll pour it into the dishpan and you can add the soap." He turned to her wife. "Let things rest a moment in here, Anna. Let's finish our coffee out on the porch."

As Molly finished the churning, Samuel and Anna sat on the porch swing, sipping silently. Anna sighed and put a hand on Samuel's knee. "Samuel, I have tried to be patient. I understand that God made all creatures for a purpose. But that fox has pushed me too far. I had twelve hens back in March. They gave us soft black-and-white feathers for our pillows. They gave us enough eggs to eat and sell. They gave us chicks to add to our brood. They loved to walk around the pasture catching bugs. They were good to us, and we were good to them. They seemed to know that we needed them."

Samuel scratched his head. "When Dan slept at the bottom of the ramp to the chicken house, no fox ever dared attack the hens. But Dan is gone and the fox has realized that fact. Mike Johnson told me he doesn't have a floor in their chicken coop, and that rascally fox dug underneath and came up inside to grab their hens."

"Well, ours has a wooden floor and a door with a latch, and he's still found a way in," Anna said, exasperation in her voice. "Now that wily old fox has grabbed my favorite laying hen, and I'm taking this theft personally. Four hens can barely provide enough eggs for this family, and the six chicks won't start laying eggs for another six months, at least—which means we can't afford to butcher any more chickens for our family to eat," she said. "I don't care how you do it, Sam, but that fox has to be stopped. Soon. Kill him, Sam."

Samuel ran his fingers through his hair. "I know, Anna. I know. Every time I open the door with my gun, the varmint is already running away, usually with a chicken in his mouth. I'll say this for them: foxes are as cunning as their reputation. I'm sure he can smell me when the wind is blowin', and if I carry a lantern, the light alerts him that I'm comin'. But what stumps me is how the fox opens the latch on that door."

Molly's churning was just about done. She looked over at her Papa and suggested, "Have you thought about standing here on the porch, hiding behind these corner roof supports with the gun cocked and resting on top of the porch railing? That way all you'd have to do is take aim and shoot."

When her father looked thoughtful, she added, "I've been looking from here, and the way that chicken house is positioned, you wouldn't hit the barn, and you probably wouldn't even hit the chicken house. By the time your finger touches that trigger, the fox will probably have started running down the hill toward the field."

"I'd only get one shot," Samuel mused as his wife and daughter waited for his response. He walked to the corner roof support on that side of the porch, surveying the landscape between the house and the chicken house. Next, he walked to the other side of the porch and stood at that corner roof support, doing the same thing. His smile took in both Molly and Anna. "It can be done," he announced. "I'll only have one shot at Red, but with luck I'll only need one shot." He handed Anna his coffee cup. "Now, if you'll excuse me, I'm off." He kissed Anna softly on the lips, and then bent over and kissed Molly on the top of her thick blond hair. "Mr. Gladstone recognized a brilliant young mind, and I'm proud to say it belongs to my daughter. Thank you for the idea, Molly."

"The dishes are done, Mama," Lillie declared, stepping onto the porch. "Can I help you push the butter into the butter press?"

The three Gilmer ladies returned to their chores, and Samuel whistled as he walked down the porch steps, heading to the barn. He arrived just as Jake was leading the two cows out of the stable and into the green pasture.

"Hi, Pa," Jake said. "Milking is done. I'm on my way to the spring house with the pails of milk."

Samuel mussed his son's hair. "Let me have one of those pails and I'll go with you. I have a problem that I think you can help me with, Jake. Let's talk on the way to the spring house."

Looking intrigued, Jake strode quickly, to keep pace with his father. The little rock building was situated on the edge of the woods. Its door could be latched and a tin roof protected the milk house from the elements. Inside its dark interior, a spring bubbled up with cool water. If Samuel had the use of a thermometer, it would have read thirty-nine degrees year-round. The pool, which measured four feet by two feet, was surrounded by rocks. In crocks submerged in the water, the family stored foods safely year-round. The foods didn't freeze in the winter and didn't spoil in the summer.

"This is my favorite water to drink," Jake said, squatting, cupping his hands together, and dipping them into the pool. At the rear of this spring house, a small stream of water flowed over rocks in a steady trickle, hurrying down to Beaver Creek.

Jake bent and lifted a sealed crock out of the water. Carefully, he poured the milk from his pail into this crock. When the pail was empty, he added the milk from the other pail. Then he conscientiously sealed the crock once more and placed it underneath the spring water. Samuel, who had remained outside, closed the door when Jake left the little building.

"Jake, we're going to rid the world of one marauding fox," Samuel informed his son. "Your big sister gave me an idea, and I'm going to show you how we're going to be a team, so we don't miss. We'll only get one chance."

Jake's face brightened. "Sure, Pa! Nothin' would make me happier than finally getting' Red."

"Exactly. You handle the Winchester well, and I'll have the Springfield. Together this could work. Come up on the porch and I'll show you where we're going to position ourselves tonight."

Unfortunately for their well-laid plans, a sudden thunderstorm and harsh rains delayed the campaign against the fox. To make certain the remaining hens and chicks were safe, not only did Anna check the door latch repeatedly, but she also wrapped a wire around the pivot of the latch and secured it to a nail she drove into the door frame.

The next night, however, was clear. Moonlight flooded the farmyard, and not a breath of a breeze was stirring. After dinner, Samuel and Anna sat on the porch swing while Jake practiced his skills with a yo-yo and Molly taught Lillie a few knitting stitches. The two girls each had a skein of yarn and two needles. "Remember, Lillie, knit one, purl one, knit one, purl one," Molly explained as she demonstrated slowly for her sister. Samuel kept one eye on the chicken house, which was barely visible in the moonlight. He hoped that when all the lamps in the house were extinguished and his eyes adjusted to the darkness, there would be enough light to make out a fox.

When the clock chimed nine o'clock, Molly and Lillie admitted they were ready for bed. Before Anna followed them into the house, Samuel spoke softly. "I have a feeling that our friend Red might consider payin' us a visit tonight. You ladies stay inside. I don't want you to be scared if you hear a gunshot. Jake and I are gonna stick around out here and watch."

All five of the Gilmers walked into the house. Samuel kissed Anna, whispering, "Wish us luck, dear." When his wife and daughters went to their rooms, Samuel turned to Jake. "All right, son. First, I want you to know that we don't shoot anything that we don't intend to eat—but this fox has been eatin' our food as well as our neighbors' food. We're gunnin' for it because it's a nuisance and dangerous."

"Do you think it's like that rabid coyote Pap-paw shot?" Jake asked.

"Something like that, though this time it's the chickens' lives, not ours, at stake," Samuel said. "Jake, are you ready?"

Jake nodded and picked up his Winchester. He pulled back on the pump action to load a shell into the firing chamber, inserted one more shell, and then closed the shotgun. Samuel opened his Springfield bolt-action rifle and loaded it with two bullets before speaking softly to Jake. "Son, we can't talk when we're out there unless we want Red to hear us. When you see him runnin' our way, take aim, then look at me. Wait for me to nod twice. That's when you fire."

They extinguished the kerosene lantern and took their positions on opposite ends of the porch. Jake sighted his shotgun and then leaned against the post to wait. Samuel sat backward in the small ladderback chair facing the chicken house, positioning the long barrel of his rifle on top of the porch rail.

An hour passed as they strained their ears. They listened to insects buzzing in the trees and the hooting of a Barred Owl off in the woods. With their eyes adjusted to the darkness, the moonlight shining through the trees was ample enough to illuminate the chicken house. However, anyone—or anything—standing down the hill from the coop could not see anything but darkness on that porch.

More time passed. Jake stifled yawn after yawn. Once, his head started to droop in fatigue. Shortly afterwards, a shadow appeared in the field, moving quiet and stealthily. The shape of a good-size fox materialized. A tiny gasp escaped from Jake's lips as the shape glided steadily and warily up the hill near the barn, then turned toward the chicken house. Onward it moved, closer and closer. Jake looked toward his Pa, who made no motion. Together they watched and waited for the perfect moment.

The fox approached the ramp leading to the door of the chicken house. At that moment, the hens began clucking nervously. They sensed the danger outside their door. To Jake's astonishment, the fox stood on his two back legs, resting his front legs against that door. One paw and a pointed nose reached upward. "I'll be switched. That rascal is actually pushing up against the latch from underneath," Jake marveled. He imagined the latch beginning to rotate just when he saw his father nod twice. Jake moved the Winchester slightly, to get the fox in his sights.

The fox's head jerked around, sensing a human nearby. He dropped onto his four paws, turned as quick as a lightning flash, and started running down the ramp.

BOOM! Jake's Winchester exploded. With a yelp of pain, the fox staggered.

BOOM! Samuel's Springfield rifle fired a split second after Jake's rifle, knocking the fox off the ramp. He flopped over onto his side. Jake could see no movement.

The world was blanketed in silence—and to Jake's ears, it was deafening. No bugs or birds sang in the trees. Jake imagined the owl had been startled off the branch where she had been watching a field mouse below.

"Let's see what we got," Samuel said in a hushed voice, striking a match and lighting the lantern.

Jake carefully propped his shotgun against the porch railing. Samuel kept his rifle raised as they ran down the slope toward what appeared to be a still, quiet animal at rest. Jake arrived first, approaching the creature from behind. Samuel moved to the head of the fox, keeping his rifle aimed directly at the animal. Jake looked for signs of breathing, and when he didn't sense any, he bent and felt for a pulse in the fox's chest. He stood quickly. "Yep, he's dead, Pa. Look! You must've shot it in the heart or lungs, because there's a hole here in the chest."

"His head was turned as it started to run, so I couldn't get a head shot," Samuel agreed. "The chest was my best chance." He pointed to the fox's hindquarters. "Jake, your shot in the hip stopped the animal as it was running, or I wouldn't've been able to get my shot off."

Jake beamed proudly. "I guess we're a good team, huh, Pa?"

"We are, for sure," Samuel said. "Because of your help, I could bring Red down." He lowered the lantern, shining it on the animal. "All right, let's look this big boy over—but be careful to stay away from the fox's head, in case it has any diseases," he warned.

As they looked more closely, Samuel pointed to the animal's swollen belly. "Jake, this fox was a female. Stands to reason that a critter smart enough to lift the latch of the chicken coop would be a female. And, look: enlarged nipples and abdomen. She was pregnant. Thank heavens we got her now. Otherwise, we'd have been in for a whole passel of trouble, if she'd given birth to a litter of kits—and that explains why she kept raiding everyone's chicken coop. She was almost ready to deliver."

Jake studied the carcass carefully. "Pa, did you ever see an animal as clever she was? She could raise the door latch with her paw and nose."

Samuel shook his head. "I know foxes are clever, but I don't think I've ever seen one this smart. Jake, can you go back to the porch and bring that sack I put under the porch swing? I want to bag Red. We'll bury her in the morning."

"Dibs on the tail, Pa!" Jake exclaimed. "And I might skin the varmint before we bury the carcass. I'd like to hammer that hide up on the side of the chicken house, to warn future foxes to stay away or face the consequences. Our chickens will rest easier after this."

As if to confirm what Jake had suggested, the clucking and flapping in the chicken house stopped as quickly as it had begun.

Samuel laughed. After the father and son bagged the beast and placed the body inside the smokehouse temporarily, they returned to the house. Samuel slung his arm over Jake's shoulder. "You are a fine hunter, Jake Gilmer," he said. "And you're an even finer young man. I'm impressed with the maturity you show—I forget sometimes that you're only ten years old. I'm very proud of you, son."

When they slipped into the kitchen and latched the porch door, Anna called softly from the nearby bedroom, "Samuel?"

"Red won't bother the chickens anymore, Anna."

CHAPTER TWELVE: *"PAPA, THAT SACK IS MOVING!"*
August 15, 1913

The air was still, hot, and sticky in the Piedmont of North Carolina in mid-August. The katydids in the trees and the grasses made a racket, indicating that the heat didn't affect them. When Jake and Lillie finished their chores for the morning, they decided to explore the creek between the dam and the mill. "That might be a good place to find arrowheads and other Indian artifacts," Jake announced to his mother before the brother and sister ran down to the water.

"Be careful to look in every nook and cranny along this here creek bank," Jake cautioned Lillie, but after a half-hour search, they found nothing more exciting than countless rocks, tree roots, and snake holes— which Lillie quickly moved away from. When she tired of the search, Lillie reached into the creek, cupped her hand, and sprayed her brother with the lukewarm water. Jake was delighted to stop the search and join the splashing. When they were both nearly drenched, they dropped onto the banks of the creek, panting and laughing, knowing their clothes would dry almost immediately in the hot sunshine.

Idly, the brother and sister watched little silvery minnows zig-zag in the water and observed the glacial progress of tiny little creek snails as they slowly moved on the rocks under the water. It wasn't long before Jake stretched out, covered his face with his straw hat, and proceeded to doze. Lillie was made of stronger stuff. Holding up her skirts, she waded through the water, bending down occasionally to move a rock and watch crayfish scoot from under her shadow and dart downstream, to find shelter beneath another rock.

"Jake! Lillie!" Pa's voice reached them, causing Jake to sit up and Lillie to stop in her tracks. They glimpsed his face at a window in the mill. "Y'all come up here. Someone wants to see you."

"All right, Pa. We're coming," Jake called to his father, standing up and brushing leaves and grass off his backside. "Wonder who it is?" he asked Lillie, who was struggling to climb up the side of the creek bank with her skirts in one hand and her other hand grabbing tree roots along the way. "Race you!"

"Hey! No fair! You got a head start." she squealed. But Lillie knew that Jake would wait until she caught up before he made that final sprint to the mill. Jake watched his little sister to make sure she didn't slide back down the creek bank as slowly she inched her way up to the top. With one last lunge and the support of a small dogwood tree, she pushed herself up and over the top of the bank.

Once on solid grassy ground, the youngsters bolted toward the building, panting when they screeched to a halt just inside the doorway of the saw mill. Walking into the shadowy interior, they blinked quickly before noticing a large man standing next to their grandfather. When their eyes adjusted to the darkness, they saw that the man looked disheveled. Dressed in bibbed overalls like their father and grandfather, the man stood silent, looking sternly at the children. He spat a stream of tobacco juice expertly into the brass spittoon on the floor before nodding at them silently. The children gulped.

"Uh, hello, Mr. Granger." Jake finally found his voice. Lillie took a small step backward, in the direction of her father's comforting figure.

"Mornin'," Will Granger replied, still not smiling. "Boy, have you been shootin' any rabbits up my way recently?"

"Oh, no, sir!" Jake spoke emphatically, shaking his head. "I ain't been anywhere near your property since that Saturday morning when I followed that fox." He hesitated, glanced at his father, and added, "I'm sorry again about that, sir." When the man still didn't speak, Jake took a deep breath and continued, "As a matter of fact, Mr. Granger, the only time since then that I've shot my Winchester was a few days ago when Pa and I both shot that red fox late at night. We killed it, Mr. Granger. And it was a mighty cunnin' fox—you shoulda seen her openin' the door of our chicken coop."

Will nodded, and his face took on a more pleasant expression. "Your Pa was just tellin' me that story. Glad you got the varmint. That rascal killed six of my own hens." He seemed to choose his words carefully before he added with a trace of awkwardness, "Well, anyway, since you haven't been able to kill any rabbits recently, I brought somethin' over that was in my lower pasture this mornin'. Take a look in this sack."

Will held the sack out toward Jake, but Jake glanced at his father for direction. When Samuel nodded, Jake reached for the feed sack with a hesitant "thank you?" and looked inside. It held the body of a fresh-killed rabbit.

Jake grinned, "Wow! That's a whopper, and a good 'un, too. Mama can make us some good stew with this catch. Thanks, Mr. Granger."

Lillie was studying a second sack just a reach away from her feet. When she leaned forward to look more closely, the sack suddenly came to life, wiggling. Squealing, she ran to hide behind her Papa. "Papa, that sack is *moving*! There's somethin' in there." When all eyes turned in the direction her little finger was pointing, the sack obediently moved once again. A tiny whimpering sound could be heard.

Jake added his voice to his sister's. "Pa, there's something little and alive in that sack!" He, too, moved closer to his father.

"Well, what do you know about that, son?" Lee Hanner asked. And the three adult men commenced chuckling.

Will Granger suddenly grinned, the biggest—and only—grin the two Gilmer children had ever seen on his face. "Jake, why don't you go see what's in there?" he suggested. "It sure-to-Betsy wants out of there."

Jake looked at his Pa for a nod of reassurance before he walked over and cautiously pulled open that old feed sack. At that moment a whimper turned into a small, high-pitched bark. Jake dropped to his knees to open the bag. A puppy dashed into his arms. "It's a puppy! A beagle puppy!" Lillie squealed, kneeling beside her brother, who was holding the happy, wiggly creature. "He has brown ears, Pa! And his face is totally brown, except for a patch of white around his shiny black nose."

"And look at this white line running between his eyes," Jake added, running his finger along the ridge of the puppy's nose. The back of the wiggly little body was black, but his chest and belly were white. "And best of all, he has a white tip on his tail—just like Dan."

The brother and sister laughed as the tiny little beagle jumped up to lick their faces, barking in delight. "Oh, this is the cutest beagle puppy in the world!" Lillie exclaimed as the little dog bounced from one Gilmer child to the next, offering fleeting licks before heading back to the other. "I've got to show Mama and Molly this cute little boy. Can I, Pa? Can I, Jake?" Before they could nod, Lillie ran to the open door and called to the puppy. With the little fellow on her heels, she headed up the hill.

"Look, Pa! He runs with his tail straight up and waving like a flag in the wind. Just like Dan," Jake said, watching the two. At that moment, a connection was made in Jake's brain. He stood tall and looked Will Granger in the eye. "I don't understand, sir. I thank you again for that rabbit, and we will sure enjoy eatin' it. But, why would you bring over this beagle for us?"

Will Granger still had the hint of a smile on his face. "Jake Gilmer, you're quite a hunter. A good hunter needs a good huntin' dog. Just before your Dan died, my beagle gave birth to five puppies, three females and two males. I'd promised three of them, and I want to keep one for myself. But this particular beagle seemed extra-special. Smart and curious. When your Pa told me the circumstances of Dan's fight with the snake, I made up my mind that this one had to come to you."

The man glanced down at his feet for a moment, then looked at the boy and spoke frankly. "I was dadgum mean to you that day you surprised me on my property, Jake. I reckon I owe you an apology. A big one. I'd been drinkin' a lot of whiskey at the time." His gaze took in Samuel Gilmer when he continued, "I want you—both of you—to know that the only things remainin' of that campsite in the hills is the stone fireplace, three walls and a roof. Our escapade convinced me I'm not makin' or drinkin' a drop of whiskey ever again."

He added, as if to change the subject, "That'll become a right nice—and safe—little campsite, a place to go if I want to hunt deer or turkeys." Samuel nodded at his neighbor. Will Granger said with a trace of awkwardness, "Well, this little guy is your dog now, Jake. I know you'll take good care of him. I hope you have many good years with him. I hope he turns into as good a hunter as your last dog. I'd appreciate it if you could use him to find every fox that comes anywhere near our chicken coops."

Jake was speechless. He'd never had a grownup apologize to him before, and he had never expected to receive a gift from his big, scary neighbor. He walked over to Will Granger and stretched out his hand. "Thanks so much, Mr. Granger. I promise to take real good care of that little puppy. I know we'll have plenty of good times together." Jake took a handkerchief out of his pocket and blew his nose. "Well, shucks." He grinned. "Mr. Granger, I was really scared of you, but not now. Sir, if you'll excuse me, I'd like to take the rabbit up to Mama and get to know Luke better."

Will Granger smiled. "Luke. That sure is a good name, son."

CHAPTER THIRTEEN: *BIG MEETING*
Sunday, August 17, through Sunday, August 24, 1913

The Rev. Ephraim C. Murray of Alamance Presbyterian Church recorded in his notes that the first Big Meeting, the congregation's week of special Revival services, took place in 1801. At that time, a guest minister who rode the circuit from church to church would come and spend the week conducting Bible studies during the day and preaching every night. In the evenings, after chores and milking were finished and folks had a chance to eat and wash up, the community would gather in the sanctuary for a revival service that generally lasted an hour and a half or so.

People came from miles around for these events. Some even camped beside the creek for the week so they wouldn't have to go all the way home each night. The final service on Sunday morning included Holy Communion, followed by a congregational dinner on the church grounds.

Each service featured the good old-fashioned gospel hymns, a special song prepared by the chancel choir, and a sermon by the guest minister. At the close of each service, an Altar Call gave people the opportunity to give their lives to the Lord Jesus Christ for the very first time or to rededicate their lives to Jesus once again. At this time in the proceedings, everyone sang a stirring hymn while the guest minister and the resident minister stood in front of the congregation to greet anyone who came forward.

By the time the Big Meeting rolled around in August of 1913, the entire community was buzzing with excitement. This was a powerful spiritual time, but it was also a chance to have relaxed fellowship with neighbors, to catch up on news with friends, share farming tips, and meet new people.

On this particular week, Will Granger was helping Samuel with a big sawmill project. After Anna delivered a basket of lunch and a cool pitcher of water for the men, Samuel pulled a chair for himself and one for Will to the open mill door. The men could hear the stream trickling below as they ate, then leaned back on their chairs, enjoying a whisk of a breeze. That was when Samuel turned to Will.

"You know you're more than welcome to ride over to Big Meeting services next week with us, Will," he offered. "We have plenty of room in the wagon, and Anna is already makin' plans for the victuals she and our friends are plannin' to cook for the picnic when Big Meeting's over."

Will paused in thought before he spoke. "Thanks for the invite, Samuel. I reckon if I decide to go, I'll just ride my horse over." Long moments later, he added in low tones, "You know, after goin' seven years without hearin' preachin' or teachin' of the Word, it's a whole lot easier *not* to go than to go. I reckon I might've forgotten what to do, even."

Samuel nodded, but remained silent. A few minutes later, the men returned to work. But Samuel did mention the conversation to Anna that night. Together, they prayed for Will.

Big Meeting began on the evening of the third Sunday in August. Once the cows had been milked, the family members fed, and everyone had washed up, Samuel Gilmer hitched the horses up to the wagon. "Let's shake a leg," he called as Molly peeked into the mirror over the wash stand one last time and Anna stored the last dish in the cupboard.

"Can we bring Luke, Papa? Please?" Lillie pleaded.

"I don't think Luke is ready for church—and I'm certain sure church isn't ready for Luke, despite his fine gospel name," Samuel said.

"He'll be much happier in his crate by the stove, Lillie," Anna said, as Samuel handed her up onto the front wagon seat. Molly took her place beside her grandfather on the bench behind them, facing backwards. In the rear seat, facing forward, sat Lillie and Jake. The three adults and Molly carried their Bibles, which Jake glanced at longingly. Anna read his mind and smiled. "Jake, it won't be long before you'll be gettin' your own Bible. It's just a few months until Christmas."

"Gid-yap," Samuel ordered the horses, and the wagon headed off down the road, bumping and rocking slowly as Samuel tried to avoid as many ruts as he could. The two horses steadily pulled the wagon up the hill from Beaver Creek to the higher and more level ground leading to Alamance Presbyterian Church. As they traveled, they glimpsed other wagons on Hanners' Mill Road. Other neighbors passed them riding horseback. The procession of horses and wagons grew when this road intersected Williams Dairy Road, and it grew again when they reached Greensboro-Chapel Hill Road. (This stretch was known as Alamance Church Road.)

"This trip always seems to take so long when I'm anxious to get there," Lillie sighed. Her grandfather heard her. "Now, Lillie, it's only a mile-and-a-half from Beaver Creek Bridge to the church. Be patient, child."

At last they reached their destination, along with neighbors and friends from miles around. The men unhitched horses and mules from wagons and led them to a patch of land just beyond the church, near the little stream that gurgled cheerfully below the cemetery. There was enough pasture grass and plenty of clean, cool water to entertain the animals while their families attended the service in the house of worship.

"I never fail to appreciate this view," Anna told Samuel as he handed her down from the wagon seat. Across the road from the church cemetery and beyond the stream, hills rolled upward toward the horizon. Behind a nearby fence, a farmer's cows and horses were grazing, bathed in the oranges and reds of the glorious sunset. Birds came to life during the early evening on hot summer nights. Their joyful songs mingled and filled the air as dusk descended.

Calls to friends, laughter, introductions, and smiles were exchanged as neighbors lingered briefly outside the church doors. But soon enough they entered the church. Because the weather was so hot and humid, all the windows and doors had been flung open, and women and old folk fanned themselves with cardboard fans decorated with pretty pictures and the logos of various funeral parlors, which had been stored in the trays on the backs of the pews.

The congregation filled every pew during this week of special services, even though brand new additions to the north and south of the sanctuary had enlarged the space considerably. Those sitting near the windows on the creek side of the church could hear the cows lowing across the hills. Occasionally a chimney sweep or a little bat flew into the church in pursuit of an insect. Children giggled and made faces at each other across the pews. But when the organ music began playing softly and the choir entered from two doors on either side of their loft behind the pulpit, everyone fell silent. Two ministers walked in together after greeting the late arrivals at the front door.

The Reverend Alexander Crawford, pastor of Alamance Presbyterian Church, nodded from side to side as he silently greeted his congregation on his procession down the center aisle. "Hard to believe he's only been here eight months," Anna whispered to Samuel. "I still miss Rev. James Wilson, though." Her husband nodded.

Reverend Crawford announced the first hymn and motioned for the people to stand. The organist worked her magic on the pump organ, and the service began with a rousing chorus of the hymn "Throw Out the Life-Line." After the final note ended, the congregation sat down in unison and returned the hymn books to the wooden pew racks. Lillie giggled at the simultaneous "clunk" sounds. Samuel raised his brows at her, and she put her hand over her mouth, quiet once again.

"Welcome to the first night of the Big Meeting." The deep, comforting voice of Reverend Crawford easily reached the far corners of the sanctuary. "This revival has been held at Alamance for more than one hundred years now, and I'm looking forward to my first Big Meeting." After thanking the choir for their diligent preparations for special music throughout this week, he reminded the congregation of the covered dish lunch the following Sunday morning after the worship service. "Now," he intoned, "Let us rise and sing 'Tell Me the Stories of Jesus.'"

"This is my favorite," Lillie whispered to Molly. "I can read all the words by myself!" She sang happily.

When the song ended, Reverend Crawford introduced the guest minister, the Reverend Bob McIntyre, pastor at Bethel Presbyterian

Church in McLeansville. After the ministers shook hands, Reverend McIntyre mounted the podium and introduced the scripture: Matthew 25:32-46. "This is the story of the separation of the sheep and the goats, reminding us all about what actions we are obliged to take when we see strangers hungry or thirsty or naked or sick or imprisoned," he said before the reading.

"Those who know about the needs of our fellow man but do nothing to help are the goats," he reminded his listeners. "Jesus tells us that when they reject the needy—whether they be friends, neighbors, or strangers—they are actually rejecting Him. Therefore, these goats will share the same punishment for eternity that Satan and his evil demons will receive at the Judgment."

"Amen," came a voice from the rear of the church before the reverend continued, "On the other hand, those called sheep are the people who see the needs of those around them and reach out to help them in the name of Jesus Christ. Brothers and Sisters, who will you choose to be?"

The minister paraphrased the scripture, reminding his congregation that the "sheep" asked, "But Lord, when did we see you hungry, sick, or naked?" and Jesus replied, *When you helped these who are my children, you were doing it to me. Enter the gates of Heaven and receive the reward that my Father has prepared for you.*

Reverend McIntyre then discussed a passage in the Book of James, chapter two, verse seventeen: *Faith without works is dead.* His words caused more than one child to squirm. "Wow! I need to do everything I can to help other folks if I follow Jesus," Lillie whispered to her sister. "I sure don't want to be a goat." Without taking her eyes off the pastor, Molly nodded.

"And now for our special song of the night, which is one of the favorite songs of Alamance Presbyterian Church," the choirmaster announced, smiling. "Dwelling in Beulah Land". Hazel Gorrell walked from the pump organ to the piano. As she began to play and the people began to sing, the harmony seemed especially beautiful on this peaceful night. Jake enjoyed the two-part chorus, where the men sang, "Praise God" after the women sang, "Underneath a cloudless sky." He smiled, thinking to himself, "After my voice changes, I'll be able to sing that low part, too."

Once this song was concluded, Reverend Crawford returned to the pulpit, to announce that the final hymn every night this week would be "Just As I Am", sung during the Altar Call. "Anyone who feels moved by the Holy Spirit should come forward, and a minister will lay hands on you and pray for you."

The week-long event was an exciting time for people living in rural stretches of North Carolina. The grownups looked forward to conversations with friends they seldom saw. Young people cast shy glances at each other, and often courtships began after the Big Meeting. Before and after services, young children played tag and hide-and-seek, laughing and squealing in the large grassy areas around the front and sides of the church and in the back where the cemetery rolled gently down to the creek.

Wednesday night of Big Meeting Week offered another worship service; this one had life-changing results for at least one hurting and lonely man whose heart was sometimes hard and cold as stone. On this night, he waited in the shadows outside the church until the singing of the first hymn, "Blessed Assurance, Jesus is Mine", ended. Then he slipped quietly up the steps and into the cloakroom, where he found a wooden chair to sit on while he listened to the evening's message. After hearing neighbors talk for two days about the Big Meeting services and how lives had been changed, his curiosity and a strange, burning hunger inside his spirit brought Will Granger to this moment.

The sermon on this night was based on the Scripture from Mark 4: 35-41: *Jesus said to His disciples, "Let us go over to the other side." Leaving the crowd behind, they took Him along, just as He was, in the boat...A furious squall came up, and the waves broke over the boat, so that it was nearly swamped. Jesus was in the stern, sleeping on a cushion. The disciples woke Him up and said to Him, "Teacher, don't you even care if we drown?" He got up, rebuked the wind, and said to the waves, "Quiet! Be still." Then the wind died down and it was completely calm. He said to His disciples, "Why are you so afraid? Do you still have no faith?" They were terrified and asked each other, "Who is this? Even the wind and the waves obey Him."*

Reverend McIntyre's message discussed storms. "We all know how, on a summer afternoon in North Carolina, a thunderstorm can build up quickly and catch one unprepared. Suddenly, instead of playing, bringing in laundry, plowing a garden or harvesting grain, we race for shelter as pelting rain, hail, or dangerous lightning crashes all around us." His kind eyes scanned the congregation. "In our personal lives, in just a moment, something disastrous can happen that can shake us to our very core, and our lives may never be the same again."

Many heads in the church nodded as the reverend continued, "During this storm, after the lightning bolts have struck, we often shout at the Lord. We demand to know, 'Where are you? Don't you care? How could you leave me when I needed you the most?' But think of the example of Jesus. He was so trusting in his heavenly father, so safe and secure in his loving arms that he fell asleep. A peaceful, blissful sleep, though the storm around him was raging. Yet his disciples—the men who knew him the best—were panicking. They feared they were all going to die. How dare Jesus sleep when they needed his help? They asked themselves. So what did they do?"

The minister paused, looked at his listeners, and continued, "They shook him awake. Yes, they were angry when they asked him why he didn't care if they drowned. Well, of course Jesus took control of the situation. He commanded the storm to cease and he calmed the sea. But more importantly, Jesus used this as a teaching moment about faith. Hadn't they been with the Master long enough to realize that they could trust him even during a raging storm? He asked them about their faith. Jesus didn't rebuke his friends because they were terrified. He simply asked them why they had chosen fear instead of faith."

The sermon pointed out that Jesus's questions astonished his disciplines and caused them additional fear because their rabbi actually had the power to control wind, waves, and any storm that came their way. "You may have missed one important aspect in this story—and this is crucial," the minister said. "Jesus didn't send the disciples out in that boat knowing they were going to be caught in a horrible storm. No. Where was Jesus? Yes, friends, Jesus was right there in the little boat *with* them. He went through that storm *with* his disciples. And this same Jesus will be with us in all the storms of our lives. Many times he delivers us from a storm, and we don't even know it."

Again, the reverend paused and looked into the congregation, making sure that all eyes were on him when he added, "Sometimes, however, Jesus has to send us into a storm. I am sure that he doesn't like to do that. No loving parent likes to see their child hurt. But, rest assured, brothers and sisters, our Lord Jesus Christ walks through the storm with us. He knows every tear we shed and feels every pain we endure!

"Have any of you been through a storm that you thought would be the end of everything in your life? I know you have. Have any of you shaken the shoulders of Jesus, demanding, 'How *dare* you sleep when I'm drowning here? Why aren't you stopping this horrible thing from happening to me?' We plead with him, 'Don't you care? Are you even here? *Do* something!'"

As this message continued, the man sitting in the cloak room shifted uncomfortably on his chair. Then tears filled his eyes. He clutched his chest, amazed to feel the coldness lessen its grip. His insides began to warm. The hardness in his heart felt as if it was beginning to melt away. Slowly and gently, a peaceful and powerful warmth began to wrap itself around him—a sensation he hadn't felt in seven long years.

Will Granger began to feel what he knew was divine love pouring into his soul. At first, the feeling tingled. And then he felt a rush of exhilarating joy. "This can only be the Holy Spirit," he murmured, clutching his chest. Suddenly he felt a strong, compelling need to do something about this. Right now.

Quickly, Will closed the door to that cloakroom, knelt beside the chair, and poured his heart out to God. "Oh, God, I've been so lost. So bitter, angry, and mean. The grief and pain have poisoned my life. An evil darkness turned me against just about everyone. Especially you, Lord. I've pushed you aside and told you that I didn't want nothin' to do with you any longer. Look what this did to me. I've been jealous of everyone who can laugh, everyone who's experienced joy, especially the joy of being married to someone they love. I've ached every time I've seen a little boy about the age Will Junior would have been. I've hurt people. I've wasted so much of my life with hatred and selfishness."

And then he apologized to Jesus and asked for his forgiveness. Tears were streaming down his face and drippng onto his shirt by the time his prayers ended.

The choir had just finished their special song for the evening, unbeknownst to Will. He didn't know that the anthem "The Ninety and Nine" tells about the good shepherd who loves all of his one hundred sheep. And how, when he discovers one sheep is missing, he leaves the ninety-nine to search for that one who was lost. And he continues searching until he finds it and he brings it safely back to the sheepfold rejoicing.

Will quietly opened the door of that cloakroom in time to hear Reverend Crawford announce, "Our final hymn, our Altar Call, is 'Just As I Am'. Remember, the title is not 'Just As I Want To Be.' Jesus loves you so much that he died for you. He wants you to come just as you are. Right now. Full of sin, fear, pain, heartache, and loneliness. If you feel the Holy Spirit whispering to you right now, brothers and sisters, I ask you to come forward. Jesus is waiting to welcome you home. Come!"

The music began. Will Granger stood, trembling. His first instinct was to walk out the front door and run for home. But the altar beckoned to him.

Several people were walking forward, and before he knew it, Will Granger joined the line, hat in hand, with tears pouring down his cheeks. He knelt at the altar of Alamance Presbyterian Church, feeling like a prodigal son returning home to his heavenly father, a loving father who had been watching and waiting for him for a very long time.

Samuel and Anna were focused on their hymn book when Jake grabbed his mother's hand, whispering loudly, "Mama, look. It's Mr. Granger!" Samuel immediately handed Anna the book and walked forward to the altar, where he laid his hands on the head of his neighbor and friend. He listened quietly as Will prayed the Sinner's Prayer with Reverend Crawford. When the prayer ended and Will Granger rose, the minister whispered, "Please stay here at the altar, Will. After the benediction, I want to spend a few minutes longer with you." He suddenly grinned at the large man who stood before him. "Congratulations, Brother Granger! Welcome to the family of God."

After the service ended, the congregation filed out of the church silently while their friends and neighbors who had answered the Altar Call spoke with the ministers and received copies of the Bible. A half hour must have passed before Will stepped outdoors in the last rays of light from the sunset. He was surprised to find that Samuel Gilmer and his family were waiting for him. Will came over to speak to them and say his goodbyes, but Samuel put his hand on the big man's shoulder, saying, "Will, we want you to stop by on your way home for a cup of coffee and a piece of Anna's finest apple pie."

Will nodded, smiling. "Sure would like that. With a full moon tonight, I'll be able to get up the hill to my home."

Laughter filled the air as the Gilmer family members and their neighbor sat on the porch and enjoyed pie and coffee. The tiny little puppy chased Lillie and Jake until they collapsed on the ground, at which time the puppy bounced between them, licking their faces. "Race you to the swings!" Jake challenged.

"I can swing higher than you can!" his sister retorted. The s
maple seats Samuel Gilmer had suspended by ropes from the la

branches got plenty of action before Lillie yawned and rubbed her eyes. By that time, countless stars were twinkling in the sky and the moon was blazing in all its glory. The last of the fireflies of summer were flashing down near the woods and the creek.

Anna smiled, "I think two young people need to get their teeth brushed and climb into bed."

"But I'm not sleepy, Mama," whined the yawning Lillie. However, she obediently walked to the big porch swing, hugged and kissed her Mom and Dad and then her Pap-paw, who was starting to stretch and yawn himself. Last of all, Lillie stood in front of Will Granger, who was sitting in a rocking chair, sipping on his second cup of coffee. The child smiled at him and reached out to give him a big bear-hug. "Good night, Mr. Granger. I'm so glad you got saved tonight, and I'm glad you came to visit us. You're a good neighbor who gives really good puppies. Good night!"

Will hesitated just a moment, uncertain how to respond, but then he embraced the little girl tightly in his arms.

Anna turned to Molly. "Will you tuck Lillie in, Molly, and make sure Jake actually uses soap and water to wash his hands and face?" Molly grinned and followed her brother and sister into the kitchen.

Will cleared his throat and looked over Anna's shoulder when he said huskily, "That—the love of a family—is more valuable than any money in the bank." And he thanked the family for their friendship.

This was the cue for Lee to rise out of his chair, grunting as his ꞁ. He stretched noisily. "I'm bushed, folks. Time ıe hay." He shook hands with Will Granger. re any time. We're mighty glad that you found ɔrd. I'm always lookin' for a Bible Study and

191

prayer partner, and I'd be happy to be yours any time." He raised his hand in farewell as he opened the screen door.

Will stayed until the last of the lightning bugs disappeared, sharing his experience with Samuel and Anna. "Finally, everything made sense. I'd given up on God, not knowin' that, during the past seven years whilst I've been grievin' with a heart broken in two, that he was right there with me. I'd pushed him outta my boat. I've been foolish, but now, with his help, I aim to live right."

"Good for you, Will," Anna murmured.

"Well, I don't know what I'm s'posed to do, but I'm convinced that God has some kind o' good purpose for my life." He rose and his hosts followed suit. Anna hugged their neighbor and Samuel took his big hand in both of his. "Thank you for being so patient with me," Will said. Then he mounted his horse, rode up the lane, and disappeared into the woods leading to his own house.

Samuel and Anna stood on the porch, their arms around each other, listening to their neighbor whistle a happy tune. "Well, that's a first!" Anna said, hugging Samuel. "Praise God!"

The katydids and cicadas in the trees and the frogs in Beaver Creek appeared to sing with extra joy and enthusiasm as the Gilmores kissed each other, then walked inside. One by one, the kerosene lanterns throughout the house were extinguished. The barred owl in the hickory tree nearest their bedroom window heard Anna's soft giggle as she settled into the arms of her husband. Then the owl continued his call, *Who-cooks -for-you, Who-cooks-for-you-all?*

CHAPTER FOURTEEN: *MOLLY'S BIG MOVE*
August 25, 1913

Two birthdays were celebrated during the summer of 1913. Molly Gilmer turned seventeen in early June, and Lillie Gilmer became seven in mid-July. They had decided on one big birthday celebration this year on the Fourth of July, inviting the two girls' closest friends from school and church for an outdoor picnic at the Gilmers' farm. On the special day, these guests dined on new picnic tables that Lee Hanner and Samuel Gilmer had built and placed in the woods just behind their home, overlooking Beaver Creek. Molly had requested pork roasted in a pit in the ground, fresh corn on the cob, and green beans, and Lillie agreed with this menu wholeheartedly. When Anna asked Lillie what type of cake they would like, Lillie declared "Your pound cake with lemon icing, of course!"

This year's celebration was joyful as well as bittersweet. It would be the last social event the girls would have together before Molly Gilmer set forth on a new phase in her life: she was going off to college at the very end of August. Mr. R.M. Gladstone, her teacher at Tucker School, had been true to his word. He recommended her for advanced schooling and had written a letter to that effect, sending along her school transcripts when Molly applied to the State Normal and Industrial College near downtown Greensboro. At the end of June, she received word that she had been accepted as a freshman.

The weeks between the birthday party and the start of school flew by for everyone but Molly, who worked feverishly to sew a wardrobe appropriate for a freshman coed when she wasn't studying the volumes on literature, science, and mathematics that Mr. Gladstone loaned her.

At last the long-awaited day arrived. On the afternoon of Monday, August 25, Molly Gilmer was expected to register at the college. That morning, Molly stood behind Lillie, who was sitting on a revolving stool in front of the dressing table in the girls' bedroom upstairs, brushing and braiding Lillie's long, thick red hair. Though Lillie was struggling to keep her emotions in check, a large tear trickled down her nose. She sniffed and reached up to wipe the telltale tear away. Molly saw her little sister's sadness, and, as she finished the right braid, she turned the stool around and knelt in front of Lillie, smiling.

"Lillie, you know nothing will ever change the fact that I'm your sister. I love you, and I always will. It won't be long before fall comes, and I promise I'll be here to visit one weekend in October and for five days at Thanksgiving. I'll write to you, and you can write to me. I want to hear all your news, so you have to write often! You can tell me about all the adventures at Tucker School and all the mischief Luke gets into."

The big sister put the finishing bows on Lillie's braid. "There, now," she said in satisfaction. "You know how to braid your hair now. I've just been doing that to spend some time talking to you early in the morning. Just imagine it: you'll have this big room all to yourself until I come visit."

That did it. The dam burst. Lillie wrapped her arms around her sister and sobbed into Molly's apron. "I don't want this big ol' room to myself. I want you! Molly, you're not just my sister, you're my best friend—even more than Susie! Now you're off to college, and pretty soon you'll be getting married, and I'll still be a little kid."

Molly leaned down to hear the words Lillie spoke that were muffled by her apron. "I don't know how to get along without you. Who's gonna sit on my bed with me every time I get scared when that coyote howls? Or when I have a bad dream? Who's gonna give me clues on how to solve 'rithmetic problems? Who's gonna teach me how to make somethin' nice with those knitting stitches you've been showin' me? Molly, I think my heart is breakin'."

As Lillie poured out her concerns, Molly wiped her own tears with a dry corner of her apron. "I'll miss you too, sweet Lillie. You bring so much joy to my heart. I don't care how far apart we are or who we meet or what we do, we'll always have that special sisterly love that no one can take from us. I'll need your happy letters to keep me going with studies, Lillie, because I know this school is going to be hard, and I'm going to get lonely. You have to promise to send me a letter every week without fail. Then I'll have something to look forward to. Jake is a dear boy and a faithful protector for us both, but he isn't one for writing, you know."

Lillie burst into a mischievous smile. "Oh, I think I can write to you. I already put a surprise inside your Bible last night after you went to bed. Oops! I wasn't gonna say that."

Molly hugged her sister. "Let's go down and eat breakfast. I expect Pa has the wagon already loaded, ready to go." The two sisters, one a tiny little girl with red braids, green eyes, and freckles, and one a slim young woman with deep blue eyes who was wearing her wavy blond hair in a grownup bun, walked down the stairs together holding hands.

Pap-paw Hanner set down his coffee as the girls walked in, "Ho! There you are. Thought p'rhaps you had changed your mind, Molly, y'all took so long gettin' down here. The rest of us're almost through with breakfast." He turned to Samuel. "I know the horses are through eatin' now. I'll go hitch them to the wagon."

Lee Hanner untied the horses from the oak tree and grunted, wincing in pain. But when the family appeared on the porch in their Sunday best clothes, he managed to climb onto the front seat of the wagon beside his daughter Anna. Samuel jumped up on the other side of his wife and, after gathering the reins, turned and winked at his oldest child. Jake and Lillie took the seat just behind their parents, facing backwards toward Molly, who was wedged in between two suitcases and a large travel bag. The Gilmer ladies wore travel bonnets to protect their hair from the wind and dust.

"Everyone ready?" Samuel asked before clicking his tongue and shaking the reins. Off the entire family headed to Greensboro.

The day was overcast, which meant it was not as hot as it otherwise would have been. Since it was a workday in Greensboro, buggies, horseback riders, and people on foot filled the road leading into the city. The long, mournful whistle of a train rolling slowly south on Elm Street greeted the Gilmers when they reached the town limits. The train was coming in their direction. A cloud of smoke billowed gently above the black steam engine. As the ground shook beneath the tracks, the big iron monster slowed to a stop, with steam hissing from the engine and its brass bell ringing a steady "Clang! Clang! Clang! Clang!" The two younger children had never seen a train this close. The coal car and the passenger compartments had the words *SOUTHERN RAILWAY* emblazoned along the sides.

The train ceased movement at the modern passenger terminal which had the words **GREENSBORO** on all sides of the covered platform. The station was a three-story red brick building with a large turret and a mansard roof. Its extended roof allowed passengers to come and go no matter what the weather might be. Jake paid particular attention to the men wearing uniforms—black pants, white shirts, black bow ties, and black hats—as they walked quickly up to the train, wooden steps in hand, to assist passengers stepping off the train before they helped board new passengers.

Wooden carts with steel handles and large steel wheels stood waiting. Some were empty, ready for baggage from these passengers; others contained baggage that the porters would load onto the train.

Lee Hanner spoke loudly enough that the youngsters could hear. "I hear tell that as many as forty trains stop here in Greensboro every day. The railroad people call this place the 'Gate City'."

Elm Street appeared to be paved, but dirt was piled on top of the pavement. Another set of tracks ran parallel to the train tracks, with wires running over them about fifteen feet off the ground, the Gilmers noticed. But their wagon continued to move in a northerly direction on Elm Street, alongside all the tracks. "What are those tracks and those wires up in the air, Papa?" Lillie called to her father.

"They're trolley tracks, Lillie," Samuel said. "Trolleys are small trains that run on electricity, which is sent through those wires are up above us. Trolleys go back and forth on this street all day, from one end of the line to the other. When the trolley gets to the end of the line, the driver just walks to the other end of the trolley car and drives back the other way. There are tracks going all the way to the north end of Elm Street, and one route goes east-west down Market Street past Spring

Garden, out past Molly's college, and to the edge of town. Another goes to the Proximity Village of Cone Mills, factories where people make cotton and denim fabrics. And I've heard that more trolley tracks are being built."

Anna interrupted. "Molly, don't you need to stop here on the main street and do some shopping?"

Molly called from the back of the wagon, "Yes, Mama. I've saved up for two new dresses and one pair of new shoes."

Anna put her hand on Samuel's arm. "I need to stop at Shoffner Brothers and Company when we come back, to buy some groceries. While Molly and I are shopping at Meyer Brothers Department Store, you and Pa and Jake can walk to C. Scott and Company to look at their seeds. I hear tell that they have something called peanut butter that you can sample. It's supposed to be made fresh here every day." She turned in her seat to smile at Lillie. "Lillie, dear, where do you want to go?"

Lillie was busy looking at all the buildings the family's wagon passed as it slowly rolled down Elm Street. She had to crane her neck upwards to see the top of some of them. The city was all new to her, and she marveled at all she saw, so Anna had to repeat her question before Lillie made her decision. "Mama, I think I'll go with you and Molly. But I sure would like to taste that peanut butter."

"Pa! Pa! What's that thing parked close to the mercantile?" Jake shouted. "Look over to your left. It looks like a fancy carriage, but where do the horses go?"

The family all turned to stare. "That there's an automobile," Samuel announced. "I don't know as much about them as I'd like, but my guess is that it's a Ford touring car—and it can't be more than four or five years old. Automobiles don't need horses because they're powered by gasoline engines."

"Look at that contraption closely," Lee Hanner added. "More and more of these automobiles are being made every day. In your Pa's lifetime, they may replace most of the wagons and horses now on the road."

The Gilmers craned their necks until they lost sight of the contraption. They passed the tall Guilford Hotel, Pages' School of Pharmacy in the Grissom Building, Wills' Book Store, Southside Hardware, and a five-story skyscraper called the Dixie Building. ("This is where they sell Dixie Fire Insurance," Lee Hanner told Anna.) The family gazed up at the top of the Southern Telephone and Telegraph building on the corner of Market and Eugene Street, the next street over. Then they passed a dry goods store called Sapps and another one farther along called Gilmers' Dry Goods.

"Are they kinfolk, Pa?" Jake asked.

"Not that I know of," Samuel said, smiling. "Funny that I didn't notice the name of that store on my last trip to Greensboro."

Slowly the wagon continued moving along, past the new Greensboro Savings and Loan, the Benbow Hotel, and another pharmacy, Porter's Drug Store. "Speaking of drugs," Anna said. "That salve I put on your chests when you get bronchitis and coughs is called Vicks Magic Croup Salve. Mrs. Forsyth told me it was invented in Selma, North Carolina, by a druggist named Lunsford Richardson. He decided the market for selling his ointment would be much bigger in Greensboro, so he moved here and bought the Porter-Tate Drug Store. They started manufacturing that salve in tiny bottles. By the time they changed the name to Vicks Chemical Company, they were using machines to pump it into containers without humans touching it. Now, this salve is shipped all over the United States."

"That's not the only interesting thing about Porter's Drug Store," Lee Hanner added. "I went to school with Mr. Porter. He's the uncle of the writer we know as O. Henry—but his real name is William Sydney Porter. He worked there for his uncle when he was young."

Anna pointed out a few more sights as Samuel pulled the wagon into a grassy space between two buildings just behind Elm Street. "I can't wait to stretch my legs," Jake announced, jumping over the side of the wagon. The rest of his family followed him down to the ground. "Meyer Brothers is just up this street, less than a block," Anna told her daughters. To Samuel, she added, "We should be back within the hour, Samuel."

He nodded. "We'll go look at the hardware store back that-a-way first. Jake and I need ammunition, and I need another sharpening tool for the new saw blade and grease for the mill. Then we'll come back to C. Scott and Company." He turned to his father-in-law. "How about you, Lee?"

"All that walkin' is not for an old man's knees, Samuel." Lee Hanner stretched painfully, his hand on his back. "I'll stay here with the horses and Molly's belongings. I can sit here on the wagon under this shade tree and watch everybody rush by when I don't have to. I appreciate not havin' to be in such a dad-blamed hurry like these city folks are!"

In just under an hour, all the shoppers were back at the wagon. They climbed aboard and proceeded on their way to the college. Samuel turned the horses' heads westward. "Now, that's a wonder," Anna murmured, staring at the breath-taking dark red brick West Market Street

Methodist Episcopal Church South. This building had been completed just two decades earlier, replacing the previous sanctuary.

As they proceeded along West Market Street, Anna was just starting to answer Molly's question about St. Leo's Hospital on Summit Avenue. She pointed northwest, "It's about two miles—"

Ding-ding-ding-ding-ding! The sound of a very insistent bell resounded from behind the wagon. Jake and Lillie screamed. On the Gilmers' left side, a trolley clanking along the narrow steel tracks rushed quickly and noisily past their wagon, nearly taking off the rear left corner. The startled horses reared and almost pulled the reins out of Samuel's hands. Despite feeling startled and disgruntled, the Gilmers noticed the long metal pole that stretched from the top of the trolley to the wires overhead. Clusters of little blue sparks flashed as it proceeded down the line.

"That trolley almost tipped us over!" Molly called out indignantly, clutching her bag and replacing her bonnet on her head. Jake grabbed one suitcase as it was bouncing off the side of her seat.

"Whoa! Whoa there, SueJean! Whoa! Whoa back, Dolly. Easy, girls, easy." Samuel worked hard to calm his team of horses. He leapt from the seat and checked the wagon after calming himself. It took long moments before he managed to calm the poor horses.

"Merciful heavens!" Anna said, untying her bonnet, which had been blown over her face. "Is everyone all right?" She shook her head. "Samuel, that was just too close."

Lee Hanner lost his hat in this near-calamity, and sent Jake to retrieve it. "We're only shaken, not injured," he reported.

"All's well, considerin'." Samuel sounded exasperated when he climbed back up onto his seat, took the reins, and spoke to the horses.

"Let's go, girls. Just a mile or so more, and you can have some water and some grass and a rest. *Haw.*" The team continued their travels, this time down a steep hill and then upward again.

"There's Molly's school!" Lillie pointed, then turned to her sister with a smile.

"But this sign reads GREENSBORO FEMALE COLLEGE, Founded 1838.*"* Anna read the words out loud, puzzled.

Molly spoke up from behind her. "Oh, I read about this college. It was Greensboro's first college, and it's just for women. Mr. Gladstone said it's a private college, a very good one. It was founded by a minister in the United Methodist Episcopal Church South."

"Methodist, huh?" her grandfather echoed, looking at the college curiously.

"My college is supported by money from the State of North Carolina, not a church," Molly explained. "Mr. Gladstone said to watch for a road called Tate Street, on the left, just past Greensboro Female College."

As soon as Molly finished speaking, they reached the top of the hill, where a sign on their left announced Tate Street. Samuel turned the horses down this small street. "Sure enough, here it is," he said, pointing to the sign: THE NORTH CAROLINA STATE NORMAL AND INDUSTRIAL COLLEGE. They had arrived.

Samuel drove very slowly as they passed through the gate and entered the school campus. They scrutinized two or three brick buildings that appeared to be classrooms, and then several wooden buildings situated under a cluster of trees. "Can those be the dormitories?" Molly wondered aloud.

The Gilmers watched clusters of young women walking purposefully, some carrying books and walking as though they knew where they were going, and some carrying personal belongings. Ahead loomed a huge red brick building three stories tall, with two imposing turrets, and a slate roof. Lillie gasped, "Mama, is that where they lock up bad people?" Everyone laughed.

"It does look rather spooky, but no, Lillie," Anna said with a smile.

Molly read the sign on the grounds leading to the building. "That's the Foust Building. The papers the school sent me mentioned a Dr. Julius Foust. He was the second president of the college. Maybe it's named for him. Perhaps—" Molly never finished her thought. When she noticed a formally dressed man walking towards them, she leaned forward and said, "Look, Papa, perhaps that man is a professor. Should we ask him for directions?"

Samuel nodded, reined in the horses, handed the reins to Anna, and once again jumped down from the wagon seat. He walked up to the stranger, held out his hand, and spoke to him. After listening to Samuel's inquiry, the man pointed to the second little white building across the commons. He spoke a minute or so longer with Samuel, and then they shook hands again, and Samuel escorted the gentleman over to the wagon. After a quick glance at the passengers, he approached Molly.

"We're delighted to have you as one of our new students, Miss Gilmer," he said, as he took Molly's hand. "I am Professor Hudgens." Then he smiled at the family. "What do you know about Miss Gilmer's new school?" he asked.

"Not as much as we'd like," Samuel admitted.

The professor leaned on his cane and swept his arm across the view in front of them. "This is the dream of Dr. Charles McIver, who felt the state had need for a school of higher education for young women, a place where they could learn skills by working side-by-side with men— here and later, in the business world. He also wanted to train young women to become teachers. Dr. McIver often said, 'Educate a woman, and you educate a family'."

"That's true," Anna murmured. Her husband smiled at her.

"Our first students arrived at the railroad station in 1892. We've had some serious bumps in the road. A few years after the school opened, a fire burned the dormitory. Later, our students suffered a typhus epidemic But those tragedies are in the past. This university is growing every year, educating fine, upstanding young women."

"Can we meet that man?" Lillie asked.

The professor smiled at the little girl. "Sadly, Dr. McIver died in 1906, when he was riding on a campaign train with William Jennings Bryan."

"Good man, Bryan," Lee said thoughtfully.

The professor nodded. He turned back to Molly. "Why don't you find your room and unpack? The incoming freshmen will meet in the Foust Building at four o'clock." Molly smiled back and thanked him for his help. The professor raised his hat and continued his walk.

Samuel drove the wagon around the little white building, stopping the horses near an even smaller building. "We'll park here, because the professor was kind enough to tell me about that hand water pump and watering trough," he announced, pointing ahead as he leapt from the wagon seat, handed Anna down, and then moved in the direction of the pump. "I'll start pumping the water. Lee, could you unhitch Dolly and

SueJean and walk them over here? Molly, Professor Hudgens said you are to enter that door and look for the house mother. She'll direct you to your room. We'll be there soon."

Anna, Molly, Jake, and Lillie walked into the building, carrying Molly's possessions. Seated at a desk just inside the doorway was a middle-aged woman who wore her glasses far down on her nose. Her gray hair was pulled up in a tight bun, and she wore a long, simple cotton dress. She was writing in a notebook when Jake whispered to Molly "She looks like a school teacher." Molly nodded, but put her finger to her lips.

Three girls about Molly's age, each holding suitcases and wearing nervous expressions, had formed a line in front of the Gilmers. The woman at the desk opened a map of the building and showed each young woman where they could find their rooms. Before they walked away, the house mother smiled and suggested, "Let me know if I can help you in any way."

Molly was next. She stepped forward, smiled, and introduced herself. "Welcome to the Normal and Industrial College, Miss Gilmer," the woman said, returning Molly's smile. "My name is Miss Foster, and I am the house mother of this dormitory." She looked down her list, and her finger stopped as she found Molly's name. "Yes, Miss Gilmer, you are coming in as a freshman. We have the second floor reserved for you young women. Your room is Number 12."

Her smile included Molly's family. "You'll find a bed, a desk, a chair, a chest of drawers, and a closet for your clothes there. Your roommate is already in the room. We will hold a mandatory house meeting tonight at eight o'clock. Let me know if I can help you in any way. We're delighted you are here!" She looked behind the Gilmers as the line lengthened. "Next?"

Samuel entered the building just as his family moved toward the stairs. "Your father said he won't do well on stairs today, so he decided to stay with the horses and the wagon," he told Anna. He relieved Molly of the heavy suitcases she was carrying. When Molly noticed Miss Foster peering through her round glasses at Samuel, she introduced her father to the house mother.

Up the stairs the Gilmers climbed. Three doors away from the staircase was a room with an open door. Jake peeked in. "Wow. Is this a real indoor privy? Look at what it has! Toilets and sinks in the very same room—and indoors!" He grinned at his mother. "Uh, it's a long ways home, Mama, and I think I need to see how one of these things works."

Anna laughed, "All right, Jake. But remember to keep that door closed. This is women's territory."

"I want to see how it works, too!" Lillie insisted.

"Perhaps we should all take advantage of that facility before we start back," her mother suggested, pointing in the direction of Room 12.

They found the door open. A tall, slender young lady who wore glasses was closing her suitcase when the family appeared in the doorway. She smiled shyly at the crowd. "My name is Rose Mary Davis. I'm from Galax, Virginia. I came in on a train at noon."

Molly extended her hand. "I'm Molly Gilmer, and these are my parents, Mr. and Mrs. Gilmer, and my sister Lillie. My brother will be along any minute now. We live on a farm on the southeast side of Guilford County, about six miles outside Greensboro."

Sam smiled at the girl. "I've been to Galax. It's a beautiful place up in the hills of southern Virginia."

Rose May returned his smile.

"Why don't we help you unpack, Molly, and you can put your belongings away as soon as we leave?" Anna suggested. When the last item was removed from the last bag, there was an uncomfortable pause and Anna saved the day. She cleared her throat and hugged her daughter. "Molly, we need to start back now, and you need to find your way to that big building in an hour and a half. Would you like to walk with us back to the wagon?"

The Gilmer family said goodbye to Rose Mary Davis and descended the stairs. Miss Foster was still greeting young women who stood patiently in line in front of her desk. Some were alone, some arrived with large families. Once the Gilmers left the building, Molly ran ahead to hug her grandfather. Lee's voice was husky when he told her, "Molly, your Mam-Maw would be so very proud of you! I know she's smilin' down on you right now. God be with you, child." Then he pretended to sound stern. "And don't forget to study hard, young lady." He abruptly turned, clearing his throat, and hitched the horses to the wagon again. They had finished nearly all the water in the trough.

Jake hugged his big sister. "Molly, you are so smart. I've always been proud of you for that. You're gonna be a great teacher. Hurry and finish so you can replace Mr. Gladstone and give me all A's!" As his family laughed, he hugged his sister and whispered, "I love you!" He hopped up on the wagon.

Samuel was the next to say his goodbyes. "Daughter, I hope your mother and I have taught you what you need to know in this adult world. You have always been responsible and mature, and I've never worried about you. Not once. You are my pride and joy. I love you. I don't have to ask you to work hard and make us proud, because you already have." He crushed her to his heart, swiftly wiped one hand across his eyes, and grinned at his wife. "If I don't get on this wagon now, I'm gonna bust out cryin'." Samuel kissed Molly's cheek swiftly and hugged her one last time.

Anna took both of Molly's hands. "My first child is now a beautiful young woman. I love you even more today than I did the day you were born. I'll write you next week, sweetheart. Always trust God to walk with you." She held Molly closely for a moment as the tears flowed down their cheeks. Anna smiled at her daughter mistily as she rummaged in her pocket for a handkerchief. Samuel handed his wife up into the wagon.

Last to say goodbye was Lillie. She stood beside her sister, eyes fixed on the ground, not wanting to act like a baby, and not knowing what to say. Molly helped her out. "Come here, Lady Bug. I need to tell you a secret." Lillie looked up at her, quietly and expectantly. Molly put her mouth close to Lillie's ear. "I have just finished a shawl. Remember the one I was making when I taught you knitting stitches?"

Lillie nodded. "The one that looks like autumn, with the colors of the forest and goldenrod."

Molly whispered again, "Honey, if you start missing me so much that your heart feels like it's breaking, I want you to put that shawl around your shoulders and just feel my arms wrapped around you. Okay?"

Lillie nodded. Molly knelt to hug her little sister. She kissed Lillie on her cheek and on the top of her head. "I love you, my Molly!" Lillie declared. Then she climbed quickly into the wagon. As Samuel clicked his tongue and snapped the reins, everyone waved to Molly, who stood there a minute under that oak tree, watching the wagon disappear. She pulled out her handkerchief and put it to good use. Then she turned to walk to the dormitory just as the long mournful whistle in the distance announcing a train arriving at the depot on South Elm Street.

"No owls hooting here or cows mooing, but I guess I'll be getting used to train whistles now," Molly murmured as she opened the door of her new home. A new adventure in her life had begun.

The Gilmers made one last stop before their long wagon ride home. At Shoffner Brothers and Company, they purchased fresh meat, fruit, and vegetables that didn't grow well in red North Carolina clay. During the fifteen minutes Anna and Lillie shopped, the three men once again heard the *Ding-Ding-Ding-Ding-Ding!* of the Elm Street trolley as it rattled by on its tracks. Although it was moving slower here because its many stops along Elm Street, Samuel held his horses' reins tightly, calming SueJean and Dolly, who snorted nervously as the metal beast approached. At least this time they could see the approach of the trolley.

That night, after Lee Hanner went to bed, the four Gilmers sat on the porch, all of them lost in thought and unusually quiet. Finally, Anna broke the silence. "One thing we can be sure of in our lives is change. Change can be a scary thing, but often good things can result." Samuel nodded. Jake looked at his mother with a puzzled expression. Lillie made a face at Jake. Anna smiled at her little girl. "All right, Miss Lillie. Let's get you tucked into bed. I'll come up with you this time."

After Lillie said her prayers, she climbed into bed and lay there quietly for a moment. Anna sat on the bed beside her youngest child, not speaking. She just held Lillie's hand. Silence for a few moments, then Lillie's face turned red and her eyes crinkled. She sat up and leaned into her mother's bosom, "Oh, Mama! I miss my Molly so very, terribly much," she sobbed. Anna rocked Lillie gently as she cradled her on her lap. She kissed her on her head, then kissed away some of Lillie's tears. She had come prepared with another handkerchief. After a big nose-blow, Lillie spoke. "I just feel so lost and empty right now, Mama."

Anna gently put two fingers under Lillie's chin to raise her face, so she could look into her eyes. "I do too, sweetie. And that's all right. It means that we love our Molly so very much. And I think Molly is a very lucky young woman to have a sister who adores her as much as you do, Lillie. But guess what? You are never, ever, alone, my daughter. When you feel lost and alone, just close your eyes and know that our Lord Jesus is always, always holding you."

Anna bent and whispered in her daughter's ear, "He never sleeps, Lillie. If you wake up feeling those empty feelings, just remember that Jesus is with you, and he loves you more than even Pap-paw, Jake, Molly, Papa, or I love you!" She gently returned her little girl to the bed and pulled the covers up to her chin. "Good night, my precious girl." Another kiss, and then she carried the kerosene lamp out of the room.

Before going to bed themselves, Samuel and Anna tiptoed up the stairs to make one last check on Lillie. With the wick of the lantern very low, only the faintest light came into the room. They looked toward Lillie's bed, but she wasn't there. Neither was the pillow. Puzzled, they looked at one another, then Samuel moved the lantern around the room. Lying on her sister's bed, Lillie slept soundly, with a new autumn-colored shawl around her shoulders and a tiny smile on her lips.

CHAPTER FIFTEEN: *TRAGEDY AT MCCOLLUM'S MILL*
September 10, 1913

"I heard you were especially busy here at the mill. Thought I'd lend a hand," Will Granger offered, appearing at the door of the mill shortly after Lee and Samuel arrived for a long day's work

"We're not fixed to pay you right now, Will," Samuel said, wiping his forehead with a checkered handkerchief after he'd hoisted a log onto the carrier.

"I didn't come for pay. Just wanted to be neighborly," Will said. He immediately set to work stacking lumber as it was cut, so it was ready for delivery to a customer. Lee and Samuel exchanged glances. They noticed that their neighbor still had facial hair but it was clean and neatly trimmed. His hair had been cut and combed recently, and though his clothes might be patched and worn, they were clean.

At the end of the first week of September, Will Granger had taken his last load of cured tobacco to the tobacco auction and was paid in cash. While he was in Greensboro, Will put the majority of his money into his bank account. Now he had extra time on his hands, so he had evidently decided it was time to repay the man who had been the organizer behind the rebuilding of his tobacco barn.

James Thacker rode up on his horse soon after the lunch Anna delivered. "Just got back from collectin' Helen at her sister's house," he said, dismounting. "It's on McConnell Road."

"Where?" Lee asked.

"About eight miles away," James said, taking a seat in a rough-hewn chair near the mill door, preparing for a friendly visit. "Helen went to help her sister for a week. Janice—she married the blacksmith over thataways—is recoverin' from surgery."

"You must be glad to have your wife back home again. I hope this means that Helen's sister is better?" Samuel asked.

Lee was pounding iron "dogs" into a log that was positioned on the log carriage, ready to go under the blade. The dogs would prevent the log from slipping while the first cut was being made. But he stood to hear James answer.

"Yup, she's movin' 'round the house well now. Helen says that other than bein' sore, she's sprightly." James remembered the reason for his visit. "Say, have y'all heard about that terrible accident at McCollum's Mill on McConnell Road? It happened over a week ago."

Lee and Samuel stared at each other blankly. "No! Can't say as we have," they answered in unison

Will Granger walked back inside the mill after placing a load of boards on the wagon just outside. "Excuse me for interruptin', Sam. I've been keepin' count, and that wagon is now full. Where do you want me to start the new pile?"

Samuel glanced toward Will. "Thanks, friend. Why don't you take a break for a minute, and then we'll start stackin' boards in the shed. It sounds like there's somethin' we ought to know. An accident at

McCollum's Mill." He nodded to James Thacker. "So what happened, James?"

Will leaned against the mill wall as he swigged spring water from his canteen and listened to the news James was eager to tell.

"Well, it seems that Old Man McCollum had been having trouble with branches, leaves, acorns, and other junk building up in the flume and buckets of the water wheel, so it was turnin' very slowly. They called in Henry Shoffner. Do y'all know him?"

When his three listeners shook their heads, James explained, "He's a tobacco farmer, but he also goes to some of the local mills when they need help with cleanin'. Anyway, Henry discovered that the problem was much worse than they thought it was. Debris was packed tight inside the buckets and under the wheel, since it hasn't been cleaned in five years. He told them the only way he'd be able to clear that clog would be to climb up into the flume and pull the mess out."

James inserted a plug of tobacco into his cheek before continuing the story. "Well, Henry got up there. Evidently that old flume and water wheel are really old, and all the collected pine needles, leaves, and algae made the flume as slippery as ice, so the work took longer than anyone expected."

Both Lee and Samuel cringed. They could guess what happened next. James continued, "Someone inside the mill didn't realize he was up there in the flume and started the water flowing over the wheel. With all the racket from the big wheel and all those gears turnin', no one heard him yell at them to stop that wheel. He slipped and fell into that water wheel, and before anyone could shut the thing down, he was thrown into the gears and the pulleys and belts."

His listeners shut their eyes when James said, "He was crushed to death before anyone could get to him."

Silence, as the men all had mental pictures of this gruesome tragedy.

"My Lord." Samuel finally managed to gasp. "How old was the man? Does he have family? Children?"

James nodded. "Henry must be close to thirty. He had a wife and two little ones—I'd guess the boy is not quite six and the little girl two years old."

"Poor little tykes," Lee wiped his hands over his eyes. "I don't know the man. Who is his wife? Does she have kinfolk around there?"

"Well," James said. "I don't know her. Helen says her sister was a friend of the woman's mother's and very fond of her. Name's Marjorie. She was born and raised in McCleansville. Her folks are nice people—the Gannons. When she finished school, she started working in the general store on McConnell Road. That's where she met Henry. She's a trifle younger than he was. And now here she is, a widow with two young 'uns and a load of tobacco that Henry was ready to take to the auction house in Greensboro the next day."

Unbeknownst to the three men who were intent on the story, Will Granger had turned white. He could feel his legs start to buckle. They looked around when he dropped his canteen. Samuel grabbed hold of Will's arm, to offer him support. With a concerned look on his face, he asked, "You okay, Will? You don't look so good. Did you know this man?"

Will shook his head. "No. But I knew Marjorie Gannon. I knew her very well." He shook his head and muttered, "Oh, dear Lord!" Then

Will picked up his canteen. "Samuel, I need to head on home. There's something I need to do. Sorry."

Samuel nodded and looked piercingly at his friend. "We appreciate all your help today. You go ahead. And God go with you."

Will galloped home, thoughts spinning in his mind. As he washed and changed clothes, he remembered the days when he courted Marjorie Gannon, the woman he once thought he loved—until he met Suzanne. He had tried to push thoughts of Marjorie from his mind for the past nine years, but now that he knew she was alone and needed help, it was time he appeared on her doorstep once again. When he was presentable, he mounted his horse Beauregard and pointed the horse in the direction of McConnell Road. He stopped at the general store in the McLeansville area to ask for directions to the Shoffner home.

A coon hound greeted the big, burly stranger with some ferocious barking and a load of curiosity. Will jumped off his horse, removed his hat, patted the dog on her head, and stepped onto the porch. When he knocked on the door, a little boy peeked out, and called, "Mommy, there's a great big man out here."

With sweat beading on his brow, Will waited for footsteps to approach the door. Marjorie Gannon Shoffner was a small brown-haired young woman with large dark eyes. She opened the door, while holding a little girl on her hip. When she saw who her visitor was, she gasped.

"Will Granger, is that really you?" She studied him carefully while the little girl smiled shyly and started wiggling in her mother's arms. Marjorie set the child down on the porch floor watched her as she toddled after her big brother, who had escaped into the yard. When she returned her attention to the visitor, she said, "For heaven's sakes, it's been nearly ten years!"

The man squeezed the rim of his hat with both hands, but when he nodded mutely, she remembered her manners and asked, "Would you like to come in?" Her face was as pleasant as Will had remembered, and her mannerisms were elegant.

Will Granger shook his head politely, "No, Marjorie. I've come to bring my condolences, and also with an offer of help. It will just take me a minute."

Marjorie Shoffner pointed to a chair on the porch, but he continued to stand, hat in hand, as she settled onto the swing.

"Marjorie, I live in the Beaver Creek area near Alamance Presbyterian Church now. This afternoon I heard the news of your…your husband's death. I was so shocked, I jumped on my horse as soon as I heard. To see how you're doing, that is. I'm very, very sorry, Marjorie." He barely managed to stop himself from stammering.

Though Marjorie tried to maintain her poise, her face registered her pain and heartbreak. "Oh, Will." She seemed to choke the words and she shuddered. "It was so horrible. So unexpected. That day started out like any other day. I kissed Henry before he left. I snapped beans, cooked, and cleaned the kitchen in between chasing these two little ones. The night before, Henry and I had talked about our plans for the future—fine plans for a happy future. But late that afternoon, the preacher and Mr. McCollum rode up on their horses together."

She swallowed again and again before she continued, "I knew when I saw them that something bad had happened. But even still…Who'd believe something like that could happen to a healthy, fit young man?"

Will summoned his courage. "I ain't here to upset you all over again, Marjorie. I'm here to tell you that I'm truly sorry that this has happened to y'all, and I want to offer my help in any way I can. I heard that your husband was preparin' to take his tobacco to the Auction House and never got the chance. I know my way 'round that place, and I know that those men can take advantage of a woman who doesn't. I'd like to offer to take your tobacco so's you won't be short-changed. I'll either take it on my own or take you and help you get the best price. It ain't safe for a young woman to be in the city there alone with a pocket full of cash."

Marjorie's eyes opened wide, but she managed a tiny smile. "Will, I can't believe you've ridden eight miles over here to offer to do that for me. Some men from my church came here the day after Henry's funeral, loaded up wagons with our tobacco, and took it to the warehouse in Greensboro. They got it weighed in and identified as ours, but they had to come back before selling it. They had their own tobacco to deal with. I could surely use some help. But I don't want to rob your wife of your time."

Will's face turned white, but he managed to say in even, colorless tones, "My wife died seven years ago, and my own tobacco crop has been taken care of. I'd be honored to help you with yours."

Before Marjorie could stammer out her own words of condolence, Will held up his hand and managed a little smile. "It's been ten years, Marjorie, so maybe you don't remember how stubborn I can be. If I say I want to do this for you, it means I have the time to give you."

Will offered to arrive early the following morning. "We can take my wagon and drive directly to the warehouse to get your tobacco sold," he offered. "Since they've already weighed it, we'll just need to carry a sample to the auctioneers and have them go ahead and bid on the tobacco."

"I don't know anything about tobacco prices," Marjorie admitted.

"I'll be a stand-in for Henry, and we'll sell it together," Will said. "Then I'll drive you to your bank. Do you want to take your children with us?"

Marjorie held up her hand. "Wait, Will. You've taken my wits away. I haven't even said that I'll go tomorrow." As Will watched her face, curious to see the changes ten years had made, Marjorie Shoffner contemplated the man's offer.

After a few quiet moments passed, she sighed. "Will, so much has happened over the last few years. Henry was a wonderful Christian man, a hard worker. We made a good life for our two children. And then…And then…" Her voice trailed away. She covered her eyes with her hands for a moment. When she spoke again, it was with forced cheerfulness. "Well, we just never know, do we?"

As Will remained silent, crushing his hat with both hands, he watched her face brighten, and she spoke with resolve. "I'll thank you kindly to help me, Will. Tomorrow is Thursday, and my neighbor across the way—the one who lives on that dairy farm—" She pointed in the direction of a well-tended farm whose buildings were clustered near a clump of trees. "—asked if my children could come play with her little ones on Thursday. She knows that there are times when having children underfoot doesn't help a woman get much done. I do believe she's paved the way for me to have an outing to the Auction House."

She stood and stretched out her hand. "Will Granger, I guess the two of us are going to deal in tobacco in Greensboro tomorrow morning. I…I thank you, Will. I—."

Once more, Will stopped Marjorie in mid-sentence. "No thanks needed. This is something that any brother in Christ would do, Marjorie."

Her eyes huge, Marjorie stared at him in disbelief, "Do you mean to tell me—?"

Will nodded. "Yup. Happened just a few weeks ago, at the Big Meeting at Alamance Presbyterian." He tried to reshape his crushed hat before returning it to his head. "Well, anyway, I'm sorry for surprisin' you like this, Marjorie, but I knew this was somethin' that shouldn't wait. I'll start for home now, before it gets dark, and I'll see you here in the mornin'." Will started walking toward his horse.

Marjorie followed him off the porch, protesting, "But Will, I've forgotten my manners. I haven't asked you about your life."

Will mounted Beauregard and glanced down at the woman who still looked like the girl he'd known a lifetime earlier. "My story isn't important right now, Marjorie. Let's deal with your situation first." He touched his hat in respect, took the reins, clicked his tongue at Beauregard, and galloped down the driveway.

"Mommy, who was that man?" asked young Charlie Shoffer with curious brown eyes, reaching for his mother's hand as he watched the very large stranger ride away.

"Someone I haven't seen in many years, my son," she responded softly. "Someone that I think God has sent to help us."

CHAPTER SIXTEEN: *BRINGING IN THE SHEAVES*
September 25, 1913

Farmers in North Carolina actually harvest grains in their fields two times every year. In May or early June, they reap grains and grasses grown to make hay for cattle and horse feed during the winter months. These include oats that are not allowed to mature to full grain—they are cut while still growing. Wise farmers plant clover to entice bees, who collect the nectar and produce honey. When clover finishes blooming, farmers cut it with their horse-drawn reaper. They spread it in the field to dry, and then compact it to make quality hay.

To make hay, farmers cut the green plants and raked them into windrows to allow the hay to dry properly. They left the hay to dry in warm sunshine and wind for two or three days, turning it at least once to bring the grasses on the bottom to the top to dry. Then the hay was ready to be stored in barns loosely or (as is now the common practice) compacted by machines, baled, and stacked in dry sheds.

Late September and early October in rural North Carolina were especially busy times in the year 1913. Children had been back in school for only four or five weeks, and now they would have an eight-day harvest break, so they could help their families bring in the grain crops—

corn, oats, and wheat—as well as loading the hay from these grains into a barn.

The lives of farm families and their livestock depended on this harvest, so teachers were flexible with their schedules during this time. Bringing in the harvest depended on good weather. If a two-week period of clear weather occurred somewhere near the end of September, that was when farmers brought in their crops—and that was when the children would be needed on the farm. They returned to school as soon as the harvest was completed. If, however, rain started in the middle of September and continued through that crucial time, harvest would be delayed.

Change and an unusual level of excitement filled the air during the harvest season of 1913 in the community around Beaver Creek, including Alamance Presbyterian Church and Tabernacle Methodist Episcopal Church South. For the first time, farmers would have mechanized assistance, using new binding and reaping machines to cut the wheat and oats and tie them into bundles. Machines would also help thresh the grains.

Samuel and Lee explained to their family that men and boys would use pitchforks to toss the wheat straw into a baling machine, which would and compressed the hay to form neat bales. Then a wooden block with channels for baling wire would be placed in a slot to hold the bale shape and provide a means of tying the bale. Men would thread pre-cut wires through channels in the blocks and around their side of the bale as it moved through the bale chute. Once the bale cleared the bale chamber, the other end of the wire would be passed through the next block and secured.

Samuel and Lee met with their neighbors to schedule their harvests so they could work together and make the best use of their time while these machines were available. The tractors, gasoline engine, threshing machine, and baling machines were expensive, and few farmers could afford them all, so one farmer would buy a tractor, another would buy a threshing machine, a third may possess a gasoline engine, and a fourth might purchase a baling machine. In order to maximize the amount of work they could get done in one day, they worked together as a team on one farm until the project was complete, and then they moved the entire convoy of equipment to the next farm.

"Someone will have to drive a horse and wagon or a tractor hitched to a wagon loaded with large empty fuel containers to the closest filling station. We'll need to load up on gasoline and kerosene for each day's work," Samuel told Jake. "And we have to go to the city for gasoline." That night he told Anna that the harvesting and hay baling could go on for several weeks because the process depended on the size of the farms in their community. "I'll ride SueJean to let our neighbors know when they can expect their turn."

"All this involves hard labor and long days," Lee sighed. "I sure hope my old joints can cooperate this year."

"In a pinch, Jake or I can drive the wagons to the storage barns," Anna said.

"But Mama, what I like best about harvest is the food," Lillie said, rubbing her stomach. "Your job is to cook and bake enough." Women were a valuable part of the team during these long harvest days. They brought cold water to the workers and prepared their choicest foods for hungry workers to enjoy.

Excitement grew as the mechanized harvesting army drew closer and closer to the Beaver Creek neighborhood. Word had spread that these miraculous iron contraptions were doing much more work in much less time than farmers had experienced up until now with human, mule, and horse labor.

The Gilmers' morning started very early. Jake had just delivered a pail of fresh milk to the spring and transferred it to the crock that sat chilled in the spring house when he saw the cloud of dust billowing up from the south. And then he heard sounds of internal combustion engines popping and chuffing. He ran to the road in time to see a steel-wheeled tractor belching smoke as it chugged slowly along, the big wheels in the rear bouncing along the dirt road but also providing good traction.

Jake moved close enough to see that the man who was driving that iron beast was battling the machinery's vibrations from the steel cleats on the wheels, so vigorous that Jake could see his arms shaking as he gripped the steel steering wheel. The tractor was painted black, with the words ***MCCORMICK-DEERING*** in large letters on its side.

The tractor was pulling a machine that had a steel seat on the right side where a man would sit and operate control levers. Later that day, Jake would watch a row of sickle bars rotate. On either side of this wheeled platform, the cut grains would fall. This machine was bright green, except for the seat and cutting apparatus which were yellow. The name ***JOHN DEERE*** was painted on one side. Samuel explained to Jake that this was a "reaper and binder" machine.

"You see, son, one man will drive the tractor slowly through the wheat field while another man sits on the reaper-and-binder machine," Samuel said, walking up to his son when the machinery stopped in the Gilmers' farmyard. "He'll start and stop the machine, which can easily slice through the ripe wheat. The wheat will be dropped onto the platform, while the cut stems will fall onto a canvas, carrying them into a binding mechanism, where they'll be tied with twine as they're bundled. Then they'll be pushed out the back of the binder by other gears. Rows of bundled cut wheat will be dropped in the fields. That's where you come in."

Jake turned his attention from the machine to his father. "We'll need you to run along these rows, standing these bundles so they lean against each other," Samuel told his son.

"Like tepees?" Jake asked.

Samuel nodded. "Wind and sun will quickly dry them, preparing them for threshing." Jake, Samuel, and Lee followed the machines into their fields.

By noon, the work was done and the farmer who drove the tractor informed Samuel that he would return after two days—"weather cooperating"—with the threshing machine. The Gilmers watched the machines move on to Will Granger's farm.

Keeping his promise, early in the morning three days after the wheat had been cut, raked, bound, and stacked in the fields, the same tractor rattled, clanked, and rumbled into the Gilmers' field, pulling a wooden machine that rolled on big steel wheels. This wooden machine was shaped much like a box, but with lots of gears, small wheels, and belts running from one wheel on the side of the machine to another. Two metal chutes were tied to the body of the machine, running from a square hole on the top. A wide belt led into a chute that disappeared down into this box. The word **RUMELY** was barely visible on the side.

Jake looked to Samuel for an explanation. "It's a threshing machine, son. An engine hooked to a long belt will be attached to this, to power the machine. You'll see it working later."

During threshing, men loaded the bundles into the top of the large thresher. For the first time, the grains would be separated from the chaff, or waste, by a machine, instead of by hand. The usable grain was blown into large bags, which the farmers hauled to a grist mill. The straw and chaff were blown out in another direction, forming a large pile by the end of the day.

On this particular day, a second tractor with the name *FARMALL F-20* painted on its side followed the first into the Gilmers' farmyard. Shiny and gray, it pulled a bright-orange *CASE* hay-baling machine. Jake had seen an older version of a hay press, which had been pulled by horses. Men shoved dry hay into the compartment, which shaped hay into bales after it was squeezed into the proper shape by compression screws. He had watched as a board was slid into position to separate the bales, which were secured with twine by human hands as the bales were pushed out of the chute. At first, hay was produced one bale at a time and stacked onto a flatbed trailer, which was pulled by horses. In later years, by a tractor would pull the baler.

When the trailer had a full load of hay, a farmer drove to the storage barn. One by one, farmers unloaded the bales and stacked them inside the barn in closed areas where they would stay dry—even young children knew how important it was to keep the hay dry and free of mildew and rot.

In the Gilmers' barn, the hay was stacked in the loft. Each bale was positioned under a hay spear or a hook, and someone on the ground would use a rope and a pulley system to hoist the hay up to the window in the hay loft. Someone up there removed the hook or the hay spear and dragged the bale to the back of the loft. Farmers always knew which side of the barn had rich oats and clover hay and which side had bales of straw. Often they mixed them together when feeding livestock. Straw would be used as litter on the floors of the barn, so it was stored closest to the animal stalls.

We return now to the Gilmers' wheat field. Following this noisy parade of machinery came a horse-drawn wagon driven by a man sitting on the wooden bench seat. Two powerful Belgian horses pulled the wagon, which had two large wagon wheels at the rear and two smaller wheels in the front. On top of the wagon, just behind the seat, perched a large cast-iron machine with a cast-iron wheel on either side; the wheels had six spokes each. On top of this cylindrical-shaped mechanism with the name **GALLOWAY** painted on the side sat a smaller square cast-iron box, open on the top and hollow. On the main part of this machine were gears, metal shafts, small glass containers filled with oil. The man driving the wagon directed his Belgians to follow the threshing machine. He reined in the horses about ten yards behind that machine when it stopped.

Samuel walked up to the driver and held out his hand. "So this is the new hit-and-miss gasoline engine!" He motioned Jake over and told him, "This Galloway is a gas engine that will provide the power to run that threshing machine. This is a first for both of us, son. I've never seen one in operation before, either."

The driver unhitched the huge horses and Jake went with him as he ushered his Belgians to the creek, where they would rest, drink cool water, and nibble on the tender grass. Before the driver returned to the field, he dipped a large bucket into the stream and carried it back to the gas engine. Jake was puzzled, and walked over to the engine to ask how it worked.

"Sir, why do you need water? I thought Pa said this is a gasoline engine."

Mr. Bowman, the owner of the engine, nodded. "And your Pa is right, son. It does run on gasoline. Even on kerosene. An internal combustion engine like this produces a lot of heat, and heat will crack the cast iron and ruin the engine if we don't have water sitting up in this sealed water hopper." He climbed up onto the wagon and poured the bucket of water into the square box. "After the engine runs for some time, you'll see steam coming out of this hopper. It can get so hot with use that I have actually floated a few eggs in there, and in a few hours they're hard-boiled. Now, I need to get two more buckets of water, and we'll be ready to run that threshing machine. Excuse me, young man."

A horse-drawn flatbed trailer was already being directed around the field, and children were throwing shucks of wheat onto the trailer. Dolly and SueJean were such well-trained horses that they remained still while hitched to the trailer until Samuel commanded them to move on. Sooner than the Gilmers thought possible, the wheat was all loaded onto the trailer and the horses pulled the trailer to the threshing machine. "Unhitch Dolly and SueJean, Jake," Samuel asked. "You can walk them back to the barn. That way they won't be frightened by the noisy engine."

Mr. Bowman pulled a large wide, flat leather belt from under the wagon seat of the Galloway gasoline engine and carefully hooked one end of the belt to the threshing machine. Then he pulled the other end to the shiny brass wheel on the side of the engine. At his command, several men pushed on the wagon slightly, so the belt tightened on the pulley. The owner of the threshing machine moved in, arranging the metal discharge tubes so one would spew out the straw and chaff, and the other would shoot out the good wheat heads. He fitted clean sacks over the end of the tube to collect the wheat. Then he climbed onto the trailer with a pitchfork and told one of the helpers to hold the first bag under the chute on the other side.

"I'm ready, Eli!" he shouted to the farmer standing at the very end of the wagon as he adjusted the carburetor of the gas engine. Eli motioned to Samuel. "Why don't you give me a hand starting it up?"

"I'll be tickled to do it," Samuel said. He had never been this close to a hit-and-miss gasoline engine before.

"All right," the mechanic announced. "We're gonna pull these flywheels over a few times, and hopefully, it will fire right up. She ran several hours yesterday just fine. Let's see…I've added oil, and there's a full tank of gas." When Samuel looked interested in the mechanics, he pointed to the shiny brass box on the side of the engine. "This here's a magneto. It produces the spark that'll ignite the gasoline each time the piston fires. Ready? Here we go."

"This here Galloway engine has seven-and-one-half horsepower," a knowledgeable farmer told Will Granger, who had come to help. "It was just built last year. The flywheels over there are three feet in diameter and I know for a fact that each weighs well over a hundred pounds."

Eli and Samuel stood on either side of the engine, holding onto a flywheel. At the mechanic's orders, the two men quickly jerked their wheels back toward the rear of the engine. First, a *CHUFF* sounded, and blue smoke spurted out of the exhaust pipe. "Keep a hold of them wheels!" Mr. Bowman called. He stuck his palm under the air intake and fiddled with the carburetor adjustment again. *CHUFF*. More smoke. Then, *POP* and another spurt of smoke. The air was full of

CHUFF...FOOM. Foom! Foom! Foom! And then the engine began running on its own.

The farmers and their sons standing nearby cheered. A few even clapped at this amazing new technology. Samuel Gilmer backed away, grinning from ear to ear. Eli Bowman signaled to the men at the threshing machine, then he walked to a round handle built into one of the flywheels of the gas engine. "Here goes!" he hollered, and pulled it outward. The brass wheel on the side of the Galloway engine where the large leather belt was attached began to turn slowly. Smoke belched from the exhaust pipe as the belt moved more quickly. The belts and gears on the threshing machine started moving and turning. Chain-driven conveyor mechanisms started rolling along inside the machine with rattles and clanking sounds.

The farmers standing on top of the flatbed trailer used pitchforks to toss the sheaves of wheat into the chute at the top of the thresher. With grinding and chopping noises, a spray of straw and chaff blew out of one chute and onto the ground just in front of the trailer. At the same time, the man holding the large bag at the end of the grain chute began to feel his bag fill, as grains of wheat were blown in.

This process continued until the last bundles of wheat on the trailer had disappeared into the mouth of the thresher. Men took turns using pitchforks to lift the wheat upwards and toss it into the intake chute. When the engine turned off, they hopped down to the ground, hot, dirty, sweaty, and covered with bits of wheat straw that had blown back onto them. Samuel looked at the bags of wheat tied and sitting beside a tree. "This is wonderful," he said, shaking his head. He reached into the last bag before it was tied, running the grains of wheat through his hand. "They're almost totally free of the chaff and stems!" he marveled. Then he shook Mr. Bowman's hand heartily.

"My whole life, I've had my grain threshed by a machine using horses for power," Samuel said, shaking his head in awe. "I knew that invention saved me time and the work my great-grandpappy had to do by hand. But what took me all day has taken you only two hours with this new equipment. I am grateful. And, in return, I'll cut those trees of yours into lumber. No charge."

At this time, the men driving the threshing machine and the man driving the wagon holding the big gasoline engine prepared to make their exit, to head to the next farm. The remaining neighbors quickly worked together with pitchforks to load wheat straw onto the empty trailer. Little boys picked the last of the loose straw from the ground. The straw was ready for baling.

The *Farmall F-20* tractor was already hooked up by a large flat belt to the Case hay-baling machine. Lee Hanner hitched Dolly to the trailer so she could pull it the short distance to the baling machine.

At last it was time for a well-deserved lunch break. Anna Gilmer, with great assistance from Lillie, had cooked a bountiful lunch for twelve hungry men and boys: platters and bowls of Brunswick stew (cooked all morning in a huge kettle over a fire pit near the field), pinto beans, cornbread, and turnip greens. Helen Thacker, Anna's neighbor across the road and up the hill, had baked four apple pies. She drove her surrey to the Gilmer farm. Anna and Helen loaded the surrey with the main meal, pies, plates, silverware, and pitchers of cold spring water, then drove her horse and surrey to makeshift tables Samuel and Jake had set up under the trees bordering the fields.

The women had spent two days preparing this feast, and the hungry men polished off all the food almost as soon as they reached the table. They told stories and shared jokes as they devoured their meal in the shade of the oak and pine trees.

The baling of the wheat straw went quickly. The tractor provided the power for the baling machine. Once again, men stood on the trailer with the wheat straw, using pitchforks to toss it into the chute on top of the baler.

After the tables had been cleared, Anna and Lillie helped Helen Thacker load her surrey with all the empty serving bowls and dirty dishes. She would transport them back to the Gilmer house before taking her leave. But Lillie took a break to watch the hay baler.

"Mama, that looks like a big arm with a hand in that baling machine. The elbow goes up and backward, and the hand gives the hay a big shove, pushing it all together to make a bale," Lillie pointed out.

Anna nodded, but added, "Lillie, we need your help now." She and Lillie walked beside the surrey as Helen drove to the Gilmers' back porch. She helped unload all the dirty dishes and serving pieces into the kitchen, but when Helen offered to help wash and dry them, Anna insisted she go home and rest. "Your surrey and apple pies were your help. Lillie has been wonderful helping me in the kitchen since Molly went to college, so we'll be fine washin' and dryin'. Thank you, Helen."

Back in the field, the bales of wheat straw were loaded onto the trailer. After Samuel paid the man who owned the tractor and baler for his work, one by one, the helpers got another drink of cold, clear spring water and started for the next farm. When Samuel made a point to thank each of them, Dr. Josiah Forsyth said, "Sam Gilmer, don't thank me. You just helped me last week in my field. That's what neighbors are for."

Samuel then accompanied his neighbors to the Granger farm, where the process would be repeated. In his absence, Jake brought Dolly and SueJean out of the barn and led them to the two flat wagons. Lee helped him hitch the horses, and they pulled their load of straw to the barn.

Jake carried a dozen fresh bales of this wheat straw to an empty stable on the ground floor of the barn, to use on the floor of the stables as soft bedding for the animals. Late that afternoon, when Samuel returned from Will Granger's fields, he helped pull the rest of the straw up into the hay loft on the second level of the barn, using the same technique of hay spear, rope, and pulley. Jake Gilmer stood on the trailer and made sure each bale was securely hooked and could be lifted to the hay loft. Lee Hanner stood on the ground, pulling the rope that lifted the bale of hay upward. Samuel grabbed each bale of straw when it arrived at the large door of the hay loft, dragged it inside, and stacked the bales. Samuel was careful to place the wheat straw in a separate area of the loft, to avoid getting it mixed in with the clover and oats hay that had been carefully stacked there in the late spring.

The quiet at the end of the day, after the hard labors were done, was nearly deafening to three exhausted men. Lee clapped his son-in-law on the back as they walked to the pump to douse their face and hands and then scrub them with Anna's best homemade lye soap. "Oh, will we ever sleep well tonight, Samuel," Lee said, stretching.

Samuel glanced at his father-in-law with a grin and noticed an unexpected melancholy expression on the older man's face. "What is it, Lee?" he asked with concern.

Lee shook his head. "Samuel, I saw the future today, as well as the end of a bit of history."

Samuel joined the wise old gentleman at the oak tree. They both bent to grab a wisp of straw and chew on it before Samuel broke the silence. "Well, Lee, I saw the future also, and it seems exciting. Our world is changing, becoming more and more mechanized."

Lee nodded, and Samuel continued, "Did you see how quickly and efficiently those machines and the tractors worked today, getting this difficult task done faster than ever before? The grain harvest is done now in one long day, and safely stored for us to use through a cold winter."

When Lee didn't respond, Samuel asked, "What do you mean about the end of some history?"

Lee pointed toward the water-powered saw mill. "Samuel, my Grandpa Hanner built that mill near the end of the War of Northern Aggression because he saw that people around here needed lumber to rebuild homes, barns, and blacksmith shops. And he knew they'd want new schools and churches. Water was an amazing source of power. It was the best and quickest way to do that hard work. What we saw here today is the beginning of the end of our mill, Samuel."

When his son-in-law looked startled, Lee continued, "You saw those gasoline engines at work today. That's the future, Samuel. Yes, there will always be saw mills and grist mills, but there will be new machines doing the work you and I do now. The mills'll run on gasoline engines and electricity, not water power. One day in your lifetime, our horses just might be considered pets, a luxury that won't be necessary for farmin'. In a few years, these rutted, muddy, rocky lanes will be paved roads like they have in the city. Automobiles, trucks, and buses will be rolling up and down all over these hills. People will go more places—and much faster. That will bring noise, dirty air, and even accidents. Electric power lines will be strung out here to us rural folks, and after that, lines for those telly-phones."

He paused in his speech-making and looked Samuel squarely in the eyes. "Samuel, time is drawin' short for our mill, I'm afraid. Perhaps in your lifetime, but definitely in Jake's lifetime, it may be regarded as a hobby. Or something people will be curious to see, like a history museum. Yup, things sure are changin' quickly, Samuel." In a low voice, Lee added, "I just ain't sure I want to change along with 'em."

"You've given me somethin' to ponder, Lee," Samuel agreed as they walked up the hill toward the house. "Things are changin' fast. But people will remain the same, basically, won't they? We all need the same things. We all want good health and happiness and success for our young 'uns. Farm folk will still rely on their neighbors for help and friendship. And we can remember that, in spite of everything else changing, the Word of God is always the same Good News." He patted his father-in-law on the back. "Well, this might be all the philosophizin' we can handle for one night, especially after such a busy day. Let's go see if Anna and Lillie managed to wash all those dishes. I'm hopin' there's hot water left for a bath. I don't know about you, but I'm itchin' something fierce!"

CHAPTER SEVENTEEN: *ENDING IN NEW BEGINNINGS*
Thanksgiving Weekend 1913: November 26-November 30

"What a glorious autumn this has been," Anna commented to Samuel early one morning as they stood on the porch with coffee cups in hand, surveying their view. "I don't ever remember colors as vivid as this."

The couple enjoyed the lovely fall colors in appreciative silence. Spring had been warm and wet this year, with the summer days of unusually abundant rain and hot sun. The fall weather had been crisp, with warm days and cool nights. Up until Thanksgiving weekend, only one or two nights had dipped into freezing temperatures. The leaves of brilliant colors had remained on the trees nearly two weeks longer than usual, so they were still falling the week of Thanksgiving 1913.

From mid-October onwards until the trees were bare, Jake and Lillie had an extra chore to do on Saturdays—raking leaves into large piles and then loading them into the wooden wheel barrow. Jake pushed the full wheelbarrow loads through the pasture gate and down the gentle hill to the brush pile. As he transported the leaves and dumped them, Lillie continued to rake. Of course, the new beagle pup, Luke, played his own special role in the activities, diving into the leaves and leaping repeatedly at the moving rakes. Every now and then Jake gave him a ride on the wheelbarrow, to the dog's delight. Brush piles were burned on cold days with little or no wind, and when the ground was still damp after a good rain.

Lillie had been even more animated than usual since school let out on Tuesday afternoon for the Thanksgiving holiday. A letter had arrived from Molly the week before, and Lillie had been the one to find it in the Gilmers' post office box at the general store a mile away. She could barely wait until dinner time, when Anna opened the letter and the family gathered close to hear Molly's news. After describing her classes and professors and new friends, Molly reported that she would be arriving home on Wednesday afternoon. She had arranged a ride, so her family didn't have to make the long trek into Greensboro to pick her up.

On Wednesday morning, Lillie woke up extra early and had her bed made and the room swept and dusted long before sunrise. "Mama, I'm so excited I might just burst!" she announced when she rushed into the kitchen. Lillie skipped all the way to the chicken house while carrying the cracked corn for the hens, and as she scattered the grain over the yard in front of the coop, she divulged this exciting information to her feathery friends.

Meanwhile on that same Wednesday at daybreak, Lee Hanner and Jake shouldered their guns and went hunting, intending to bag a nice turkey for Thanksgiving dinner. They crossed Beaver Creek at its narrowest spot and followed the twists and turns of the stream into the edge of the woods. There, they both sat down on a large flat rock, leaned back against a tree, and loaded their weapons.

"Jake, we need to be very patient and quiet now," Lee told his grandson. "This turkey huntin' can take some time. The only sound I want to hear from you in this—." He reached into his pocket and pulled out a little wooden object shaped like a kazoo, with holes on both ends. "This is a turkey call I made years ago."

He put the instrument in Jake's hands. "I want you to blow into this several times and then listen carefully. Hopefully, a turkey will think he's hearin' the sounds of a potential sweetheart. Or his competition. And when he does, he'll start returnin' the call and come this way. You just keep soundin' the turkey call, and then when we see the rascal, we aim for the head." He reminded Jake—not for the first time—that turkeys can only fly about eight feet, far enough to reach a low limb where they can roost at night. "They don't fly like a bird," he added. "Whoever gets a good shot at the head will shoot first. Ready?"

The boy nodded and started to blow. The sound that came out of the wooden turkey call startled him, but he continued blowing until he produced a facsimile of a male turkey's gobbling. He continued this for a minute or so, and then paused so they could both listen. Nothing. He continued off and on for the next ten minutes. He took a swig of water from his canteen and blew again. He was a persistent and patient hunter, thanks to his father's and grandfather's training, so he kept on blowing and listening. Nearly an hour passed before his efforts were rewarded.

GobbleGobbleGobble? rang out from a briar thicket in the distance. Jake looked out the corner of his eye at Lee, who nodded slowly, fingering the Springfield rifle. Jake blew the turkey call again, and once again, the turkey answered. He was closer this time. Jake continued, relentlessly.

At last they saw the top of a cluster of tail feathers, and then a pink, skinny little head with beady eyes and a long, pink wattle appeared. Jake blew even more vigorously, and the turkey walked slowly closer, looking around for the source of the sound. Though his mouth was as dry as sawdust, Jake sounded the turkey call one more time, watching his Pap-paw raise his rifle, quietly sighting it. Suddenly, the turkey saw the two humans. He started to run back into the trees, but it was too late.

BOOM!

"Great shot, Pap-paw!" cheered Jake. He helped his Pap-Paw onto his feet when Lee Hanner said he was stiff from sitting on that hard rock. Then the boy sprinted to the area where they had last seen the turkey. Lee limped slowly behind him, arriving in time to see Jake pulling limbs, briars, and thick grasses out of the way. Jake ignored the thorns that scraped his skin as he searched and found the turkey's body.

The creature was absolutely intact, except for the fatal wound to the head. "It's a young male, but he looks big enough for all of us to get our fill," Lee said with satisfaction. He tied the turkey by its feet upside down from a tree limb. Then he pulled his Case hunting knife out of the leather sheath and cut her throat, to drain all the blood. He washed the knife in the creek before tucking it back into the sheath. After that, the grandfather and grandson put their guns on safety, packed the turkey into a sack, and started for home.

At the smokehouse, Lee placed the turkey tom on the large oak stump that served as a butcher's block. One again, he unsheathed his hunting knife. The elderly gentleman, an expert hunter and butcher, started at the breastbone, splitting open the body and removing all the entrails, much to the interest of a certain beagle puppy. Luke had left Lillie's side in order to investigate this new game. After dashing down the hill, he was busily eating the treat the hunters tossed to him.

"Jake, go ask your Ma for salt and a roasting pan big enough for a ten-pound turkey," Lee said as he continued his work. By the time Jake returned, Lee had removed the neck, liver, heart, and gizzard from the bird and rinsed them off with clean water. These went into a little cheesecloth sack, which Lee tied with burlap string and hung from a small tree limb nearby. "Your mother will use these for stuffing and for gravy," he told the boy. And then he gave him a lesson in removing all the feathers.

When the plucking was complete, he washed his hands with strong soap and water and rubbed the turkey carcass vigorously with salt. Then he carefully rinsed this turkey hen inside and out, twice. The turkey and the small sack fit perfectly in the pan. As Jake placed the roaster into the cold spring water, to wait until the next morning, Lee Hanner scoured the old stump and rinsed it well.

At that moment, a horse-drawn surrey came up the driveway from Hanners' Mill Road. Lillie saw the visitors first, from her perch on the front porch. She opened the door squealing, "Molly's home, Mama!" before she ran into the yard to greet the travelers. Her little feet barely touched the steps as she flew toward the surrey. Anna wasn't far behind. Instead of using the back porch door, she took the shortcut, coming out the front door, which was only used on very special occasions.

Meanwhile, Samuel had been cleaning the mill and sharpening the saw blades in anticipation of the mill's official closing until Monday, but when he saw the surrey arrive, he immediately left his chores. As he headed up the hill, he noticed the horse pulling the surrey, and he vaguely remembered seeing it before. When the horse came to a stop, a handsome dark-haired young man climbed down from the driver's side and walked around the surrey to hand Molly down. Lillie danced in excitement by his side.

At last, Molly was home again. She removed her hat quickly, smoothed the wrinkles in her long skirt, and held her arms out toward her mother and sister.

"You're here. You're home!" Lillie squealed, but she was nice enough to let her mother kiss Molly first. While they joyously greeted each other, Molly's driver removed a suitcase and travel bag from the rear of the surrey. Lillie noticed him for the first time. "I like that man's twinkly eyes and smile," she whispered in her sister's ear, as Molly bent down and hugged her closely.

"Sweetie, I just saw you seven weeks ago, but it seems like forever," Molly told her. "I have so much to tell you!"

"It feels like you've been gone for a year," Lillie said. "I'm so happy to have you home, my Molly!"

"We all are," Molly's mother agreed, hugging her firstborn for the second time.

Samuel rounded the corner in time to hear Molly introduce the young man who had brought her home from college. "Mama, Papa, Lillie, you remember Joe Thacker." The Gilmers all took turns shaking his hand.

"It seems like just yesterday you were in short pants, dangling upside down from a tree limb," Anna said, smiling up into the young man's face. "If you ask me, you young folk have grown up much too fast."

Lillie, having never been one to keep her opinions to herself, took Joe's hand "I like you. You have a nice smile!"

Samuel reached out one large, strong hand to this young man who had delivered his daughter home. Silently, he promised himself he would have a talk with James and Helen Thacker later. "Y'all come right on in and sit a spell, won't you?"

"Thank you, sir, but I just have time for a glass of water. I have to get home to Mom and Dad. I just arrived on the train from Raleigh late yesterday, and I borrowed Dad's surrey to go pick Molly up in Greensboro this morning."

When the family looked intrigued, he added, "There's a Thanksgiving community service tonight at the Tabernacle Methodist Episcopal Church South, and they'll need this surrey. Meanwhile, I need to do some serious studying tonight and Friday because I know I won't get any done on Thanksgiving. Plus, Saturday night is the big End of Harvest Celebration at the Foust's farm." He explained that he was in his fourth year at North Carolina State College, and he would have to board the train back to Raleigh on Sunday afternoon.

"Good school!" remarked Samuel. "Are you studying agriculture? Or mechanics and engineering?"

"Actually, I'm studying engineering," Joe said. He hesitated, then explained, "You probably didn't recognize me because I've been working at the Cone Mills White Oak Denim plant for two summers now. In fact," he added with a hint of pride in his voice, "Mr. Caesar Cone has offered me a full-time job when I graduate next May, maintaining all the machines and designing new ones." Samuel smiled, nodding approval.

Joe Thacker finished his water and handed Anna his glass, thanking her. "I better head up the hill to our farm now, or Pa will come lookin' for me," he said. The group stood up, and walked out the front door. Lee Hanner and Jake, who had cleaned up after working on the turkey, were now in the front yard and introduced themselves. After shaking hands all around once again, he clasped Molly's hand for a long moment, gave her a wink, and climbed into the Thacker surrey. Clicking his tongue to the horse, he departed.

Molly and Lillie raced indoors, while Samuel and Anna watched the surrey depart with thoughtful expressions on their faces.

Thanksgiving morning arrived. Lillie was like a whirling dervish in motion around the dining room and kitchen.

"Lillie, calm down, child, before you bump into the table and knock off those dishes that you just set so nicely," warned Anna. "Why are you so excited today?"

"Mama, I can't help it," Lillie said with a big smile. "I love Thanksgiving! I love all the smells—the food, the spices, the piles of leaves burning outside, the tingly fall air, everything. I love the beautiful fall colors. I love playing in the leaves. And I love the pretty frosting on the ground on cold mornings. I love being with my family, especially now that Molly's home again. But most of all, I love telling God, 'Thank you.' This is one of my most favorite days of the year."

"I'm so glad, Lillie," her distracted mother managed to say. "But if you really must jump around, please go outside until you get all your wiggles out, honey. Molly and I have hot things coming out of the oven, and I'm worried you might get burned."

The Thanksgiving meal was delicious. There was plenty of turkey, thanks to Lee Hanner's successful marksmanship and Jake's turkey-call assistance in the hunt. Molly and Anna cooked, sautéed, roasted, and boiled a record number of mouth-watering dishes, and Lillie mixed all the ingredients for the pumpkin pie before she set the table with Anna's wedding china. Conversation was lively. Everyone noticed that Molly's cheeks wore a perpetual blush, and she was humming softly with a mysterious smile all the time.

"My classes are quite grueling, but my grades are fine," she reported. "I'm definitely going for the four-year diploma instead of the two-year certificate. As long as I promise to work in a private or a public school in North Carolina for five years, my tuition is paid for. But I sure do miss all of you. Very much."

The days seemed short and exciting. Before the Gilmers knew it, Saturday night arrived. The biggest social event of the year, the End of Harvest Celebration, would be held in the Foust family's barn and in the newly-harvested hay field in front of the barn on the east side of the road across from Alamance Church. After Alamance Church Road makes a sharp turn to the left in front of the church and crosses a small stream just below the church cemetery, it meanders up a small hill past the Foust farm on the right, then extends several miles to the outskirts of Greensboro, where it intersects with Highway 421, a main highway.

The Foust family owned a large and prosperous farm, with the newest, largest, and most modern barn in the community. They were known for their hospitality and were always the first to offer their home and barn for events such as this one. On this Saturday night, everyone brought food to share, arriving in time to greet their neighbors before the festivities began.

A bluegrass band filled the air with hand-clapping, toe-tapping excitement. Many neighbors brought their clogging shoes and were guaranteed several opportunities to show off their dancing skills. The rhythmic beat of the clogs resonated beautifully on the wooden barn floor built on a rock foundation. The band showed a surprisingly wide repertoire. They alternated bluegrass with slow country music, square dancing, and other familiar old-fashioned Southern country dances throughout the evening.

Lillie and her young friends danced with each other during some of the lively bluegrass songs and the Virginia Reel. When the grown-ups danced to slow music, the children munched on mouth-watering foods and enjoyed cold cider and cold water from the well. When the first slow song began, Lillie ran to her Mama and Papa, who were sitting on a picnic bench watching the action. She tugged both of them by the hand, urging them to dance. "Come on! You two need to get up there and dance all snuggled up. I like watching you!" Samuel and Anna faked reluctant complaints, laughing as they went with her. But soon they were in each other's arms, looking in each other's eyes, smiling and whispering. Lillie stood off to the side, clapping.

As Samuel and Anna made a dip and a turn, they glimpsed Molly dancing with Joe Thacker on the far side of the barn floor. Molly's cheeks were bright pink, and the young people were talking softly as they danced closely together. The song ended, and Samuel and his wife, also a bit pink in the face, returned to an empty bench beside a picnic table and sat back down. Suddenly, Samuel's brain made connections. He finally tied together the facts about this man who appeared to be Molly's beau. And he was incredulous:

"Not little Joey Thacker!" he sputtered. "Not the little boy who irritated Molly so many times! Isn't he the boy who tossed sweet gum balls at her on the playground? Didn't he put a sharp pine cone on her seat at school just as she was sitting down?"

Anna smiled and nodded. Samuel shook his head. "Isn't he the boy who actually put a frog down her back one day when she walked home from school and she was so mad it took you all afternoon to calm her down?" When Anna nodded again, Molly's father protested. "You can't be serious!"

"One and the same" was Anna's calm answer. "That was years ago, Samuel. Looking at him now, I'd reckon he's grown up and abandoned the idea of sticking frogs down a girl's back." She glanced with a flirtatious look at her husband. "And, if I recall, once upon a time, a boy caught a black snake and chased me around the playground, waving that snake at me. In fact, that same boy would have dipped my braid in the inkwell if my best friend hadn't stopped him. And, that was the same boy the teacher was talking about when he handed out report cards and said, 'If I gave grades for hunting, fishing, and climbing trees, this student would receive highest marks.'"

"What a rascal he was!" laughed Samuel. "What did you ever do to stop him?"

"I married him," she replied calmly. "In fact, I married him despite having my father snort, 'I don't know if that boy will ever settle down and amount to anything.'"

"Hmm…Why did you marry that boy, Anna?" Samuel asked, taking her hand between his two.

She smiled at him mischievously. "My mother saw another side of you and promised Pa that things would be all right. More than all right."

"Can you explain to me why you girls put up with such behavior as children and still love us enough to marry us in later years?" Samuel asked, squeezing her hand.

The song was ending now, and people were clapping and catching their breath, but the two Gilmers didn't notice. Anna's eyes smiled into his. "Darling, women do not see the rough, irritating, uncut diamond that you once were when we fall in love. We see the sparkling-like-fire diamond you become after you are touched by the Master Craftsman. We see you at your best, at your fullest potential. And we love you for that."

Samuel stared at his wife, awed at the wisdom of the female brain as well as the love and grace of the Heavenly Father. A revelation hit him, and he told himself, "They disregard all the garbage of our past and all our mistakes. They see right through them, right into our hearts, and just love us for who we are. It's a wonder."

But the wonder of this evening was just beginning. A surrey pulled into the parking area, driven by a very large gentleman who sported a neatly trimmed beard. He was dressed in new store-bought clothes and a fashionable hat, Anna and Samuel noticed as they watched him jump from the driver's side and help a young boy out of the back seat. Next, he lifted a tiny little girl out of a woman's arms and gently set the child on the ground beside the boy. Then he walked to the passenger side of the surrey and chivalrously extended his arm to a young woman with soft features, shoulder-length black hair, and large brown eyes.

As more people turned to watch curiously, the little girl held hands with her mother and the little boy walked beside the man as they came forward to join the festivities. The well-groomed man was wearing a slight smile as he whispered something to the woman on his arm.

Anna gasped, "My stars, Samuel! There's Will Granger, looking decidedly handsome! I never thought I'd see the day. I wonder who the young woman and two children are."

Samuel looked quizzically at his wife before he twisted around in his seat. "Well, I'll be!" he said, standing and heading over to the little family. Anna could tell that he was inviting them to join the Gilmers at their table. Meanwhile, Lillie came skipping over, and Will Granger introduced her to the boy named Charlie. "Come play with us," she invited, and Charlie followed her into the yard, where a cluster of children prepared for the next game.

Anna turned to Will's friend and smiled broadly. "I'm so very glad to meet you!" she said, as she introduced herself. "Our daughter Molly is seventeen, and she's off dancing somewhere. Our son Jake is over there, threatening to eat everything on the food table, and the little ball of fire who just went running off with your son is our youngest daughter, Lillie."

Then she smiled at her neighbor. "Mercy sakes, Will. You're a handsome man. And you've brought us a lovely new friend." Slightly flushed, Will Granger deftly removed his new hat and placed it on the table. He nodded shyly, but it was the newcomer who spoke first.

"Thank you. I'm Marjorie Shoffner. I'm a…a…friend of Will's from 'way back. We hadn't seen each other in ten years, but one day, out of the blue, he came knockin' on my door. I live on McConnell Road." She told the Gilmers that her daughter's name was Elisabeth and her son's name was Charlie.

"We've had some…ah, some sadness this summer, and Will has been very kind helping us out," Marjorie told Anna when the men offered to fetch drinks and dessert for the ladies. "This week, Will told me I needed to get out and attend something happy, so he invited us all here." She paused and added, "Will has told me that you're not only his neighbors, but you're also very good friends."

As Marjorie was talking, Anna's mind put two-and-two together. She studied Marjorie's face more closely and then glanced at Will, who was returning to the table. Anna spoke warmly to the woman. "I have just figured out who you are, Marjorie. I am terribly sorry about the loss of your husband. Samuel heard the awful news from James Thacker after he returned from McConnell Road, bringing his wife home from her sister's." She told Marjorie that Will had been in the mill helping Sam at that time of James' visit. "Samuel told me that Will got quite upset when James mentioned Henry Shoffner's wife. We haven't seen Will much since then. I suppose he's been helping you."

Marjorie sighed softly, and Anna saw a flicker of her grief and hurt in those large, expressive eyes. After a moment, Marjorie responded, "The day that Will arrived on my doorstep, I was feeling totally alone, helpless, and without hope. My parents are elderly and they'd just left for their own home, which is in Virginia now. Our tobacco crop had been harvested, but my husband hadn't found the time to sell it. After he died, kind neighbors had taken the load to the Auction house; it was sitting there, and I didn't know what to do about that. The enormity of what I was facing as a widow was crushing me."

She wiped tears with a bright white, embroidered handkerchief before she continued her story. "Will surprised me that same afternoon. He said he rode over as soon as he heard about Henry's death and the tobacco. He came to extend his sympathy, and he offered to help me get Henry's tobacco to market, making sure I got a fair price for it."

She smiled at the memory. "I admit I was a bit wary at first, because it had been so long since I had seen Will. I didn't know what his purpose was in his sudden appearance and offer of help. But I stepped out in faith—and I'm so glad I did. Not only did Will take me to Greensboro and negotiate a good price for the tobacco, but he drove me to our bank and entertained the little ones while I went in and deposited the money.

While I was in there, I followed Will's suggestion and removed Henry's name from the account—he knew enough to tell me that I should bring my identification and Henry's death certificate in my purse."

Since then, she said, Will had visited frequently, making a few repairs on the house, plowing her garden, digging the potatoes, cutting the corn stalks, and fixing a hole in her fence. "The children just love him, and gradually…well…our relationship has changed." She blushed in a very pretty way, looking toward Will, who had overheard the last part of her story.

"I told Marjorie when I surprised her that afternoon that I was just respondin' to her need as a Christian brother. The Good Book says we're s'posed to help widows and orphans," he said, running his finger under a collar that suddenly felt too tight. "I was followin' those commands, Anna. But as time went on, both of us realized that somethin' else was happ'nin' here."

Samuel slapped his friend on the back. "Good for you!"

"I didn't want to take her out over yonder because it's only been three months since Henry died, and courtin' that soon just wouldn't seem proper," Will explained. "But Marjorie and I have known each other for years, so it's not like we're startin' from scratch. We had lots o' catchin' up to do, you understand."

Will continued that he told Marjorie the story about his life with Suzanne and her death in childbirth and how mad he was at God and the world after his wife and baby died. Marjorie had shared about her life with Henry and what a good man he was. "I messed up with Marjorie years ago by taking her for granted and bein' a stubborn cuss who refused to get serious about God," Will confessed. "When we went our own ways, God brought Henry Shoffner into her life, and he was just the man she needed then. And, though I sure didn't deserve it, God put a wonderful woman named Suzanne right in front of me, and she was such a blessin' to me."

Will took Marjorie's hand and held it firmly as he gazed at her. "I have no intention of ever trying to replace Henry Shoffner in Marjorie's life—I can't. I want the young'uns to remember their father. Marjorie isn't Suzanne, and she ain't s'posed to be. But I can be honest with you two: that night in August at Big Meeting, Jesus took all the sin and bitterness out of my life, and somethin' that I thought had died inside my heart found its way back. I'd gone into a shell to protect my heart from being broke again. Now that hard shell's gone and I find I can live—and even love—again."

Will Granger took a deep breath. "I figure it's time for me to celebrate life and all that the Lord has brought me in this year. You good neighbors rebuilt a barn for a grouch like me. And now God brought me a wonderful woman. I'm a man blessed by God." Will smiled at Marjorie, rose, and bowed, inviting her to dance. "It's been a long time. I'll try not to step on your feet."

Marjorie stammered a moment, "But Will, what about Elisabeth?"

Samuel grinned. "The little lady is safe right here with us, Marjorie."

Will whisked Marjorie off the picnic bench and onto the barn floor as soon as the music began. Jake walked to his parents' table as this was going on, bringing a friend from school. Munching a juicy red apple, Jake asked happily, "Howdy! Are you folks having fun? They've got some good food here this year. Oh," he added, turning to his friend. "This is Freddie Coble. We're hidin' from Geraldine Gladson and Cindy Allred. Y'all ain't seen 'em over here, have you?"

Samuel raised his eyebrows and Jake said sheepishly, "We just sneaked up behind 'em and dumped a big ole pile of straw over their heads. Anyway, I'll meet y'all back here when the last song is over. Bye!" The boys sped away, laughing.

Anna winked at Samuel, "See what I mean? It must be a disease common to most young males." Samuel just shook his head, chuckling.

Joe Thacker and Molly arrived at the table, pink-cheeked and out of breath, with plates loaded with good food. They sat opposite each other, beside Molly's parents. Anna and Samuel held hands, watching Will Granger and Marjorie Shoffner square-dancing together, spinning around and clapping. Marjorie had a lovely smile on her face, obviously enjoying the moment. As they watched, Will turned the wrong way and came close to crashing into Bubba Forbis. Both men laughed heartily. "Oh, what wonders the Lord hath wrought" Anna said in a whisper only loud enough for Samuel to hear.

He whispered back, "Amen!" leaning over and kissing her.

On a bright Thanksgiving Sunday morning, Reverend Crawford focused on the theme "An Attitude of Gratitude" at the worship service. Molly's belongings were already loaded in the wagon outside, because the family would be dropping Molly off at the Thacker home on their way back from church. Helen Thacker had asked Molly to come for Sunday dinner, since James would be driving Molly and Joe to Greensboro. His first stop would be Molly's dormitory, and then James would turn the wagon back toward the train station on Elm Street. Joe already had his ticket; he would be taking the five o'clock train back to Raleigh and North Carolina State College.

Hilda Gorrell, the organist at Alamance Presbyterian Church, launched into the last song of the morning service with her feet pumping the pedals enthusiastically. In contrast to the soft music during the prayer time, she made the volume swell with joy in this final hymn of the morning:

Come, ye thankful people come,
Raise the song of harvest home;
All is safely gathered in,
'Ere the winter storms begin.
God our Maker doth provide
For our wants to be supplied;
Come to God's own temple, come,
Raise the song of harvest home.

Hours later, the horse clip-clopped up the hill from the Thacker farm, along the rutted red-clay road leading to Greensboro. Molly and Joe sat together in the back seat, deep in thought. Their suitcases, the books they brought from college, and Molly's travel bag filled the front seat and floorboard beside Mr. Thacker. As the surrey reached the top of the hill and the road curved so that the land of their childhood was no longer visible, Molly broke the silence.

"Joe, look around us. There's no electricity out here. No running water. No indoor toilets. No automobiles, trolleys, or telephones. I heard about this year's harvest, how for the first time steam tractors, steel-wheeled gas-powered tractors, and gasoline engines worked on our farms.

Most of the fruits and vegetables we grew up eating were grown on our own land, and the meat was either slaughtered or brought home freshly killed. Fish was carried home in wicker baskets from local ponds, lakes, and streams."

Joe nodded. "Most of my friends at college attended city schools. We were taught in one or two-room school houses."

Mollie took his hand. "After sayin' all that, Joe, I can honestly tell you that I feel truly blessed that I was able to grow up in the community of Beaver Creek and Alamance Presbyterian Church. We had a lot of very hard work and heartaches. But, Joe, the peace and quiet, the clean fresh air, the love of my family and my church, good neighbors and friends, the beauty and power of nature, and feelin' so close to God out here has filled my heart with such happiness that I'll treasure as long as I live."

Joe Thacker gave her a broad smile, nodded, and squeezed her hand in agreement.

Beside the surrey, a young colt raced along the rail fence, whinnying and kicking up his heels in pure joy. Things didn't need to change so very quickly here in the country, after all!

Jobe-Haines

EPILOGUE:

More notes about the farm equipment from Chapter Sixteen

My father, Garland Jobe, was the son of a skilled mechanic, Mr. Albert G. Jobe, who taught Dad everything he could about engines and machinery. Daddy was so interested in equipment and in designing machinery that he graduated with a degree in mechanical engineering from North Carolina State College of Agriculture and Engineering (now N.C. State) and worked many years for Bell Laboratories. He always had a love of farm equipment, and in 1970 he started collecting and restoring old farm machinery and engines that dated from the early 1900's. He actually brought home two antique tractors. One was a Farmall "F-20", built around 1912, which is where I got the idea for including a tractor in this story. When Dad restored it, I helped by painting the gray primer paint on this big beast. I can't imagine how uncomfortable this old steel-wheeled tractor must have been to ride, but, at the time it was used, it was the best equipment available and many farmers yearned to have one.

The other steel-wheeled tractor that my father had, but never finished restoring, was a McCormick-Deering "10-20." This old tractor is still in the large shed below the house where we lived, and my nephew has dreams of restoring it. Newer than the old Farmall, the McCormick-Deering was built in the early 1920's.

My father also brought home a threshing machine built around 1912. The actual threshing machine Daddy had was called "The Champion" and was made by Ellis Keystone Agriculture Works, but I know that Advance-Rumely was a famous company producing early threshing machines. Sadly, my Dad did not live to restore this threshing machine. It was sold at the estate sale, and I was pleased to learn that the gentleman who purchased this fragile old apparatus said that he planned to restore it to working condition.

When Dad was young, he had been told about a 1912 7½-horsepower Galloway hit-and-miss engine that was bolted onto the flatbed of a horse-drawn wagon. He said it was still powering threshing machines in rural southeast Guilford County when he was a little boy in the 1930's. About forty years later, after Dad started restoring antique gasoline engines, he asked around about this old Galloway, and he managed to find this apparatus in 1974. It had been pushed into a gully by a bulldozer and broken into many pieces. It was rusted and the wagon was nearly rotted through, but Dad brought all the pieces he could find to our home in barrels and boxes. I think even my mother had doubts about his ability to make something of all this wreckage. But, over several years, Dad performed a miraculous restoration of this engine and the wagon to their original splendor. He took photographs during the long process and wrote an article about this challenging restoration. Sometime around 1978, this appeared as the cover story in one of the issues of *Gas Engine Magazine.* Daddy enjoyed showing this rig at antique farm equipment shows for many years. Of all the engines that he restored and the scale-models that he built, the Galloway was his biggest challenge, and I think it gave him the greatest feeling of accomplishment.

Not only did Garland Jobe restore full-size gasoline engines, he also built scale-model gasoline engines, milling and fabricating all the parts in his shop. At antique farm equipment shows, folks love to see the engines "at work." Dad built three different scale-model machines that operated just like the full-size originals performed years before, doing specific jobs. Daddy built many scale-model engines, but these three were hooked to miniature machines that he also built, that worked! One crushed rock and another ground dried corn into meal. His favorite, however, was the CASE hay-baling machine that actually made little bales of hay or straw. He would attach the hay baler to his best-running, favorite scale-model gas engine, a Fuller-Johnson. At the shows, my Dad would demonstrate how the hay baler worked by starting the engine and then connecting the small leather belt to the hay baler. As the miniature hay baler ran, he gently pushed straw or hay into the chute on top, then carefully threaded wire through the holes near the end of the baler, as farmers had done in the past to secure the bales. At first, Daddy gave away the little hay bales to interested spectators. Later, my mother convinced him to charge $1.00 per bale. Many people bought these at his exhibit, walking away with big smiles on their faces.

Appendix A

REFERENCES THAT HELPED IN WRITING THIS STORY

Lynn May Barnes, Administrative Secretary Alamance Presbyterian Church, Greensboro, NC
4000 Presbyterian Road 27406   Phone: (336)697-0488

A History of Alamance Presbyterian Church 1762-2000: Her People and Their Stories, by
Edna Smith Jobe, 2008.

Book of North American Birds, The Readers Digest Association, Inc. Pleasantville, NY 1990.

OUR STATE: Down Home in North Carolina. August 2013 Edition. Volume 81, Number 3.
Mann Media, Inc. 800 Green Valley Road, Suite 106, Greensboro, NC 27408

Greensboro, A Chosen Center—An Illustrated History, by Gayle Hicks Fripp. American Historical Press, Sun Valley, CA.

Making of America Series: *Guilford County, Heart of the Piedmont,* by Lynn and Burke Salsi. Arcadia Publishing, Charleston, SC 29401, published in 2002.

Websites also utilized:

ncgenweb.us/nc/guilford/alamance-presbyterian-history

www.findagrave.com/cgi-bin/fg.cgi?page=cr&crid=2129828

library.uncg.edu/map/details/Foust_Building.aspx

www.wmsumc.org/our_history